A MATTER OF LIFE AND DEATH

ANDY MARR

ALSO BY ANDY MARR

Hunger for Life

For my daughters, Malin and Anja, without whom I'd have finished this book years ago.

ONE

Sally is tied to a chair at the dusty farmhouse dinner table, screaming out in pain and terror as the family of demented cannibals sits around, tormenting her. Dressed in a wig and an apron, Leatherface, the baby of the family, is serving a dinner of human casserole. Watching all of this, Sally knows she's going to be next on the menu...

I know it, too. In the agonising tension of the moment, I've almost forgotten I'm trying to get tipsy. The wine glass I'm holding rests coolly against my lip.

I wish I'd left the curtains open.

Suddenly, Sally comes face to face with the desiccated body of Grandpa. He's asleep, but when his family presses a cut in Sally's finger against his dry lips, his milky eyes open and he sucks hungrily at the blood. Sally watches as Grandpa is handed a hammer with which to smash her head open. But Grandpa is too weak, and in the ensuing confusion, Sally breaks free, runs across the room, and –

BRRRRRRRRRRING!

I jump so violently that the contents of my glass spill down my t-shirt. Gasping at the sudden cold against my skin, I glare accusingly at my phone, which vibrates indifferently against my left hip on the sofa. I'm half tempted to launch the thing across the room, but then I'd only have to fetch it back again in time to order dinner, which seems like a lot of work. Grumbling, I pick it up and answer. 'Yes?' I ask. 'Hello? Who is it?'

It's my sister, Sophie. 'Tom?' she says. 'What's wrong? You sound breathless. Oh no, wait... have you been... were you... Eeew!'

'For goodness' sake,' I say, immediately reading Sophie's one-track mind. 'I was watching a film.'

'Yeah, right,' she says. 'Like the one you used to hide behind the stuffed toys on your bookcase?'

'What? No. What?' How the hell did she know about that? I squeeze my eyes shut, suppressing a cringe. 'Sophie, do you always have to make things so awkward?'

'Yes. It's the only way I can enjoy our conversations. I mean, it's two o'clock on a Friday afternoon and you're sitting indoors watching some crap movie. And it's not even a porno. You live in London, Tom. The world's greatest city is literally standing outside your door.'

'It's a very good film, actually,' I say, sulkily.

Sophie sighs. I can almost hear her eyes rolling. 'My god, you're about as much fun these days as a dose of crabs.'

I should probably be offended by this, even if it's completely true. Beneath Sophie's impatience, though, I hear strains of genuine concern. 'Were you *only* calling to lift my spirits?' I ask.

Sophie sighs. 'I'm sorry. I know I'm grumpy. But... Dad just called. He had some news. Some bad news. He... uh...' There's a noise from the other end of the phone. It sounds like a sob.

'Sophie?'

'It's... He... Oh, for Christ's sake, Tom. Aren't we supposed to be able to do all that twin telepathy shit? Couldn't we start that now?'

'I'm getting nothing.'

Sophie exhales, takes a deep breath. 'Tom, it's Mum. It... It's come back.'

I feel as though the wind's been knocked out of me. Shutting my eyes tightly, I lean forward and rest my head against my knees. It feels nice down there. Feels safe. And dark. I want to stay like that until all my problems have melted away, and I would, except that my back's already beginning to spasm.

'Tom?' Sophie says. 'Are you still there?'

I tell her yes, though my face is pressed hard against my jeans so it comes out more like DRUUUFF.

'She saw her doctors last week for some tests,' Sophie says. 'The results came back this morning. It's not looking good.'

With eyes still closed, I move back to a seated position. 'How "not good" is it looking?'

'Very, very not good. And it's not about to get any better. We're talking weeks rather than months.'

Part of me has been waiting for this, I suppose. When my mother was given the all clear two years ago, it was with the warning that the cancer was likely to return. As she herself put it, her last treatment had offered a stay of execution rather than a new lease of life. Even still, I'd expected that it would take a few more years at least for the cells to gather together with enough force to wage a second war against her weakened body.

'How was Dad?' I ask.

'I don't know. Quiet. Distracted, too, though I guess he was just in a hurry to get back to Mum.'

'Is she in the hospital?'

'Nope. And won't be going, either, if she has anything to do with it. She's going to kick the bucket at home or nowhere at all, she says. Dad's hiring a couple of people to look after her.'

'What kind of people?'

'I don't know.'

'Yeah, but are they nurses or what?'

'Christ, Tom, I don't know. Maybe you should give Pete a call if you're so desperate to find out.'

'I'm not calling Pete,' I say.

'Right,' Sophie says. 'So, we'll just have to wait and see. Because I'm not calling him either.'

Pete, incidentally, is our brother, older than us by precisely three years. Sophie and I caused quite a stir when we decided to enter the world on our brother's birthday. The news spread so fast, in fact, that my mother was still high on morphine when the county newspaper arrived at the hospital to take what would be the first Halliday family portrait. The reporter, clearly excited about the story, asked Dad how he felt about his three children beating odds of 1 in 55,000 to share a single birthday. My father replied that the real odds were actually far shorter than this, given that two of the three siblings in question were twins. The reporter sniffed once before turning her attention towards my mother, who was sufficiently stoned to confirm all the 'facts' required to put together a nice, juicy article.

The article that appeared the following morning excitedly announced the arrival of 'Myreton's miracle children', and would surely have been offered pride of place on the wall of our lounge had the photographer not made such an exquisite job of capturing my mother's blank, open-mouthed expression. Her little miracles had fared no better,

Sophie and I struggling, red faced and wailing, in her arms and Pete standing grimly at her side, furious with the two noisy impostors who'd sabotaged his long-awaited birthday party. Whenever Pete got rough with Sophie and me as kids, I used to think back to that photograph and imagine that he was punishing us for this early act of selfishness. Now that I'm older, though, I'm able to understand the truth; my older brother was simply born to be a dickhead.

'So, what do we do now?' I ask Sophie.

'We go back home to Myreton.'

'I guessed that. But how long are you planning to stay?'

'Until after the funeral.'

'What about your work?'

'I can do it from there.'

'And you think you can stand it that long?'

'Of course. I can do anything with my darling twin brother by my side.'

'Ah. Now...'

'Oh, come on, Tom. It's not like you have a proper job.'

'Excuse me. I'm writing a book.'

'Of course, you are,' Sophie says drily. 'In any case, it's nothing you can't do back home. You're coming with me, and you're staying for the duration. I've booked you a ticket from King's Cross tomorrow afternoon. Twenty-four hours gives you more than enough time to pack your pencil case.'

'And you? You're driving down with Bill?'

Sophie laughs. 'Ha! Can you imagine what Mum would say if Bill rocked up in Myreton for a whole fortnight? She'd die on the spot just to get away from him. No, I'm going alone. Bill's flying out to Australia on Thursday anyway.'

Bill, Sophie's husband, is the chief engineer of a large oil company in Aberdeen. A tall, bespectacled man who looks like a schoolmaster and behaves like an amiable one, he's spent the past twenty years accepting ridiculous sums of money to fly around the world and embrace his obsession with drill bits and suction anchors. The result is that he spends a lot of time away from home, but the arrangement seems to suit both him and Sophie perfectly. When he's travelling, the two go happily about their own business – Bill doing whatever he does on his oil rigs and Sophie running a small mental health charity in the north of Scotland. Then, when Bill returns home, he takes a few days off work and joins Sophie in her office to help with whatever fundraising or programming work she's been saving for him. Bill undertakes each of these tasks without complaint, happy just to be by Sophie's side, proud of the work she continues to do. That he dotes on Sophie has been obvious from the moment I met him. That he'd do anything for her cannot be denied. He's kind, and loving, and if he's not the absolute perfect husband, then he's as close to perfect as a husband can be.

And yet, despite his very obvious qualities, my mother's always hated Bill. She never liked any of the men Sophie dated, but Bill she gives her special ammunition, a steady stream of unprovoked criticism that he's too good-natured to take as anything but mild teasing when it is, in fact, genuine hostility. Deep down, I know she doesn't really hold anything against him as a person, that she might even have found something to like about him had he not had the audacity to marry her daughter. Nevertheless, Bill's so unbelievably kind that it's impossible not to feel offended when she starts to poke fun at him.

'Anyway,' Sophie says, 'talking of spouses, how's your own stinking car crash of a marriage coming along?'

Until recently, I always rather enjoyed being the butt of Sophie's tactless joshing. Even on my worst days, it was a fun challenge to ensure that I emerged unscathed from her latest assault. But the last few months have left me battered and bruised, and my defences have been exhausted.

'I have to go now,' I say, trying hard to disguise the lump that's suddenly appeared in my throat.

'That's fine,' Sophie says. 'I'll have a quick chat with Lena instead.'

'Ha-ha,' I say, without laughing. 'You're truly hilarious. Bye bye.'

'What? No, tell me! I'm asking how you are!'

'Later, alligator...'

'Tom, don't you dare hang up on m–'

I punch the *end call* button on my mobile and smile as I picture my sister, red-faced and screaming, on the other end of the phone. Then I refill my glass of wine and return to my movie. After my conversation with Sophie, Leatherface and his clan suddenly seem far less terrifying than they did only a few minutes before.

TWO

THE DOORBELL RINGS AT EIGHT O'CLOCK THE FOLLOWING morning. I realise that by this time most of London's bright young things have already enjoyed a brisk morning jog and an artisan coffee, but my routine died completely when Lena left and it's been months since I fell asleep before three in the morning. Last night was no different, and I'm very tempted to curl back under my sheets. But the doorbell rings again, and in any case, I need to pee, so I know there's no way I'm going to get back to sleep. Groaning, I roll out of bed and pad bare-footed to the front door of my apartment.

It's my wife, Lena. She takes one look at me and involuntarily moves a hand to her mouth. 'My god, Tom.'

The surprise is mutual. I haven't seen Lena in a while, had begun to wonder if I'd ever see her again. Yet here she is looking as beautiful as ever in a designer trench coat, her long blonde hair worn in a perfect bun, her blue eyes sparkling even in the gloom of my hallway. I wish, as I'm sure she now does, that she'd called ahead. The truth is, I've experienced an unhealthy amount of solitude and free time since Lena left me six months ago. I've been eating crap, drinking heavily, and neglecting to shave, bathe or change clothes for days at a time. It's not been a problem until now, because I've more or less cut my ties with the world outside my window. This morning, though, Lena's clearly disturbed by the look and smell of me, and for the first time I begin to regret my new lifestyle.

'Um, it's a little chilly?' Lena says from the doorstep. I step awkwardly to the side, allowing her to move ahead of me into the apartment. She's about to enter the living room when I remember that the place hasn't been properly tidied in months.

'WAIT!' I shout. Lena freezes, her hand resting on the handle of the living room door. I run to her side and, taking her by the arms, manoeuvre her away from the door. 'Sorry,' I say, trying unsuccessfully to smile. 'Just give me one second.'

As soon as I set foot in the room, I know I'm faced with an impossible task. There's so much mess in here that it would take hours to make the place even remotely presentable. Panicked, I gather up a few armfuls of clothes and books and blankets and crockery and stuff them all behind the telly. It's an exceptionally poor choice of hiding place - the pile I've created is three times bigger than the TV screen - but at least it's cleared some kind of path between the door and the sofa.

'Okay,' I say. 'Ready.' Lena appears at the doorway and immediately freezes again. I watch as she glances around a room which, in the eighteen months she lived here, was never less than spotless. It's some time before she gathers herself sufficiently to tiptoe around the remaining debris towards the sofa, where she perches between some DVDs and a pile of books. She continues to fire nervous glances around the room, as though she half expects to find a corpse or two hidden among the detritus. Her eyes finally settle on my small coffee table, which has become the final resting place of a fusty Pot Noodle and an old sock that I've been using as a coaster.

'Sorry about this,' I say. 'I've been meaning to give the place a wee tidy.'

Lena turns to me, her face a picture of intense concern. 'Tom, what the hell's happening? Are you okay?'

'Yeah,' I say, wincing at the fake cheer in my voice. 'I've just been taking some time out. Re-evaluating and, uh, stuff. Do you want a coffee?'

'No. I want you to tell me how you are. I had no idea you... I mean, it's been six months...'

'Honestly,' I say, dishonestly. 'I'm fine. You just caught me on a bad day.'

Lena glances once more around the room. She's calculating how many bad days it's taken to fill the room with this much shit. 'Have you even found a job yet?' she asks.

'Well, not quite. But I'm working on it.' I'm not sure if the use of the word 'working' constitutes a play on words here, but I laugh a little anyway just to show Lena that I'm okay, that I'm happy, that everything is absolutely hunky-fucking-dory without her.

The fact is, I was lying when I told Sophie I'm writing a book. What I am in fact doing is considering thinking about possibly beginning to write a book. And I'm only considering thinking about it because three months ago, while on the phone to Sophie, I finally grew so sick of people enquiring about my job hunt that I invented a career for myself there and then. It was a snap choice, made simply because I was holding a Nick Hornby paperback at the time. Had I been holding a fish supper or a handful of dirty underwear, I might easily have become a chef or a gigolo instead. But no. I am now officially a writer of books. It's a decision I may well come to regret, given that my last foray into creative writing was back in high school English, when I wrote a sonnet that ran to twenty-seven lines.

Perhaps I should have kept up the charade for Lena, but there's a chance she'd have taken the news badly. She doesn't want to hear about comic books. She wants to hear about salaries and promotions and benefit packages and success. That's how things were when we met for the first time, back in the summer of 2008. We were in Munich for a conference that had been arranged by the bank we'd recently started working for. The conference was really more of a 48-hour party, an opportunity for a carefully selected troupe of rising stars within the company to meet, greet and get drunk with one another in the sort of lavish settings that would end so abruptly when the banking bubble burst the following year.

Lena's star was rising faster and shining more brightly than almost any other in the room. In her first twelve months with the bank, she had already earned two promotions, and was already close to managing a team of her own in the company's Stockholm office. Next to hers, my own efforts were pretty mediocre, but I'd done well enough back in Glasgow to earn a promotion of my own, and this, in itself, was apparently enough for me to be invited to Germany.

I'm stating the obvious, I suppose, but I'll never forget the moment I first saw Lena. It was on the first morning of the conference, just before our Chief Executive was due to give a presentation in the hotel's main suite. I'd arrived late, and was taking a seat by the door when I saw Lena in the front row, laughing at someone's joke, tucking her hair behind her ear. I stared at her. She was like an angel straight from heaven, so beautiful that she took my breath away. I realised that I had never known true beauty until that moment.

The Chief Executive soon took to the stage, where he chattered excitedly about ways to supercharge value-based pricing strategies or some such thing, but my attention never moved from Lena. Towards the end of the speech, Lena happened to look around and to see me. After staring at me for a few seconds, she smiled and lifted her fingers in a wave, before returning her eyes to the stage. I felt a strange flutter in my chest, like the glow of a fireplace or the warmth of a summer day. *If there is such a thing as love at first sight,* I thought, *then this is it.*

When we broke for lunch, Lena was one of the first out of the door, offering me no chance to improve upon the goofy half-smile I'd offered her a few minutes earlier. By the time I caught up with her in the restaurant, she was already surrounded by a group of Romeos, all fighting desperately for her attention as she smiled politely from her chair. Things were even worse a few hours later, when the lunchtime crowd was joined by a second group of men who'd found the Dutch courage they required to approach her in their after-work drinks. The attention was presumably overwhelming, because Lena left the bar after a single glass of wine, her handbag filled with business cards of wannabe suitors, and did not reappear for dinner later that evening.

The second day followed the same pattern, and by the time the bar opened in the early evening I turned my back sulkily to Lena's crowd of admirers and made the firm decision to get squiffy on the free wine that was being served. Because I was pretty unused to drinking back then, I was tipsy within the hour, and by the time I'd finished my third glass the room had started to spin. Rising from my table, I tottered outside and pressed my damp forehead against one of the heavy stone columns that stood either side of the hotel entrance. A few moments passed before I noticed Lena watching me from the other side of the doorway.

'Are you alright?' she asked, more tickled than concerned by my appearance. 'I guess the free bar got the better of you, huh?'

Actually, I'd sobered up considerably the moment I saw Lena. I was now standing straight and searching desperately for something clever to say. Nothing clever came to mind, so I nodded instead to the unlit cigarette she was holding and said, 'I didn't know you smoked.'

'I didn't know you knew me at all,' Lena said, with a grin.

The heat returned to my face, but this time alcohol wasn't to blame. I was blushing so hard that I thought my cheeks might explode.

'To be honest with you,' Lena said, holding the cigarette out in front of her, 'I don't actually smoke. I just needed an excuse to get out of that room, so I bummed this from a friend.'

'The fan club getting you down?'

Lena scoffed. 'So, you noticed.' Sighing, she flicked the cigarette into a nearby plant pot and turned to face me. 'You know, I've hardly spoken a single word to any of them all week, and yet they're still hanging around me like a pack of hungry dogs. I'm starting to wonder what I'll have to do to get rid of them.'

Without thinking, I laughed. 'Well, I think you might struggle there.'

Lena tilted her head to the side, her eyes curious. 'Why's that?'

'Oh.' I blushed a third time. 'It's just... your dress, and, uh...' *Don't look at her cleavage.* 'Uh...' *Don't look at her cleavage.* 'Your...'

'My what?'

'Face,' I said, and sighed with relief.

Lena's smile turned mischievous. 'You think I should change my appearance?'

I smiled back at her sheepishly. 'It might be worth considering. You could throw on a clown suit. Or have a tooth removed.'

'A tooth?'

'Yeah.' I pointed to my front tooth. 'This one. Get rid of this one.'

Lena covered her own front tooth with a finger. 'What do you think?'

'Oh!' I said, shielding my eyes with a hand. 'Oh Lord! You look absolutely repulsive.'

'Aaw,' said Lena, punching me playfully on the shoulder. 'I bet you say that to all the girls.'

God, I felt smug as Lena and I stepped back inside and took our seats at a quiet table for two. Every pair of male eyes in the room were watching her every move, but I knew that nobody would dare interrupt us while we shared such an intimate setting. For the next three hours, we remained locked in conversation. I told her of my life, and she told me of hers: about her childhood in Malmo with her book-loving mother and ice hockey obsessed father; about how she lost her virginity in the bathroom of a grubby French youth hostel while traveling Europe; about her years at university in Berlin, where she had her heart broken by the lead singer of a famous German punk band; and about how she fell in love again two weeks after arriving in Stockholm, only for the relationship to end when her boyfriend emigrated to New Zealand.

'Oh,' I said, at this last news. 'So, you're single?'

Lena nodded. 'For eight months now. I quite enjoyed it at first, you know, once my heart had begun to heal. But I never liked to be alone for long. I guess I'm getting ready to meet somebody again.'

'You are?' I said, a little too eagerly.

Lena smiled. 'What? Are you planning to move to Sweden for me?'

I laughed at that because I was supposed to, but at that moment I was so entirely spellbound that I'd have followed her to Mars if she'd asked me to. But it wasn't to be. The night was already drawing to a close, and within minutes Lena was standing up from the table, readying herself to leave. She kissed me softly on the cheek, smiled one final, beautiful smile, and then turned from the room. A moment later, I sank back into my seat, fully aware that I'd fallen head over heels for Lena Sandberg.

We were to meet again, of course, and far sooner than either of us could have expected. Later that summer, Lena received the transfer to London that she'd requested more than a year earlier. Two months after that, the company expanded its London office and I was asked to move south to take up a role in junior management. Being strangers in a new city, Lena and I were delighted to bump into one another in the office a week after I arrived in London, and that night we ate dinner in a Chinese restaurant that we'd visit together countless times over the next ten years. There was less to catch up on this time, but still we talked for hours, about how we were settling into London (not too badly, we agreed), and where we were living (Lena in a flat with two students from UCL, myself in an apartment my parents had owned since the '80s). I felt beyond happy. I loved the way she looked at her hands when she talked. I loved how her mouth opened slightly and her eyebrows knitted together when she was listening. It seemed like a joke that I should have her attention all to myself. After all, here was a woman who glowed so bright that she seemed to take up an extra layer of attention everywhere she went.

'And have you made any friends yet?' Lena asked, as our main courses arrived at the table.

Ah. There was a more difficult question to answer, if I wanted to hold her interest. In fact, I hadn't really been terribly close to anyone for a very long time. I'd always been well enough liked, always well regarded and respected, but having few enemies was not the same as having friends, and there was no denying that I'd been, for many years, more solitary than most. In Glasgow, I'd lived alone, and it wasn't unusual for me to say goodbye to my colleagues on a Friday evening and then not speak again until I greeted them hello the following Monday morning. I was by no means miserable – there was satisfaction in my work, a cinema half a mile from my door, the occasional pint with a few colleagues on a Friday night – but there were certainly times when I found myself wishing for a little more excitement in life.

This wish came true soon after Lena and I were reunited. Lena made friends quickly and easily, and from our first day together in London she was keen to involve me in all her social activities. There were dinners with colleagues and many late nights, and for the first time in years I found myself having tremendous fun.

As the months passed, Lena and I began to spend more and more time alone together, grabbing lunch at our favourite cafés, or catching a movie after work, or spending an entire weekend walking around the city. Somehow, by Christmas, we'd fallen in love, and by the following summer things had become so serious that Lena moved in with me. I couldn't believe it. Within a year, we'd gone from being perfect strangers living in separate countries to lovers sharing the same apartment. It was a relationship that should never have worked. But it did.

Except, of course, when it didn't.

Which it hasn't.

For months.

I'd hoped that Lena might have made herself comfortable on the sofa in the few minutes since she arrived at the door, but she still looks tense. I'm about to try and offer her a coffee again when she clears her throat and tells me she can't stay long. 'I was really just looking to grab the last of my stuff.'

Ah. So, she's here for her clothes. And here I was thinking that maybe, just maybe, she'd come here for me. Stupid Tom.

Stupid, stupid, Tom.

I must look as disappointed as I feel, because Lena immediately offers an olive branch. 'I'm free next week if you'd like to meet for coffee.'

'I can't,' I tell her. 'I'm going home.'

'Home? To Myreton? Why?'

'Cancer. Again.'

'Lorraine?'

I nod. 'It's here to stay this time.'

'Oh god, Tom,' Lena says. She stands and moves towards me, her arms outstretched, but I shake my head and turn away. I want more than anything to be held, but if she holds me now, I know she'll cry, and if she does, then I probably will, and I can't let that happen, can't let her see me with my defences down. Lena lets her arms fall back down to her side, her chin beginning to tremble as the first tears start to well in her eyes. We are standing only a yard from one another, but neither of us can bear to look the other in the eyes.

My god, how did it come to this? It hardly seems possible when I think back to the first few freewheeling years of our lives together. Back then we talked endlessly about how close we were, about the strength of our connection, about how no other couple had ever been so entirely *made* for one another. What did it matter if I left stubble in the bathroom sink, or Lena slurped her cup of tea each evening? Who cared if I sang the same line of a song for three days straight, or Lena pronounced the 'L' in salmon? Not us, that's for sure. We were *perfect* together. Nothing either of us did could have taken the shine off the other's contentment.

Time could, though. And it would. Before too long, the sex that had previously dominated our relationship became less urgent, and it wasn't unheard of for us to postpone it in favour of a new series on Netflix or a quick snooze on the sofa. Dinnertime moved from the kitchen table to the living room sofa, where conversation was quickly replaced by the Channel 4 News. We stopped bothering to suppress our farts and gave up timing our toilet breaks so we wouldn't inflict our smells on one another. Phone calls to friends grew longer and more frequent, and when we left the flat alone for a night out with mates we secretly rejoiced at the promise of a few hours of freedom. This isn't to say that things were any worse than before; it was just no longer the free ride that we'd enjoyed during those first heady months of our relationship.

But then, last winter, things *did* get worse. I don't know if it was the recent stress of my mother's illness or the pressure of working in the post-crisis banking industry, but I sank into a sort of depression. For more than a month I dragged myself out of bed and endured the stress of work, feeling sick with anxiety, sitting unhearing in meeting after pointless meeting. I wasn't getting a good night's sleep any more. I fell into bed exhausted, I tossed and turned for hours, and woke up even more exhausted. It wore me down. It wore Lena down. It wore us both down until, one morning in early December, I took a taxi to my doctor and was signed off work for a month.

Lena was an angel throughout. She would call me every day from the office, knowing that I was at home and knowing that I would not pick up. At night, she would return home to find me lying on the sofa in old clothes, sometimes with the television playing too loud, sometimes in silence with a bottle of wine by my side. She'd tidy up after me as best she could, then cook some healthy meal for us and join me on the sofa.

It was just after Christmas that I began to think seriously about leaving my job. It had taken me a long while to fully realise how unsuited I was to the finance sector. The whole industry was based on a lot of things like passion, initiative and driving ambition that I simply didn't possess. I think I'd come to suspect this a couple of years earlier, but I'd managed to push the doubts to the back of my mind by forcing myself to stay busy, burying myself in my meaningless work. But then I reached my breaking point, and I was finally forced to put my life in perspective. That's when I realised I was extremely unhappy, and that I had been for some time.

I was terrified of the way Lena would react when I finally told her how I felt. Lena loved her work. It made sense to her. It bent to her will and her sense of logic, and the thought that anybody might fail to share this devotion to their career was almost alien to her. I wasn't surprised, then, when Lena flew into a rage on hearing of my plan. Was my job really so unbearable, she asked between sobs. How the hell did I expect us to survive in London on a single salary? Had I considered how much more pressure my decision would place on her? Was there any goddamn limit to my selfishness?

Over the next few weeks, something gave way. Our relationship became a Jenga tower, and one by one we began pulling out the pieces, the structure increasingly fragile. We argued furiously and relentlessly about everything, shouting insults that left us both hoarse the next morning. When, on the first Monday of April, I handed in my notice at work, the tower tumbled, blocks spilling everywhere. Two days later, Lena packed her bags and left the flat for good.

Now, after six months, Lena's so desperate to escape the flat all over again that she practically leaps from the sofa when I give her the green light to collect her things. Thankfully, it's a good deal tidier in the bedroom. This is partly because most of the clothes that should be here have somehow found their way into the living room since Lena's departure. But also...

'Tom, what happened to your things?'

Yes, it's also because everything else I used to keep in here is now gone. All through our time together, this bedroom played host to my separate collections of movies, books, music, comics and coins, lovingly assembled over a period of fifteen years or more. The collections were my pride and joy, extravagantly displayed in a variety of custom-made folders, shelves, frames and boxes. I used to joke that they'd be the first thing I rescued if ever we suffered a fire, that I'd still be cradling them on the street outside our home when Lena's charred remains were wheeled from the building on a gurney. How, then, to explain their absence? I decide to tell the truth.

'You *sold* them?' Lena says, incredulous. 'My god, I didn't... Are you struggling? For money?'

I tell her I'm not, though in truth my finances are rather less than tickety-boo. After I quit my job, I'd assumed that, with a bit of careful planning, I'd manage to keep my head above water for a year with the savings I had in the bank. But London has an incredible knack of gobbling up money in ways you never thought existed, and now, less than six months later, I'm down to one meal a day and genuinely considering selling a couple of body parts to make ends meet. I could try to find a flatmate, of course, but I don't want to do that for the same reason that I don't want to find somewhere cheaper to live. Any change to my living arrangements would signify moving on, and I don't want that. What I want is to forget the past few months ever happened and go back to living my life the way it was before.

While Lena gathers her things from the wardrobe, I walk over to the bedroom window. The street outside is empty except for a well-dressed man who's drumming his fingers against the steering wheel of his idling convertible. It's a cold October morning, so I wonder why he hasn't bothered to put the top back up. For appearances, probably. He certainly looks like a show-off, what with his expensive suit and cashmere scarf. He's probably sporting some designer stubble too, I think, and sure enough this is confirmed a moment later when he glances up at the building and...

I squint my eyes, press my nose to the glass. 'Is that... Jeff?' I ask. 'Oh. Lena, look, it's Jeff. What's he doing here?'

I look around to Lena, who's standing, frozen, by the bed. All colour has drained from her face. After a moment my brain reaches the obvious conclusion, and the colour drains from my face too.

'Tom,' Lena says, but I'm not listening. I stumble across the room and sit down on the bed. If I don't, my legs are going to buckle.

'Tom,' Lena says again. 'I'm so sorry,'

'Oh my god,' I hear myself say. 'Oh my god. I can't believe this is happening.'

And I really can't. This is an absolute nightmare. I mean, Lena and Jeff. Lena, my wife, and Jeff. Hot Jeff from main office. Jeff the Boss. A thousand images run through my confused mind until it settles on one, a picture of Jeff and my wife on Jeff's expensive mattress in the bedroom of Jeff's expensive bachelor pad. Lena and Jeff. Lena, my wife, and Jeff. Fucking. I shake my head as hard as I can, but the image fails to disappear.

Jeff swaggered into our lives seven years ago, when he was promoted to manager of the building Lena and I both worked in. Billed as one of the brightest stars within the company by the director who introduced us on his first morning in the job, Jeff's penchant for dispensing the inspirational truisms he'd accumulated during his twenty years in the trenches, coupled with his phenomenally short temper, had made him universally despised within the office by the end of his first week. He was forever touching base, always asking to be kept in the loop. He was all about closing the deal, making the sale. 'Any performance I give, I give 110%,' he'd say. 'Never forget to think outside the box,' he'd say. 'The journey of a thousand miles begins with a single step,' he'd say. And my particular favourite: 'Success is rented, not owned – and rent is due every day.'

Yes, this was a man who knew he was the shit, who believed entirely in himself and was not afraid to show it.

The fact that he was a complete moron who'd already been promoted way above his station wasn't going to stop him from continuing his clichéd rise within the company. After all, he'd never been afraid to reach for the stars. His dreams would come true because he had the courage to pursue them. He'd thrown off the bowlines. Sailed away from the safe harbour. Caught the trade winds in his sails. He was king of the world!

Jeff quickly became a figure of fun for Lena and I. Some nights we would sit for hours, a bottle of wine between us, laughing ourselves hoarse over his latest attempt to motivate his people. I was able to do a half-decent impersonation of him that frequently reduced Lena to tears of laughter.

But then, as time wore on, Lena seemed to grow tired of the jokes. At first, she simply refused to laugh at them, but later, as our problems deepened, she began to offer some words in Jeff's defence. She had a point, of course; at their heart, the jokes were really just the cheap attempts of an insecure beta-male to counter the charm and good looks of his alpha rival within the office. Still, Lena and I were a team, had always been a team, and so I felt more than a little betrayed by the change of allegiance when it began to appear. Now, I realise that I should probably have been a little suspicious, too.

The fact is that Jeff is not without charm. In fact, providing he holds his temper, he has charm in abundance. He's tall and rugged-looking, with silver-fox hair and dark eyes that make women go weak at the knees. His teeth are several shades whiter than anything you can find in nature, and he shows off his muscles by wearing clothes so firmly fitted that the slightest unintentional movement risks setting off an explosion of stitches.

'So, I guess you got the kind of rich, successful man you always wanted, huh?'

Lena stiffens. 'I don't know what you mean,' she says. But she does. I can tell she does.

'Just tell me. How long has it been going on?'

Lena shifts her weight nervously from one foot to the other. 'A while.'

'A while,' I find myself repeating. 'So, did it start before or after you left me?'

'I never slept with him while we were together.'

'But it started before we broke up,' I say. 'I mean, he's the reason you left me, right?'

Lena lifts her gaze, forces it to meet mine. 'There were a hundred reasons I left you, Tom.'

I wasn't expecting that, and it hurts.

Lena throws out a couple of long sighs while I try not to burst into tears, or vomit over my duvet, or both. 'You know what really sucks,' I say, when I'm able to speak again, 'is that you had him drive you here to collect your shit. I mean, you couldn't even do *that* much alone.'

'I asked him to wait for me around the corner.'

'Well, that was very thoughtful of you, wasn't it? If he wasn't such a cretin, he might even have followed your instructions.'

'Tom, please...' Lena says.

But I wave a hand at her, begging her to stop talking. 'No,' I say. 'No. I think you should just leave. I think you should just... get the fuck out of my home.'

Lena's face looks as though it's been freeze-framed in one of those movie special effects that lets the rest of the world just carry on as usual around the frozen object.

'NOW!' I yell.

It gives me some comfort to see Lena wince at this. She's

seldom seen me lose my temper, and she could count on one hand the times the anger's been directed at her. I see that her pride is hurt, that she's desperate to offer some words in her defence, but she can sense my fury and balks at the challenge. Swallowing back her own anger, she grabs her bag of clothes, swings it over her shoulder and storms out of the room. When I hear the front door slam a moment later, I run to the window and throw my curtains shut, desperate to put as much of a barrier between me and that bastard Jeff as I possibly can.

When I finally remember to start breathing again, I walk over to the wardrobe and examine the space where Lena's clothes used to be. For the past six months I've felt nothing but hatred towards those clothes, for the memories they held and the feelings they forced upon me. Now that they're gone, I suddenly realise that, for the first time, there's nothing to show that Lena ever lived in this apartment, not one thing to show for all the happy years we spent here together. I want nothing more than to go into hibernation in this dark, lonely room, but I'm due to catch a train in less than three hours. With something approaching panic, I drag my own suitcase out of the wardrobe and begin packing for my journey home to Myreton.

THREE

IT'S RAINING HARD WHEN I ARRIVE IN EDINBURGH'S WAVERLEY Station, which makes the thought of standing on Princes Street in wait for the notoriously unreliable bus service to Myreton even less appealing than usual. Since quitting my job I've been careful not to spend any money unless it's absolutely necessary, but I'm tired and the rain's already begun to soak my clothes, so I throw up a hand and hail a taxi to take me the final twenty miles of my journey home.

There's another reason why I've chosen the solitude of a taxi: I'm panicking. This is my first visit home in eight months, and the first I've made without Lena in nearly a decade. Since Lena left, I've continued to insist to my family that the break's temporary, that Lena and I are just taking some time out to consider our relationship. But in recent times, it's become increasingly difficult to convince them this is still the case. After all, how much time can a couple need to think about their future together? Even I know that six months is pushing it.

According to Lena, I should even have finished grieving by now. 'It's been six months,' she said this morning when she became fully aware of my unhappiness. It hurt to hear that, almost as much as it hurt to see the accompanying look of confusion on her face. Couldn't she at least have made some effort to hide her surprise at my misery? Didn't she feel any misery of her own? Could she truly be over the worst of it already?

Well, of course she was. Quite possibly, she was already over the worst of it when she first jumped ship. Until yesterday, I always imagined that she'd taken up with one of her girlfriends after she left me. I pictured her crying into the armrest of an unfamiliar sofa each night, mourning the loss of her husband, terrified by the probability of spending the rest of her life alone. Now, I think about the night she left me and imagine her making a beeline for Jeff's apartment, falling gratefully into his arms. Yes, six months was certainly enough time to get over a relationship when you had a new and better model waiting in the wings.

Before I know it, the taxi has reached the summit of Myreton Hill. The hill is home to the entire village nobility, lawyers and bankers who commute to Edinburgh each day from their Victorian mansions and Edwardian villas. There are forty or fifty of these buildings, each leading onto a wide cul-de-sac that's long been known in the village as Millionaire's Row. At the very end of this road, where the tarmac gives way to miles of green grass, stands my parents' house.

I walk up the driveway, the familiar crunch of gravel beneath my feet. Ahead of me stands the towering three-storey building, its white walls shining even in the gloom of this dingy afternoon. Standing proudly at the centre of my mother's garden, its elaborate bay windows and high tower have long made it the envy of Myreton's more materialistic residents. It's beautiful, for sure, and many men far richer than my father would be proud to own it, but with eight bedrooms and an acre of garden, my overwhelming thought when I arrive home is always the same: what do my parents possibly need with all this space?

I'm still considering this when an old car, too small and rusty to belong to my father, makes its way from the side of the tennis court and down the driveway towards me. The girl at the wheel looks vaguely familiar, but the car's moving quickly and she has a handkerchief pressed against her eyes, so I don't quite manage to put a name to the face. As she passes me, she waves, unsmiling. I put up a hand and wave back, continuing to gaze stupidly at the car until it turns from our drive onto the main road.

As I approach the main entrance to the house, I see my father's peafowl huddled by the stone fountain. Dad bought the birds around twenty-five years ago. The flock used to be larger, but it's dying out now, and all that remains are seven females and one colourful male, Christopher.

Peafowl, by nature, are fairly placid birds, but Mother Nature forgot to inform Chris of this fact. Chris has been angry his entire life, a feathered ball of rage who unleashes his full wrath on anything or anybody that appears in his line of vision, regardless of its size and strength. Given this, I'm rather surprised he's managed to survive for as long as he has, though his years of fighting have come at an obvious cost. His beak is chipped in more than one place, and his once-proud tail is now missing as many feathers as it holds. There's a crusted lump where his left eye used to be, and a scar runs across his throat from a fight he once had with our resident fox. There was a time, many years ago, when the sight of Chris's feathers had visitors clasping their hands together in wonder; nowadays, his ravaged form more often has them recoiling in horror.

I've always known the birds are incredibly dim-witted,

and confirm this once more by taking my hands out of my pocket and making a flicking motion, at which point the entire group starts towards me. I'd half hoped that they might know better, that they are capable of perceiving from only a few yards that I have nothing for them, but instead they walk towards me, bobbing around on the gravel in search of the crumbs I've pretended to throw. They can see there's nothing there, but they continue searching anyway.

'Stupid creatures,' I grumble, and immediately, as if offended by the remark, Christopher lifts his head and sets his big, black eye on me. Spreading out his enormous tail, he opens his beak, his dark, toothless maw surprisingly menacing, and takes a few steps forward. I've had enough encounters with Chris over the years to know when it's time to run away. Offering a parting bow to him and his lady friends, I turn on my heels and make quickly for the front of the house.

It's Dad who answers the door. He's a tall man, six two or three, and despite his age his posture is still good. He stands strong and upright, with a straight back, and his eyes still gleam with life. Despite this, there's something different about him today. Though he's as smartly dressed as always, his hair is ruffled and a shirttail is hanging down beneath his jumper. His white beard, I realise, has grown so long that the fraying tips are touching the front collar of his shirt. *Oh god*, I think, *she's not even gone yet and already he looks dishevelled.*

I step forward and surprise us both by throwing an arm around Dad and pulling him into an embrace. I can count on my fingers the number of times we've hugged like this since I finished school, and we're both clearly out of practise. My stubble brushes against his cheek and he stiffens, putting one hand on my shoulder instinctively as if to fend off an attack. After a moment, though, he appears to remember that I'm his child, and draws me closer to him. 'It's good to see you, Son,' he says, into my neck.

I nod my head, then step back to sneak another look at my father. 'How are you?' I ask.

Dad sighs. 'Well, Tom, we've been better. A good deal better. But we're making the best of things.'

It's the answer I expected. Dad has the very stiffest of upper lips, the result of a strict upbringing and a decade as the director of a fast-paced investment firm, a role that would have sent lesser men crazy with anxiety.

'How is she?' I ask. Perhaps he'll have something positive to say.

Dad's eyes fall to the ground. 'She's not so great, Son. I'm afraid the situation's rather advanced.'

'Oh,' I say. 'And the chemo?'

Dad shakes his head sadly. 'It's too late for all that. In any case, your mother already told me she had her fill of poison last time around.' He presses his lips together, and the lines grow long down the side of his face. 'Listen, Tom, I hate to say it, but time's not really on our side here. I'm sorry, but we need to start preparing for the worst.'

I give him a slow nod and open my mouth to speak, but can think of nothing to say, so shut it again and swallow. After a moment, Dad clears his throat, passes his hand over his jaw. 'Anyway,' he says, 'your mother's up in her room. I'm sure she'll be delighted to see you.'

I haven't been home for a while, but the house remains unchanged. The large hallway is beautifully furnished and impeccably neat. I cross the heavily-waxed floor to the foot of the wide staircase, where I'm greeted by the same collection of photographs, representing a kind of loose chronology of the Halliday family, that crowds the pastel-coloured walls. When I reach the first floor, I creep cautiously towards my mother's room, not particularly eager to reach my destination. When I reach the door, I poke my head inside to find my mother lying in bed, her head propped up by a mountain of pillows. She appears to be asleep, but when she hears me by the doorway her eyes open and she pats the bed, beckoning me to her. I tiptoe across the room and perch self-consciously on the edge of her mattress.

'Lorraine,' I say. 'How are you?'

My mother smiles, as though smiling itself has become an effort. 'The doctors have been very kind,' she says, skilfully avoiding an answer to my question.

I can hardly believe how much she's changed in the eight months since I saw her. Her wrinkles, kept expensively at bay for so many years, have become more visible, like little ploughed lines, and her hair has come loose in places and dangles on her cheeks and forehead. Stupidly, I was expecting that she'd have lost her hair just like last time, but of course there's been no therapy since the second diagnosis.

Something else has changed. All my life, my mother carried with her the scent of expensive perfumes and sweet-scented toiletries. Today, though, the air around her has a far more primitive odour, a hospital smell that's almost more disturbing than my mother's appearance.

I'm trying hard to hide my distress, but I'm obviously doing a bad job. 'There's no need to look so glum,' my mother says. 'Cheer up a little, won't you?'

When my mother gives an order, it's best to follow without question. Lorraine Halliday is a woman the winds and tides obey. 'I'm sorry,' I say, swallowing down my emotion. 'I'll be stronger.'

'I should think so. These things happen when you get old, Tom. I'm no spring chicken, you know.'

'You're sixty-four,' I say.

My mother considers this for a moment. 'Well, I feel old.'

It's not easy to hear her talking like this. Breathing hard, I stand up from the bed and walk towards the large bay window at the foot of her room. From there, I look out onto a picture-postcard view of Myreton, with its rows of pretty houses, charming little shops and ancient church, whose ivy-coated ruins provide a centrepiece for the high street. From the same window, you can also see the long, sandy shoreline to the north of the village, while to the south a final row of old stone cottages gives way to miles and miles of patchwork fields. You can't see the golf course that lies to the east of this room, but if you want to do so you only need to step through to Dad's office, which offers a perfect view of the eleventh tee. It's always been one of my mother's great pleasures to own the only house in Myreton with a three-sixty-degree view of the village.

'So how long are you planning to stay?' my mother asks, after a moment.

I look back at her, and realise that she has no idea why I'm here. 'I'm home for a while,' I tell her. 'Sophie too. We're going to help take care of you.'

'Home?' she says. 'Here?'

I nod.

'Oh, no, Tom. You can't. What about your work?'

'I don't work.'

'Yes, but surely you're looking for a job.'

I shrug. 'I'll put the search on hold for a while.'

My mother shakes her head. 'No,' she says, adamantly. 'No no no no no. Not you. Sophie, I can understand.

Anything to get away from that awful husband of hers for a few weeks. But not you. Not you. You have your career to think of.'

'Nevertheless,' I say. 'I'm staying.'

My mother stares at me for a long moment, and then sighs. 'Can we at least expect Lena to join you here at any point?'

'What do you mean by that?'

She folds her hand across her chest. 'I'm simply asking whether your wife has chosen to take you back yet.'

My head snaps back as though I've been slapped. 'Take me back? You make it sound like everything that happened was my fault.'

My mother raises her eyebrows.

'Well, she hasn't,' I tell her. 'And if you must know, it's not looking terribly likely that she will.'

'What do you mean?'

'Just what I said. I wouldn't raise your hopes of a reunion if I were you.'

My mother looks crestfallen. She might never have liked Bill, but she's always loved Lena. I remember how bewildered she was the first time I brought Lena home to Myreton. Who was this beautiful, glamorous, outspoken creature holding hands with her son? 'Presumably she got tired of sleeping with film stars and models,' she whispered when Lena nipped off to the toilet, leaving me in no doubt, from the first possible moment, that she considered me to be punching well above my weight.

Still, she's clearly not ready to give up hope just yet. 'Have you tried speaking about it with Peter?'

'I can't see how that would help,' I say, testily. Though only three years separate us, Pete's already married his college sweetheart, fathered two beautiful young children, and built up an unassailable lead over me on the career path, achievements that have all helped to further cement his status as the successful son. My mother has never actually said it out loud, but it's clear what she's suggesting; if I want to get ahead in life, I should learn to take a leaf or two out of my brother's book.

I'd begun to feel calmer in the past couple of minutes, but now my chest starts to fill with resentment, the way it always does when I'm forced to think of my brother. I begin to search for a way to change the subject, and as if by magic the name of the girl I saw in the car outside the house suddenly returns to me.

'Emma Barnes,' I say, looking to my mother. 'I could swear Emma Barnes just drove past me as I walked up the drive.'

'I'm sure she did. I've hired her to look after me for the next few weeks.'

I'm surprised by this. I spent my first seven years at school with Emma, but I've seen her only a handful of times in the past twenty years. A few years back, all sorts of rumours spread around the village about her, whispers about a breakdown and an eating disorder and a spell in hospital in London or Glasgow or something like that. The last time I saw her was about six years ago, walking along the beach with her older brother, James. She'd looked terribly skinny back then.

'I'd no idea she'd qualified as a nurse,' I say.

'She hasn't qualified as anything,' my mother says. 'I've plenty of doctors and nurses around me. Emma's here simply to provide me with some company until... until I no longer need it.'

Right on cue, Emma re-enters the room, carrying a bag from the local pharmacy. Her eyes are red and blotchy, so I realise the handkerchief she was holding earlier must have been to blot out tears. She looks almost as tired as my mother, yet when she sees me, she stops in her tracks and smiles. 'Tom! My god, I *thought* it was you I saw before. How are you?'

'I'm not so bad,' I say. And it's true. I really do feel better now she's here. It was always like this, even back at school. When she smiled, you could never help but smile with her, and your body filled with a warmth that would carry you through the rest of the day. She never believed it, but she was easily one of the most popular kids in class. Everybody liked her. She was just the sort of person you couldn't help liking.

'How are you doing?' I ask.

'Oh, I'm just fine, thank you.' Even after all these years, her manner is the same. There's a shyness to her, a hesitation in her movements and a softness in her voice.

'And the job?' I ask. 'How's that going?'

'I'm enjoying it. Very much.'

'She's been an angel,' my mother says. 'It's been wonderful to have her around.'

Emma's cheeks flush slightly at this compliment, but she nods in gratitude to my mother. Despite her obvious weariness, I'm relieved to see that she looks a great deal better than that afternoon on the beach. With her long hair pulled up in a swinging ponytail, it's easy to see how her face has filled out, how it now resembles that of the happy little girl I knew in school. She's dressed in a thick black jumper and a pair of faded jeans tucked into Doc Martens, and while she's still slim – probably a little slimmer than it's healthy to be – her clothes no longer hang off her like they did a few years back. She appears to be wearing no make-up, and the only jewellery I can see is a thin silver bracelet on her wrist.

Everything about her is plain and understated and ordinary. It's a wonderful thing to find her looking so well.

'So, how are you enjoying London?' she asks me.

'Oh, it's fine,' I tell her, 'Despite being noisy and polluted, and chock-full of pigeons with warty feet.'

Emma grimaces. 'Doesn't sound so good.'

'No. They get infections, from all those hours standing in their own crap. Still, they seem happy enough, so whatever.'

Emma bites her lip, stifling a smile. 'I meant your life there generally.'

'Oh! Well, that's not so bad. I mean, it's not perfect but, you know, I'm alright. I have my home. And my health.'

'And your feet,' Emma says, helpfully.

'Yes,' I say. 'And also, I have my feet.'

Emma smiles, then looks down at the chemist's bag she's still holding. 'Well, I'd better go and sort these pills with the others. It was nice to see you, Tom. I'll catch up with you again soon, maybe.'

'I hope so,' I say, and wave a hand goodbye.

When she's gone, I turn around to speak once more with my mother, but her eyes are closed.

'Lorraine?' I ask. 'Are you there?' But she only snuffles in reply.

I have to admit I'm relieved, though it's a relief that can't be shown. 'Alright,' I say, with an attempt at nonchalance. 'See you later, then.'

I pray that she'll continue to sleep until I'm safely out of the room.

FOUR

NIGHT COMES QUICKLY TO MYRETON, WHERE STREETLIGHTS
are at a minimum and frequently obscured by the huge
trees that line the village streets. By the time I've unpacked
my suitcase and thrown on some fresh clothes, it's
completely dark outside, the meagre light emanating from
our neighbours' houses barely making a dent in the thick
blanket of surrounding darkness. Still, the rain seems to be
holding off for now, and it's only a short walk from my
parents' house to the home of my brother, so I refuse Dad's
offer to lend me his car and set off on foot instead.

I feel the benefit of being outside almost immediately.
After spending months buried in the city, I'm delighted to
find myself surrounded once more by countryside. Here
there's a clarity in the air, a sense of space and vitality that
makes me feel like I've shed something on the road to home.
The confinement of the city, the staleness, the grime - they
all seem to have fallen away from me in the hours since my
return.

It's not long until Pete's house comes into view. Pete
returned to Myreton within a year of graduating from

university, complete with an impressive job, a sharp new wardrobe and a ferocious determination to surpass the achievements of his father. Now, fifteen years later, the fire of ambition continues to burn so bright that he's working fifteen-hour days and will presumably continue to do so, either until he's made director of his investment firm in Edinburgh or the stress of reaching this goal finally kills him.

Pete still has some work to do before he even comes close to matching Dad's success, but he's undoubtedly on track. He's been promoted four times in the past decade, and on the past three occasions has rewarded himself by moving house, each one a little larger, a little more elaborate, and a little closer to the foot of Myreton Hill than the last. He's so close to the hill now he can almost smell the caviar from his neighbours' kitchens. Without a doubt, his mouth's already watering at the prospect of taking his place back among the Myreton elite. Without a doubt, he's already planning the parties he'll hold when he finally sits down on his throne.

He could not be more like our mother if he tried.

I walk through Pete's gate onto a long driveway, at the end of which sits a large, two-storey property, designed with the look and feel of a Tudor country house. The building is a pleasant white, with a gabled roof and decorative timbering on its walls. To one side sits an old converted stable, which acts as a guest quarter, and to the other is a double garage, home to Rose's beloved Saab and Pete's showy BMW.

Just about anyone on the face of this earth would be satisfied with the house Pete lives in, and why Pete can't just make himself comfortable here is beyond me. It's certainly big enough; he has more bedrooms than he needs, a second reception room that he never uses, and a garden he rarely visits. I suppose some people just have such exceptional taste that it's impossible to enjoy anything.

When I ring the bell, it's not Pete who answers but his wife, Rose. 'Tom!' she says, beaming. 'What a lovely surprise! Pete didn't tell us you were coming to Myreton.'

Even though she's most likely been up since dawn and wearing a bobbly sweater that's at least ten years past retirement, Rose, as always, looks stunning. She's cradling her baby daughter, Ellie, in her arms, while Crawford, her three-year-old, races wildly around her legs with a plastic dinosaur. 'Darling?' she says, grabbing at Crawford's collar. 'Darling, do you remember... Darling? DARLING, WOULD YOU SAY HELLO TO YOUR UNCLE!'

Panting frantically, Crawford throws down his dinosaur and runs up to my thighs, his little hands raised for me to pick him up. I do, kissing each of his soft baby cheeks. 'How you doing, little man?' I ask. But he's already squirming to get down. As soon as his feet touch the floor, he gathers up his dinosaur and disappears into the depths of the house. Rose watches him disappear, sighs, and returns her attention to me. 'He had some chocolate buttons with lunch,' she explains. 'I thought they'd have worn off by now, but...' She shakes her head, before looking down towards the little bundle she's holding in her arms. 'At least one of them knows the value of silence.'

'She's sleeping?' I ask.

Rose nods. 'I know. It's hard to believe it's possible with a foghorn for a brother. Take a look.'

I crane my neck and look towards Ellie, who's sleeping peacefully in the crook of Rose's elbow. 'Wow. She got so big.'

Rose smiles proudly. 'She'll be eleven months tomorrow. She's just getting herself ready to walk.' She beams down at the face, gives the chubby little cheeks a gentle pinch.

'And how's Pete?' I ask.

'Fine, I think, though I haven't seen him since yesterday. He'd already left for work when I got up this morning.'

'And he's still working?'

Rose raises an eyebrow. 'He's *always* working. But come in, won't you? He already called to say he was leaving the office, so he shouldn't be long.'

When we reach the lounge, Rose motions for me to take a seat, but my legs are still so restless after my journey from London that I choose to remain standing.

'I was sorry to hear about you and Lena,' she says. Her soft Irish accent fills her words with such touching sincerity that I feel close to tears.

I don't know what to say, so I make do with a shrug. Rose understands, and smiles. 'I know it's hard now,' she says, 'but one day you're going to love again, and it will be magnificent. Like Rumi said, the heart is the place that the Light enters... GAAAAGH!'

Now, I'm pretty sure that Rumi never said that. I'm not precisely sure what Rumi did say, but I'm certain that whatever he said didn't include the word 'GAAAAGH'. I'm certain that Rose knows this too, and that she really didn't mean to say it. And I'm pretty sure of that, because 'GAAAAGH' is exactly the same thing I scream when Crawford suddenly jumps in front of us from behind the living room table, baring his teeth and letting out a yell that would put a banshee to shame.

Crawford's clearly delighted by the outcome of his little trick. 'I fightened you!' he screams, giggling.

'Yes, you did,' I say, gripping my chest.

Crawford lifts his chin, proudly. 'Shall we play cats?' he asks.

I've always hated role-play, but I'm eager to curry favour with my nephew, so I nod politely. However, just as I'm about to deliver my best kitty impression, Crawford cocks his arm backwards and launches his dinosaur towards me. I haven't even had time to blink before it cracks me square on the temple. Clutching my head, I stare dumbfoundedly at Crawford, who only looks disappointed. 'Aaw,' he says, his shoulders slumping. 'You didn't cats it.'

Pete arrives home a few minutes later. Throwing his briefcase onto a nearby chair, he plants a kiss on Rose's cheek and makes little cooing noises at Ellie, who began to stir following Crawford's recent rebel yell. Crawford himself has wandered off to the fireplace, where he sits crashing his T-Rex over a pile of matchbox cars. If he's noticed that his father has returned home from work, he's doing a marvellous job of hiding it.

Pete spends an age kicking off his shoes and loosening his tie before finally strolling over to my side. 'Hey Tom,' he says, hugging me hard with one arm. 'You look like shit.' I feel irritated that he's not more touched to find me in his home, though I know this is irrational, because I'm not exactly overjoyed to see him either.

'Can I get you boys a beer?' Rose asks. I nod and so does Pete, though he'd clearly rather just fall asleep. I glance at him and instantly feel annoyed because, despite his obvious weariness, he still looks fantastic.

This isn't to say that I'm unattractive. In fact, you could probably call me handsome, if you bothered to look hard enough. I've inherited my mother's blue eyes and thick brown hair, as well as my father's jawline, which is just about strong enough to make up for a somewhat pasty complexion. I'm of average height, and have an average build, and my years of football training at school have ensured that I'll carry a decent muscle definition into my forties.

With Pete, though, it's different. He doesn't even have to try to look good. Despite having worked out approximately zero times in the past fifteen years, he stands just a little bit taller, has shoulders just a little bit broader, and a face just a little bit squarer than anybody else in the family. Two years shy of forty, he still has a full head of hair and heavy, solemn brows that are offset by deep blue eyes and a boyish grin. On my best day, I'm lucky if I look like Pete with the flu.

Rose arrives back with two bottles of beer and hands one each to Pete and me. She acknowledges my thanks, then turns to Pete. 'Our son just smashed his tyrannosaurus against his Uncle Tom's forehead.'

For the first time this evening, Pete smiles. He turns proudly toward Crawford, who's adding a crushed strawberry to the mess he's created on the carpet, and shakes his head admiringly. 'What's he like?' he says.

Challenging, I want to say. *It's no wonder Rose looks exhausted.*

Pete's spirits have clearly been revived by my injury, because he stands up and makes his way back over to little Ellie. 'Aww, look at you,' he says. 'Look at you all wide awake. Who's Daddy's little tiger?' He holds his hands out towards her, making his fingers into claws. 'Uhr!' he says, baring his teeth. 'Uhr, uhr!'

Ellie pulls herself tight against Rose's shoulder. 'Pete,' Rose says. 'She doesn't like it.'

'Nonsense,' Pete says, laughing, and to prove his point he bares his teeth again. 'Uhr!' he says. Ellie shakes her head tearfully, buries her face between her mother's breasts.

'Pete,' Rose warns, but the conversation ends there, because Crawford, suddenly aware of the game playing out on our side of the room, cannons towards us and launches a foot between his father's legs. He doesn't connect quite right, though I doubt Pete would agree. He glances fleetingly at each of us, his whitening face awash with fear and confusion. Then the pain hits and he crumbles, cross-eyed, to his knees.

'Uhr!' he says, again. It's clear this time that he really means it.

For a moment, we all watch as Pete squirms on the carpet, simultaneously gasping for air and clutching his groin. Then Rose plops Ellie on the sofa and moves to bring Pete up to a sitting position. 'No!' Pete rasps. 'Here... Fine... Take them.' He motions to the kids. 'Bed... Go.'

Rose gives Pete's head a sympathetic pat and then stands up to gather Crawford and Ellie. In fairness to Crawford, he looks almost as traumatised by what's happened as his father. 'I only wanted to kick his bum-bum,' he says, as Pete slides into a foetal position by his feet. Rose strokes his arm and tells him not to worry, that Daddy will be fine. When Crawford nods, she kisses me goodnight and turns to take one last look at her husband. 'Feel better soon,' she says. And maybe I'm projecting here, but I would swear, in that moment, that she's fighting back a smile which, left to itself, would split her face in two.

Left alone with Pete, there's nothing to do but sit down with my beer and watch as the colour begins to return to his face. He's breathing normally now, but once in a while he makes a strange whimpering noise, like a crying child, or a wounded puppy. It's fascinating and disturbing in equal measure.

After a few minutes, Pete wobbles to his knees and clambers up to join me on the sofa. Now the pain's lessened somewhat, the look of confusion has returned to his face.

'Are you okay?'

Pete wipes the sweat from his forehead. 'It's like a brain freeze. In my balls.'

'Is it that bad?'

Pete looks up at me curiously. 'What? It never happened to you?' When I shake my head, he clicks his tongue. 'Well, that's one thing you've got on me.'

There follows another silence, longer and more painful than the last. An entire age seems to pass before Pete finally asks whether I've seen Mum since I got back home. When I nod, he asks how I found her.

'Tired,' I say. 'And small. I can't believe the change in her since February.'

Pete sighs. 'She was doing really well until last month. Then the nausea arrived and she just... stopped eating. We told her to see a doctor, but you know what she's like. She said it was just some passing illness, and to mind our own beeswax. So, we did.'

I look at Pete, confused. 'Wait a minute – you've known for a month? Why didn't you tell me?'

'She said it was nothing,' Pete says, defensively. 'How was I supposed to know what was going on?'

'Because... look at her! You must have noticed how much weight she was losing.'

'I see her almost every day, Tom,' Pete says angrily. 'It's not so easy to notice these things about a person when you actually bother to spend a bit of time with them.'

'What's that supposed to mean?'

Pete sighs, throws a hand through his hair. I notice for the first time that patches of grey are collecting around his temples. 'Nothing,' he says. 'Forget I said anything.'

I shake my head. 'I should probably go, anyway. It's been a long day.'

Pete nods and rises tentatively to his feet. Clutching his stomach, he limps ahead of me to the front of the house. He pushes the door open and then rests against the frame, allowing me to pass. I'm a few yards across the driveway when he calls out from behind me. 'I'd have phoned you, Tom, if I'd known how bad things really were. She told me nothing, though. I swear it. I knew nothing.'

I look Pete in the eye for a long moment before nodding, first to him and then to his crotch. 'Go get some ice on old Itchy and Scratchy. They'll be glad of it in the morning.'

Pete makes a move to wave goodbye, but his hand darts back to his stomach before it's even halfway level with his eye. Usually, I'd have rejoiced in the level of suffering he's experienced since I arrived at the house this evening. As things are, though, I simply turn on my heels and begin the walk back home.

I've stood as much company as I can by now, so I creep into my parents' house and tiptoe through the hallway towards the long offshoot behind the main building. This was originally the servants' quarters, back in a time when servants were still required in houses like this, but for the past twenty-odd years it's played host to me and Sophie.

The switch from servant to sibling quarters was far from seamless. The space was long-deserted by the time my parents bought the house, and remained empty for more than a decade after we arrived, the sheer size of the main building rendering it entirely surplus to requirements. But then, during our first term at boarding school, Dad secretly brought in a group of handymen to restore the old annexe to its former glory. Sophie and I were shocked when we arrived home for the Christmas holidays to find water running and toilets flushing in the old dead space. For the past twelve years, we'd hardly dared to venture more than a few feet into the gloomy main corridor of the annexe, having terrified ourselves with a thousand invented stories of the murders and suicides that made up its tragic history. But now, with the rooms transformed, it was impossible to imagine a better place to live. So, when we were done looking around and Dad announced that the entire space was just for us, we literally screamed with joy.

Though it never occurred to us at the time, it was no coincidence that Dad began planning the renovation the very same summer that our family went to shit. Perhaps Sophie and I could have figured it out if we'd calmed down long enough to notice Dad's relief as we shifted our belongings to our new rooms, but more likely we were simply too young at the time to put the pieces of the puzzle together. It was only years later, when we looked back on that miserable period in our lives, that we began to understand Dad's reasons for arranging the work, and to fully appreciate the size of the gesture.

I went in for classic rock in a big way during my mid-teens, which is obviously the last time I redecorated my room. On the far wall, above my bed, hangs an enlarged poster of Kate Bush, in bed with a couple of very lucky dogs on the front cover of her *Hounds of Love* album. Beside the window, which looks out over the garden, is Milton Glaser's classic portrait of Bob Dylan, the young Bob's abundant hair rendered in psychedelic colours against a silhouetted background. Above my oak dresser in the corner there's room for both Debbie Harry, cool as a cucumber in her Camp

Funtime t-shirt, and a stoned but happy-looking Simon and Garfunkel.

It's not only the artwork that's remained untouched in the seventeen years since I fled to university. There are the same CDs by the Hi-Fi, the same crappy knick-knacks by the window. My collection of university textbooks, crisp and unread and a testament to the complete lack of effort I made during my four years in Glasgow, gather dust on the bookshelves. And in the wardrobe, my old, stained gym clothes are hung neatly in a row alongside the kilt I wore for my school leavers dance and an assembly of jumpers and jeans that I'd no longer be seen dead in.

On my desk, there's a photo album. I give it the old stink eye as I spy it from across the room. I haven't looked at a single photograph in all the months that Lena's been away, and I don't intend to start looking again any time soon. It's not an act of bitterness. It's an act of self-preservation. There's simply no way to carry on with my life as it is now if I have to remember how much better things used to be.

But I've seen it now, and there's no putting it out of my mind. It's there, right in front of me, and however much I try to distract myself from that fact, I can't stop looking at it, picturing the photos that lay inside it. I shouldn't go near the thing. There's no way I should go near the thing. And yet...

Before I can think better of it, I grab the album from the desk and throw myself onto my bed.

It took me an entire weekend to put the album together three years ago, and I'm surprised once more by how good it looks. Everything's there; weekends in the garden, summers by the sea, birthdays, holidays, Christmases and Easters. There's me aged nineteen in a club with Gemma, my first girlfriend, who'd leave me the following summer for a tattooed skater boy. Two years later, I'm standing in the pelting rain on the day of my graduation, clutching a certificate that would never completely recover from its soaking. Later still, I'm on a beach in Spain, looking sick and hungover on the final morning of my stag weekend.

Finally, there's me on my wedding day, running with Lena through a sea of confetti, our friends and families cheering wildly to either side of us. I look young and handsome in my family tartan, and Lena is stunningly beautiful, her ivory gown and blonde hair shining like gold in the summer sunshine. We both wear radiant smiles on our faces, flush with the promise that married life supposedly has to offer. I spent the remaining hours of that day as though lost in some wonderful dream. It simply didn't seem possible that I could feel such intense happiness. What had I done to deserve such joy? I could think of no answer to this, and yet here it was, filling my soul, forcing my pulse to quicken and my head to spin.

These memories only serve to remind me of one thing; I'm excruciatingly lonely. I'm lonely in a deep and horrible way that seems almost catastrophic. I no longer know what to do about it. Every night, I have recurring dreams about being with Lena again, holding her peacefully the way I used to when we were tired, speaking with her in low voices. It all feels so real, for a moment or two. Then I remember what happened and wake up feeling so depressed that it's almost impossible to breathe.

I continue to stare dumbly at the photo until a wave of self-pity suddenly washes over me. I'm about one inch from full-on hysterics when, thankfully, there's a knock on the door. Without waiting for an answer, Sophie enters.

'Where have *you* been?' I grumble, sliding the photo album under my pillow with one hand and brushing the tears from my eyes with the other.

'I've been busy.'

'We were expecting you hours ago.'

Sophie bugs her eyes and blows out her cheeks. 'Okay, Mum. Christ, who lit the fuse on *your* tampon?'

I sigh wearily. 'It's been a very long day.'

Sophie grins mischievously. 'You should have spent the afternoon with me in Edinburgh. A bit of retail therapy might have calmed you down.'

'You went... Jesus, Sophie. Have you even seen Mum yet?'

Sophie nods. 'Just now. She looks like shit, huh?'

'Worse than last time,' I say.

'Bet you it almost makes you feel sorry for the old cow.'

'Christ, Sophie, of course I feel sorry for her.'

Sophie considers this and nods slowly, her eyes looking me up and down. 'To tell the truth, you look almost as bad as she does.'

I run a hand self-consciously across my stubbly jaw. 'Well, shit. Thanks a lot.'

'Oh, come on. I didn't mean it that way.'

'Yeah? How did you mean it?'

She's silent for a moment. 'I guess I did mean it.' She shrugs a half-hearted apology, then reaches into her pocket for a packet of cigarettes and a lighter. 'You want one?'

I don't usually smoke, but after such a shit day it seems just the thing to do. Closing the door behind us, we each grab a cigarette and open the window just a crack, taking turns to blow the smoke into the garden. Already, Sophie's presence has begun to lift my spirits, as I knew it would. All my life, Sophie's ability to place things in perspective has been a great help to me. I've always been prone to taking life too seriously, so Sophie provides a natural antidote to my brooding.

'So, what were you doing in Edinburgh?' I ask.

'I met Nilla Hansen for a coffee. There's a place just opened on Rose Street.'

'Nice. Did you have anything to eat?'

'A scone. I wasn't going to 'cos they were out of raspberry jam, but then the waitress suggested I try it with apple sauce instead and, actually, it was really tasty.'

I nod my head, impressed. 'Sounds lovely.'

But Sophie's smile has faded. 'Oh my god,' she says uneasily. 'We're discussing condiments. When did we become so boring?'

I look to her, confused. 'I was always boring.'

Sophie considers this statement for a moment, then makes a mumbling noise of agreement. I'm not remotely offended. Sophie spent her entire youth going from party to party, dressed in clothes that were specifically designed to upset my mother. She was notoriously rowdy, but smart enough to get into Cambridge, where she drank and slept around prodigiously, getting out of bed only long enough to earn a first-class degree in psychology.

I, however, was never wild. I never stayed out late or got way too drunk more than five or six times in my whole life. I didn't sleep around. I had such conservative desires. I liked going to the library. I liked eating too much. I liked making my way through lists of movies they said to watch before you died. This isn't to say I've ever been jealous of Sophie's popularity, or resentful of the hobbies I chose for myself. It's simply to point out that, while Sophie was always fascinating to others, I've always remained rather hopelessly dull.

Still, at least for once I have some interesting news of my own. 'Hey,' I say. 'You'll never guess who I saw yesterday.'

Sophie looks around to me. 'James van der Beek.'

'Ha-ha,' I say, without laughing.

'Prince Andrew,' Sophie continues. 'Jacob Rees-Mogg. St Bernardino of Siena...'

'It was Lena.'

That puts an end to Sophie's game. In fact, for once she seems almost lost for words.

'She came around to collect some things,' I say. 'She... she had Jeff with her.'

Sophie blinks in confusion. 'Jeff? Cheesy Jeff? Jeff of the Thousand Platitudes? That Jeff?'

I nod.

'And you're sure that him and Lena are...'

I nod again.

Sophie lets out a deep breath. 'Ouch. That's got to hurt. What are you going to do?'

'Well, mostly I'm planning to not talk about it. At all. To anybody.'

Sophie nods her head thoughtfully. 'Well, that sounds productive.'

I tap the ash from the end of my cigarette, try to decide whether to take Sophie's bait. Part of me dearly wants to, but after today I've hardly the energy to stand, let alone hold my own in an argument with a seasoned quarreller. Fortunately, Sophie decides to drop the subject, and takes up a new one instead. 'Hey, did you hear Dad's hired Emma Barnes to look after Mum?'

'I know. I already saw her.'

'You *saw* her?' Sophie says, her eyes widening. 'Ooh, I want the gossip.'

'There is no gossip.'

Sophie has been with Bill for fourteen years. Neither of them ever looks at anybody else. They will grow old together. Sophie loves gossip.

'At least tell me how she looked,' Sophie says.

'She was fine,' I say. 'She looked just fine.'

'You know she had a raging eating disorder a few years back, don't you? She was in all kinds of hospitals. I'm pretty sure she even tried to kill herself. Didn't work, though.'

'It didn't? Are you sure?'

Sophie ignores this. 'It must be more than a decade since I spoke to her. The last time I saw her, she looked nearly as awful as Mum does now.'

'My god, Sophie. Don't hold back, will you?'

Sophie smiles and stubs out her cigarette on my windowsill. 'No chance of that,' she says. 'I leave all of that crap to you.'

FIVE

WHEN I WAS SMALL, MY PARENTS WOULD TELL ME THE STORY of how they fell in love. It happened in the spring of 1975, while they were both students at the University of Edinburgh. My father was in the final year of his business degree at the time, while my mother was in her first year of an accountancy course that she'd ultimately abandon when Dad gained his first promotion at the bank a couple of years later. While Dad was being bankrolled through university by his father, my mother's parents had tried everything possible to prevent their daughter from attending university at all. My mother, however, was never going to let a small thing like that prevent her from getting her way; when her parents refused to contribute any money towards her studies, she simply went out and found three jobs, which she worked between classes to pay her tuition and the rent on a tiny flat she shared with five other students. She was working one of these jobs, as a waitress in a Rose Street casino, when Dad first set eyes on her.

As is often the case with these stories, the first encounter between my parents almost never happened. A born introvert and compulsive bookworm, Dad had planned to spend the evening studying for his end-of-term exams, but he'd hardly had time to open his books before his flatmates arrived home from an afternoon's drinking and demanded that he join them for a night on the town. Dad tried to argue, but his friends were stupid with drink, and within seconds he was being manhandled into a taxi that lay idling outside the front door of the flat. Within five minutes, the party had arrived at the casino, and Dad found himself bundled into a chair by the roulette table; a heavy hand remained on each of his shoulders, cutting off any remaining hopes of escape.

Dad was still coming to terms with his kidnapping when he spotted my mother from across the room. He had a 50p bet riding on black number 17 at the time, but never stirred when the number came up. Noticing this, his friends followed his gaze towards the pretty blonde waitress by the bar. Exchanging glances, they began to formulate yet another drunken plan. It was already firmly in place when my mother arrived to take their drinks order a few moments later.

It was Rufus, the alpha-friend, who took charge. 'My friend here has something he'd like to ask you,' he said, nodding towards Dad.

My mother looked up from her notepad. 'Oh, yes?'

Dad stared daggers at Rufus. 'Shut up, you fool,' he hissed.

Which only served to encourage Rufus. 'He's a little shy,' he told my mother, in a stage whisper. 'So, let *me* ask – is, um, *everything* in this place on the menu?'

A general explosion of mirth ran among the men at the table. My mother glanced towards Dad, his face burning with embarrassment, before returning her eyes to Rufus.

'You're suggesting your friend finds me attractive,' she said. It was not a question. 'Do you find that odd?'

Faced with my mother's stony blankness, Rufus's smile began to falter. 'Huh?'

'You think it strange. Is it something about my appearance that bothers you, or do you simply feel that your friend deserves someone better than a lowly barmaid?'

Rufus's face had turned the colour of a bad sunburn, but he tried smiling at his friends. 'Don't mind her,' he said. 'She's on her period.'

'Oh, please,' my mother told him. 'If I had to bleed to find arseholes like you annoying, I'd be anaemic.'

There was another explosion of laughter; louder this time, even without Rufus contributing.

'Anyway,' my mother continued, 'I'm going to stop talking to you now, so let me just assume you'll have a whisky like your friends here. I'm afraid we're all out of sippy cups, but perhaps someone will show you how to use one of our big boy's glasses.'

And with that, she turned away from the table, smiling to herself. When she arrived back to the table a few minutes later, my father was the last to receive his order. 'I *am* free tomorrow, by the way,' Mother said, fixing him with her warm blue eyes. 'You can meet me here at seven, if you like.'

And so, my parents' story began. After two years they were married, and moved to a small house in Myreton. The couple was well-enough received, but it wasn't until five years later, when Dad bought the house on the hill for him and his wife, now pregnant with their first child, that my parents were elevated to the head of Myreton society.

While Dad immediately shunned every invitation that began to flow in from the most prestigious clubs and societies throughout the region, my mother quickly learned to relish every moment of her new-found position. She lived a life above reproach, chairing church committees, organising charitable events and hosting afternoon teas and evening cocktail parties for her well-heeled friends. She was a popular character in Myreton, walking the streets like a politician, greeting everyone she passed by name. She would draw the women into long discussions about their latest business, and knew to ask after their husbands, children or parents with perfect specificity.

But for all the kindness she bestowed upon the citizens of Myreton, she was not an affectionate mother. I know plenty of people who insist that mothers are born with love for their children and place them before all other things. I do not think this was the case with us. Mother was always patient enough, but in a way that seemed to suggest her mind was elsewhere, that she had better things she could be doing. From time to time, she would examine us, as if to make certain we still had all of our fingers and toes, after which she would return to whatever job she'd been engaged in. On special occasions, she might take us to the beach or for a little drive around the county. For the most part, though, we were left to entertain ourselves in the confines of our home.

There were other children, occasionally, but they always arrived as if dressed for a night at the opera, and were never keen on the rough and tumble style of play Sophie and I craved. Most times, we ended up huddled around a Ludo board with these 'friends', glancing longingly out of the window towards the tree house that beckoned us from the garden.

When Sophie and I finally began school and got to meet the other children of Myreton, we were overjoyed. We each had to take two time-outs on our first day because neither of us would stop talking. That was fine, though, as far as we were concerned. For the first time in our lives, we had actual, real-live friends.

After that first day, we would bound out of bed bright and early each morning, urging Mother to hurry up and make our lunches, desperate to be the first at the gates to welcome our classmates as they arrived. For seven wonderful years, from the time we were five until we turned twelve, Sophie and I lived in a state of blissful ignorance, away from the past, unaware of what waited for us in the future. But then, with a month to go until we finished primary, my parents sat us around the kitchen table and dropped a terrible bombshell.

'Tom, you're going to St Edwards with your brother after the summer. Sophie, you're going to Mary Stewart.'

The statement was the last we'd expected to hear, and arrived so suddenly that it stole the breath from us, leaving us speechless.

'Now, don't sit there staring at me with those awful puppy-dog eyes,' Mother said. 'This is a wonderful opportunity for you both. Look at your brother. He's been thriving at St Edwards for three years now.'

'But he wanted to go,' Sophie said.

'And you will too,' our mother told us. 'Once you've adjusted to the idea.'

Sophie shook her head. 'I want to go to Cranston High. We both do. All of our friends are there.'

'Friends!' Mother sniffed. 'You'll make better friends at your new schools, I assure you.'

Sophie and I had never been stabbed before, but we guessed that this was probably how it felt. We looked pleadingly at our father, who couldn't quite bring himself to meet our eyes. 'I'm sorry, kids. Your mother and I agreed a long time ago that you could attend Myreton Primary on the condition you then moved onto private school in Edinburgh.'

'Will we at least be travelling into Edinburgh?' I asked.

'You'll be boarding like your brother,' Mother said.

'But it's only a twenty-mile drive. Dad, please...'

'That's *enough*,' my mother snapped. 'I won't listen to such ingratitude. Your father and I are paying good money so you can finally get a proper education. You're going to Edinburgh in September and that's the end of it.'

And that really was the end of it. Try as we might, there was simply no way to change our mother's mind. We attempted everything; bribery, flattery, blackmail, manipulation and, though it hurt our pride, schmoozing. Finally, when it became clear that there was nothing we could do to change our destiny, we sulked. For two months, we punished our mother with a stony silence, immersing ourselves in a stormy sea of self-righteous fury. Outside of mealtimes and a few of our mother's unbearable tea parties, we barely spent a moment in her company.

I felt strange all summer, but it wasn't until I left for St Edwards, Mother at the wheel as we pulled away down the road from Myreton Hill, that I registered for the first time in my life the full level of hurt, injustice and displeasure that amounted to a betrayal. When we reached the school, I begged my mother not to leave but she refused to listen to a single word I had to say. 'You're a very lucky boy,' she told me, as she steered me through the main entrance, her thin fingers pressing tightly into my shoulder blades. 'It's a wonderful school, so be sure you don't make any trouble. And stop that silly crying. You'll settle in soon enough.' A few minutes later, she turned from me, leaving me alone in the company of strangers for the first time in my life.

For the next three months, I was just about as lonely and wretched as a twelve-year-old has ever been, which is very lonely and wretched indeed. There were around four hundred boys at St Edwards, aged between twelve and eighteen, serving time in the north of Edinburgh because their fathers had before them, or because their parents were working overseas, or because – as in my case – one or both parents believed such an incarceration was seen as a necessary prelude to a successful social and professional career. Of these four hundred boys, some were bright and others dumb, some fat and others tall, some bullies and others victims. But they all shared one thing in common – not one of them showed the slightest bit of interest in talking to me.

This was undoubtedly my own fault. I had early opportunities to join various sports or recreational teams, but I tried not to involve myself whenever possible. It wasn't so much that I lacked interest. It was simply that all the other boys seemed so much more confident, so much happier than I was. I was trapped in a world that I did not belong to, on the sidelines of the jokes and the laughter, feeling strange and out of place.

I made an attempt to approach Pete during my second week at the school. We had never got on particularly well, but he was the only family I had for miles around, and this, in my mind at least, made us closer than we'd ever been. But Pete was not interested in playing the role of supportive big brother.

'I don't understand why you're complaining,' he said. 'What do you have to complain about? Look around you, Tom. You're at one of the best schools in the country. Don't you understand how lucky you are to be here?'

'It's just, I'm lonely,' I said, feeling my chin begin to wobble.

'So, go make some friends. For Christ's sake, Tom, don't be such a wimp.'

Actually, I didn't consider myself a wimp, but next to Pete I might easily have been mistaken for one. It was one of the things I'd always envied about my brother; his almost complete invulnerability. No amount of travelling or disruption seemed to make any difference to him. He was strong and popular among his schoolmates. He was certain of his entitlement to be part of the next generation of St Edwards success stories. In this respect, we were not so much unalike as polar opposites.

'Can't I come to your dorm tonight?' I asked. 'We could watch a film together.'

'Don't be an idiot. That's not how it works.' He sighed. 'Look, trust me, Tom – you're fine. In a couple of weeks, you'll never want to leave.'

'Pete –'

'I'm serious, Tom. Just fuck off. And unless someone dies, don't bother me again.'

I stood in front of him a moment longer, praying he'd have a change of heart, but he didn't. He just told me again to fuck off. And so, I did, silently, and with grave bitterness.

If Pete made my life at the school more difficult, then Jeremy made it almost impossible. From the first day, he made a hobby of terrorizing the weaker boys, the boys without friends, the tearful ones. He tripped them and laughed at the ensuing tumbles and slapped them around when he could get away with it. He bombarded them with missiles as they walked the corridors and invented nicknames that would haunt them the rest of their lives. He ran them so ragged that they began to yearn for bedtime and a few blessed hours of escape from his torment.

I managed to avoid Jeremy for two weeks. Then, on the

third Monday of term, I was in the school toilets when he entered the room. Another boy, Robert Benson, was with him and they sauntered up, smiling like we were the very best of friends.

'Alright, Halliday?' Jeremy said, on reaching my side. Up close, he was even more terrifying than he appeared in the school corridors. At twelve, he already had the look of the classic alpha male, a look that told you he knew how to handle himself, and that he could destroy you in a heartbeat if he ever felt inclined to do so. Even smiling, he seemed to carry an air of threat.

'What do you want?' I managed to ask.

'Calm down,' he said. 'I just thought it was about time we got a little better acquainted.' Robert giggled and looked around nervously, but Jeremy was clearly in his element. His expression was a mix of anticipation and pure pleasure. I made an attempt to run, but Jeremy caught hold of my shoulder and began to drag me towards the nearest cubicle.

I determined right then that there was no way I was going to let Jeremy flush my head down the toilet. I kicked and thrashed and screamed blue murder as he threw me into the stall and forced me towards the basin of the toilet. Robert remained by my side the whole way, whispering frantically for me to shut up and take my punishment. His fears were well founded, because moments later my chin connected hard with the toilet seat and I slumped onto the cold tiled floor, tasting blood. I clutched at my mouth, speechless with pain, and for a few seconds, the room was completely silent; then we were joined by a fourth, almost deafening, presence. Groggily, I looked up to find Jeremy and Robert being lambasted by Mr Pritchard, the school's terrifying Head of Geography, who appeared to exist in a perpetual state of fury. The two-week detention Jeremy received that day was the longest to be handed out at St Edwards that year.

After that, Jeremy rarely left me alone. He continued to taunt the other boys for sure, ordered them around like he was lord of the manor. But because he considered me responsible for his own punishment, I received special treatment. Within days, he'd taken to putting a shoulder into my ribs in the corridors between classes, knocking me into the lockers and scattering my books. A week or two after that, a series of rumours began to circulate about me. First came the whispers that I was the illegitimate child of Adolf Hitler. When that one died its inevitable death, word quickly spread that I had E. coli, and that I was highly contagious, and that people should stay at least three feet away from me if they didn't want to catch it too. There were also separate reports that I kept a bright pink dildo under my pillow in the dorm room, that I enjoyed putting clingfilm up my bum, and that I was an aquaholic, who couldn't be trusted around water fountains. By December, nobody was able to look at me without bursting into laughter.

The final straw, like the first, came in the school toilets, a fortnight before Christmas. I was in one of the cubicles at the time, so Jacob and Fergus had no idea that I was only five feet from them as they walked into the room and fell into conversation.

'Have you heard the latest about Tom Halliday?' Jacob asked.

Fergus considered this for a second. 'I think so. He got run over by a milk float, yeah?'

Jacob clicked his tongue impatiently. 'No, I mean about him and his twin sister. Apparently, they've been going at it together for years.'

Fergus gasped. 'No!'

'Yeah,' Jacob continued. 'She had an abortion in the summer. That's why he was sent here.'

'Impossible,' Fergus said. 'It can't happen at twelve. Not to anybody.'

'Works different when you're related, though, doesn't it? I'm telling you, it happened. Jeremy Acker knows the doctor who got rid of the baby.'

When the boys left, I sat down on the toilet and stared at the door for a couple of seconds, trying to catch my breath, feeling like someone had my head underwater and was holding it down. I'd known for long enough that Jeremy was the architect of the ridiculous rumours, but hearing it confirmed filled my chest with an anger so hot and fierce that I felt it might explode.

Things came to a head the following week. I was putting my books away after the day's classes when I looked into the mirrored door of my locker and saw Jeremy standing behind me. I turned around to face him.

'Not dead yet, Halliday?' he asked.

I tried, and failed, to hold his gaze. 'No thanks to you.'

'Oh?' He was smiling, as if this was a friendly conversation in the street, but I could see the muscles tightening in his neck. 'And how do you work that one out?'

I glanced around self-consciously. We were in the school's main corridor, with other boys coming and going. 'I know you've been spreading rumours about me,' I said.

Jeremy folded his arms across his great, flabby chest. 'Is that right?'

I nodded.

'You've got no proof it was me.'

'I bet I can find some, though. And when I do, I reckon the headmaster will want to hear about it.'

With a few swift steps, Jeremy planted himself directly in front of me. 'You wouldn't dare.'

'I would, if I had to. If you won't leave me alone, then I'll tell.'

Jeremy narrowed his eyes. 'Do that,' he said, grimly, 'and I'll make your life a living hell.'

I swallowed. My locker was only a couple of inches behind me, and I had nowhere to go. 'Listen,' I said, spreading my hands placatingly. 'Can't we talk about this?' I offered a smile, which unnerved Jeremy so badly that for a moment I began to hope I might escape his wrath completely. But then I made my mistake. I took a step towards him.

Later, Jeremy would claim he'd acted in self-defence, that the fight had only started when I wrapped my hands around his neck and began knocking his head against the nearest vending machine. His testimony went rather against the witness accounts, which all agreed that I'd spent the first part of the skirmish on my knees, pleading for mercy, and the second half in a foetal position on the ground as Jeremy laid into me with astonishing gusto. When the teachers arrived, Jeremy, far from being a gibbering mess, was attempting to moonwalk beside my prone figure, hands raised in victory.

An hour after being plucked from the cold linoleum of the school corridor, I was ushered into the office of Archibald Clements, the school headmaster. Mr Clements was a cadaverous man in his mid-sixties, with thick glasses, a dark linen suit and the welcoming air of a medieval executioner. He had a narrow face that drew everyone's attention to his long nose and dark circles under his eyes and thick bristly eyebrows. When I entered the room, he immediately stood from his seat and made an attempt at smiling, an action that was clearly alien to him.

'Come in, come in,' he said, pointed to a chair by his desk, which I accepted groggily. I'd just been released from the nurse's station, where I'd spent the previous sixty minutes having my head bandaged and a dislocated thumb popped back into place. Already, my left eye was half shut and a shadow of purple swelling was spreading from the corner of my eye socket down into my cheekbone. A smattering of minor cuts and grazes covered the left side of my face. 'Hmm,' Mr Clements said, inspecting my injuries from the opposite side of his desk. 'Unfortunate, don't you think?'

I agreed that it was. Very unfortunate, indeed.

'Yes,' he said, shaking his head sadly. 'Quite regrettable. Then again, I, ah, see no reason to worry your parents unnecessarily about the recent, um, altercation. I shall telephone them in a few moments to advise them that there was some, ah, difficulty, but I think that's all that needs to be said on the matter.'

Even at twelve, I knew what he was saying. *We don't want any trouble over this. Let's sweep the whole sorry episode under the carpet.* I disagreed wholeheartedly, of course. I wanted revenge on Jeremy for all the hurt and suffering he'd so gleefully put me through. But, again, I was twelve. What could I do but nod?

'Good lad, good lad,' Mr Clements said, clearly relieved. Then, feeling he should offer some kind of olive branch: 'You, ah, have an older brother here. Peter, am I right? Would you like to see him?'

I shook my head. I'd seen Pete only a handful of times since our conversation at the beginning of term, and always from a distance. I saw no reason why he should care any more about my problems now than he had two months earlier.

'Very good,' Mr Clements said, rising from his chair. 'Very good. Well, off you go back to your dorm. Your friends will no doubt be eager to get a look at your war wounds. I can assure you that Mr Acker will not be bothering you again today.'

Mr Acker would not be bothering me because he'd already been sent away from St Edwards. In the days that followed, there was a great deal of excited talk of his being expelled, and I prayed to every god I could think of that this was the case. But Young Mr Acker was the son of *the* Mr Acker, a prominent Tory MP, and therefore practically untouchable. In the end, he was given a token suspension until after the Christmas holidays. I remained at the school, licking my wounds and feeling even more despondent than ever.

I arrived home for the holidays simultaneously elated by my freedom and concerned by how my parents would react to my bruises, which had faded to a sort of yellowish purple but were still clearly visible to anyone who looked even vaguely in my direction. My mother was sitting with a cup of tea by the fireplace when she saw me. 'They told me you'd been involved in a small classroom scuffle,' she said. 'It looks more like you've been off to war.'

I told my mother what had happened and, to my surprise, she seemed genuinely sorry for me. I decided to take advantage of this rare display of empathy. 'Mum,' I said gently. 'I can't do this anymore. I need to come home.'

My mother shook her head. 'You're staying exactly where you are.'

'But I'm not happy.'

'You'll be happy enough when you get used to the place.'

'I won't. I –'

'Tom,' my mother said. She took a sip of her tea, then put her cup down and looked at me warmly. 'Sweetheart, you need to stop thinking that there might be some way to change my mind over this. I assure you that it's not going to happen.'

'Fine,' I said, stubbornly. 'I'll ask Dad, then.'

My mother's expression turned to ice. 'Don't even think about worrying your father! He's working all hours to keep you at that school, offer you some kind of future. I can't believe I gave birth to such an ungrateful little man.'

'But –'

'Shut up!' my mother shouted. 'Just shut up. I've had enough of your ridiculous snivelling. You're twelve years old. Get a grip, for God's sake.'

My natural relationship with my mother finally ended with that conversation. Every subsequent encounter I had with her was shadowed by her words, and despite the occasional, public signs of affection between us, I remained cold towards her. A chasm had begun to open between us, a chasm that quickly grew so deep that my father was forced to renovate a whole section of our house just to put some breathing space between his wife and her progeny. The bonds between us were broken and all that remained was the official designation – a mother, a son.

SIX

IT'S THE END OF MY FIRST FULL DAY IN MYRETON WHICH, ALL in all, has been pretty unproductive. I spent an hour with my parents this morning, and another sorting through some of the clutter in my room, but for the most part I've been sitting in front of the telly watching a *Flog It* marathon on HGTV. Elizabeth, from Winchester, has just sold her great-grandmother's china doll at auction, a decision she's quickly coming to realise she will regret for the rest of her life.

'So, Elizabeth,' the presenter says. 'The doll has sold. How do you feel?'

'Lovely,' Elizabeth croaks. She's remembering the day she was given the doll, seventy-two years ago. She cherishes the memory almost as much as she cherished the doll.

'So, what are you going to do with your eighteen pounds?'

Eighteen pounds? Elizabeth thinks. *Is that all I got?* She nails a smile to her face. 'My husband's been looking to buy a new toaster. I expect we'll put it towards that.'

'Ah, just when he *yeast* expected it, eh?' the presenter says, waggling his eyebrows for the viewers at home.

Elizabeth forces a laugh. She's picturing Grand-Nana spinning in her grave. 'That's right, Paul,' she says.

'Poor Betty,' I tell the TV. 'She'll feel that one in the morning.' I have a quick scratch and a yawn and then the adverts come on, so I decide to set off on another raid through the kitchen cupboards. I'm halfway there when Emma appears at the end of the hallway with her coat and her bag.

'Oh,' I say. 'I didn't know you were here.'

Emma shrugs. 'Well, I'm like that. A thief in the night. Or the early evening, anyway.'

I smile. 'Is that you off home now?'

Emma nods. 'Your mum's all set now till tomorrow. Apart from her cups of tea, but your dad will sort that.'

By now, Emma's crossed the hall, and we're standing only a few feet from one another. 'You don't fancy a drink yourself, do you?' I ask.

Emma's eyes rise to meet mine. 'Now?'

'Yeah. We could head down to the Myreton Inn, if you like.'

Emma hesitates for a moment, as though afraid to answer the question, then nods. I breathe a short sigh of relief, then grab my coat and lead the way out of the house.

In just a few minutes, we arrive at the Myreton Inn, a quiet little pub that sits in the heart of the village, directly opposite the children's golf course. In summer, the entire place is packed with golfing tourists, fresh from their day on the neighbouring courses, but at five o'clock on an October evening, it's practically empty. The most noise in the place comes from a couple of old men settled in by the bar, sipping half-and-halfs and grumbling about the weather. Emma and I make ourselves comfortable at a table by the fireplace and a bored-looking barmaid arrives to take our order. I order a beer, while Emma asks for a black coffee. It's not exactly what I meant when I invited her for a drink, but it's fine.

The place has hardly changed since I was a child. Back then, Dad used to bring me, Sophie and Pete for ice cream after we'd played a round of golf on the kiddies' course. It was chock-full of knick-knacks – old maps, ancient photographs, taxidermied animals, and Chalkware statues of 1930s movie stars – which kept us well entertained during the hours we spent here. These same curios are still there today, and while they're less fascinating now than they once were, there's something deeply comforting about their continued presence.

Emma leans back in her chair and begins searching the room's various nooks and crannies with her eyes. 'I love it here,' she says, with a smile. 'When my parents used to take us out for Sunday lunch, they always let my brother and I choose where to eat. I doubt it ever took us more than a second to decide to come here. It got to the stage where they practically begged us to try somewhere else, but there was never any danger of that happening. We were addicted to this place.'

I smile. 'How is your brother?'

'He's good,' Emma says. 'He's in Edinburgh these days.'

'Married?'

Emma nods. 'Two kids.'

'Two…? Wow, so you're an auntie now?'

Emma grins proudly. 'The oldest one's… she'll be eight in March.'

'Wow,' I say, guiltily. 'I really am out of the loop, aren't I?'

But Emma just shrugs. 'It's not just you. Sometimes I blink my eyes and three months pass by. With the world moving so fast, it's difficult even to stay in touch with the people you're closest to.'

The barmaid brings our drinks and we both lean back, our knees knocking beneath the small table.

'My mum warned me it would happen,' Emma says after a moment. 'When you're a child, she said, every day seems to last a lifetime. Then, suddenly, time starts to get ahead of you and, poof, before you know it, you're thirty-five years old and wondering what the hell you're supposed to do with your life.'

'I'd say she hit the nail pretty perfectly on the head there.'

'Yeah, she did,' Emma says. She lifts her mug thoughtfully, takes a sip of coffee. 'So, come on. What pearls of wisdom did Lorraine have to offer when you were young?'

I consider this for a moment. 'That children should be seen and not heard? That was one of her favourites. That I'd never amount to anything? She loved that one, too.'

Emma raises an eyebrow.

'I'm serious. She's a real charmer, my mother.' I say this with a smile to show her that it's no big deal, except of course it is.

Emma continues to hold my gaze. 'I'm sure she's not *that* bad.'

'Actually, she kind of is. I mean, she hides it well but, truth be told, I really don't think she's a particularly pleasant human being.'

Emma tilts her head to the side, and her eyes turn gentle. 'Lorraine's not a bad woman, Tom. She's... principled, maybe. Stubborn, perhaps. But she's spoken a great deal about you since I started working with her. She loves you very much.'

I find this difficult to believe, and impossible to answer.

It's lucky, then, that the barmaid chooses this moment to arrive at the table with a pair of menus. I make a mental note to tip her double at the end of the night.

'Would you like a bite to eat?' I ask, when the barmaid leaves. 'Shall we order some dinner?'`

Emma starts, and I realise my error. I should have figured it out when she ordered the coffee. 'Emma, I'm sorry. I didn't... I wasn't thinking.'

Emma shakes her head. 'You don't have to apologise. It's fine. The thing is that I'm a good deal better now. Really, I am. There are just things I still can't bring myself to do.'

'You don't eat out?'

'Never. To be honest, it was a bit of a challenge just to make it out here.'

'Oh my god. I feel terrible. I...'

'It's fine,' Emma says, gently. 'I wanted to come.' She takes a sip of her coffee, smiles as she puts the mug down again. 'I always knew it would be this way. After all, there's no such thing as a magic cure for an eating disorder, you know? There's no making it all go away forever. But there's always some small step I can take towards a better day, some minor victory that I can win. And that's okay. I'm okay with that.'

'And the doctors? Are you still seeing them?'

'Oh, yes. They've been my constant companions for fifteen years now. Fifteen years of new medications, treatments, doctors, hospitals, nurses, psychologists. Some of them were useless, others helped me a little. None of them have transformed my life completely, but when I think back to how terrible things were... well, I feel lucky. I have a lot of things to be grateful for.'

'So, no more hospitals?'

'No. I don't think so.'

It's incredible to hear Emma speak this way. There's a real gentleness to her: a special sort of sweetness that you find sometimes in people who've been hurt badly but who don't want revenge.

I'm about to speak again when, suddenly, a voice calls from behind me. 'Emma?' it says. And then, more tentatively, 'Tom?' Emma, facing the stranger, is already smiling by the time I turn to find Mike Campbell, one of our old classmates from school, standing by the side of our table. 'Oh my god,' he says, beaming at me. 'Tom Halliday! Come here, you!'

'Hi Mike,' I mumble into his shoulder as he wrenches me from my seat.

'Good God,' he says. Having released me, he's now looking me up and down. 'You look great. How the hell are you?'

'I'm good,' I say. And it's true; I'm delighted to see him. 'What are you doing here?'

Mike points to a name badge, attached upside-down to his shirt. 'Barman. For my sins. Ha-ha. No, but really. Four years now.'

'You like it, then?'

'Oh, a lot. The hours are crap and the pay's just terrible, but I get to work with Resting Bitch Face over there. Which is a privilege. Really it is.'

Resting Bitch Face is standing by the bar, wiping a damp cloth across a row of whisky bottles. 'I can hear every word you're saying about me, Mike,' she calls, without looking up from her task.

'There'd be no fun in saying them if you couldn't, Amy,' Mike calls back. Then he smiles at Emma and me. 'She's not so bad really,' he says. 'It's just that smiling makes her look like an angry serial killer, so she never, ever does it.'

Amy throws the cloth into the sink and shakes her head, trying to hide the smile that, despite her best efforts, has begun to spread across her face. Mike, meanwhile, continues to study me, hands on hips. 'My god, Tom, I can't believe it's been so long.'

'Me neither,' I tell him. 'You've hardly changed a bit.'

Mike tries to wave the compliment aside, but it's true. There are a few lines around the eyes, perhaps, a touch of grey in his temples, but his chubby, boyish face is still chubby and boyish, and his thick hair's as wild as it always was. He dresses younger, too, though his clothes are so shabby that this is presumably not so much an attempt to recapture his youth as a failure to update his wardrobe more than once every decade. You could argue that he's a bit scruffy for a barman, I suppose, but then why would you? The guy's so intensely likeable that it would be ridiculous to hold anything as trivial as his appearance against him.

Mike was the poorest kid at our school, and got a lot of grief for it. Kids flicked mud at his shoes and threw his packed lunch in the bins. They bumped the legs of his chair during class, jeered at his second-hand clothes, sang 'Will He Know it's Christmastime' as soon as he was in earshot. A few of the gentler kids made some efforts to shield him from the sticks and stones that were thrown at him, but in any case, he was given a hell of a time.

'Will you join us for a drink?' I ask.

'I'd love to, but I start work in...' He checks his watch. 'Oh. Fifteen minutes ago.' He grins sheepishly, and I see once more the self-conscious young boy who stood loyally by my side throughout primary school.

Mike walks over to the bar, where he's greeted warmly by the two regulars. 'How're you doing, Fraser?' he asks.

'Aye, brand new, son,' Fraser says. 'Here, did ye ken ye had a bear in here earlier this afternoon?'

Mike shakes his head and sighs. Presumably, he knows what's coming. 'Is that right?'

'Aye,' Fraser says. 'A big broon yin. It walked right in here and it came up tae the bar and it said, "Give me a whiskey... and a cola." Well, Amy looked at him for a second and said, "Why the big pause?" And then the bear shrugged and said, "Ah'm no' sure, hen. I wiz born wi' them."'

Mike closes his eyes and groans. 'Oh dear. They don't get any better, do they. Alright, Angus, let's get this over with. Your turn.'

It's the moment Angus has been waiting for. He takes a quick swig of his pint, then sits up straight in his stool. 'This mornin' ah'm in Edinburgh and ah cannae for the life of me get parked. After an hour, ah says, "Lord, ah cannae stand this. If you open a space for me, ah swear tae quit the drink and go tae church every Sunday." Well, the very next second, the clouds part and the sun bursts ontae an empty parking spot. Christ, ah've never felt such relief – quick as ah can, ah roll doon the windae an' shout, "Never mind, pal, ah've found yin after all."'

That brings a laugh, and for a second the jokes look like continuing, but then the front door swings open. I'm facing away from the entrance, so I don't see who's arrived, but Emma does, and at the sight of them her face immediately pales. Confused, I turn around, following her eyes to the middle of the room, and see Daryll Cockburn, another of our old classmates, blowing into his hands to warm himself.

'Uh oh,' Mike says. 'Here comes trouble.'

Daryll shakes off his jacket as he approaches the bar. 'Aye, aye, very funny, Campbell. Just pour us a pint, will you?'

Mike doesn't answer, just smiles and shakes his head as he follows Daryll's order. Daryll stares at him for a long second, then turns his attention to the rest of the room. When his eyes reach Emma, he does a quick double-take; then his lips part into something resembling a smile, and he begins walking towards us. I don't like the smile, or the walk. It's barely seven o'clock, but it's clear from his general demeanour that he's been drinking for some time.

It's been a decade or more since I set eyes on Daryll, and it's immediately clear that the intervening years have been less than kind to him. He's prematurely stooped, with a ruddy complexion and a nest of black hair that's going thin at the crown. His once-proud nose has been broken at least once, its bulbous tip stained with a frantic network of purple veins that run through his skin like rivers. But then he's three inches taller than me, and at least six inches bulkier all round, so in some ways he's actually rather impressive, a sort of angry bulldozer on legs.

Daryll was a holy terror when we were growing up. A year older than me, he bullied pretty much everybody at school, including most of the teachers. It was him who wrote 'MiKes hoLadaY howSe' on a salt bin by the old railway yard one morning while everyone was making their way into school. When it was discovered later that day, we were all called into a special assembly where the head-mistress lectured us on empathy and kindness. She'd hoped the guilty party would own up, or at least be turned in by one of their peers. But Daryll wasn't the type to take responsibility for his actions, and none of us were brave enough to speak out against him, so his cruelty, as usual, went entirely unpunished.

'Emma Barnes,' he says now, standing by our table. 'I'm surprised to see *you* here.'

Emma tries to smile, but she's clearly unnerved. 'Hello, Daryll.'

'Did you get my letter?'

Emma blinks. 'Yes. Thank you.'

Daryll nods slowly, his angry gaze fixed on Emma. 'But you didn't bother to reply.'

Emma shuffles uneasily on her seat. 'I haven't seen you.'

'You know where I live.'

'I'm sorry,' Emma says, anxiously. 'I've been busy.'

'Too busy to drop a note through my letter box?'

Daryll's working himself into a rage, his cheeks glowing red with anger, and I can see it's all he can do to stop himself taking Emma by the shoulders and giving her a shake, so I choose this moment to join the conversation. 'She's been working at my house,' I tell him. 'My mother's been...'

Daryll gives me the once over, as though it would be a waste of eyesight to look at me twice. 'Who's this?' he asks Emma.

'It's Tom,' I say, standing up from my chair. 'Tom Halliday. We were at school together back in –'

'I know who you are,' Daryll says, leaving me to wonder why he bothered asking in the first place. 'You can sit down now. And shut up.'

'Hey! There's no need to talk to me like that.'

I don't so much actually, voluntarily say this as hear myself say it, and I'm shocked. From the way the muscles in Daryll's neck tense, I can tell it's taken him by surprise, too. He moves a step closer to me; instinctively, I take a step back, which brings a smile to his face. 'That's right,' he says, so pleased by this move that he starts to advance further towards me. 'You'd better back off.'

'Daryll, stop it, would you,' Emma says.

'What, so you can carry on your little affair?'

'You don't know what you're talking about.'

'Oh, I don't, do I? When I come in here and see the two of you sitting across from one another, staring at each other like a couple of lovebirds. Don't tell me there's nothing going on. I know what my own fuckin' eyes are telling me.'

'And what if something is going on?' Emma says, raising her voice now, the colour coming to her cheeks. 'What business is it of yours, anyway?'

'What business...?' Daryll stammers, disbelieving. He glares at Emma, and then at me, breathing so heavily through his nose that for one moment I think he might attack us, but then a hand lands on his arm and the fury he's directed at us suddenly transfers to his right.

It's Mike, our knight in scruffy cotton, come to rescue us. 'Alright there, Mr Banner,' he says, pulling Daryll towards him. 'What have I told you about Hulking out in front of the regulars?'

'Fuck off.' Daryll growls.

'Well, no,' Mike says. 'But you probably should, you know? Before I have to call the police.'

Daryll gives a snort of laughter, but he's clearly disturbed by the suggestion. 'Whatever,' he says. Then, turning to Emma, 'Don't be a stranger, okay? I'll see you soon.' And with that he half staggers, half swaggers out of the building.

'Are you okay?' I ask Emma.

Emma nods, but it's obvious she's been upset by the encounter. She reaches for her mug of coffee and takes a small sip. The china rattles on her teeth and she brings up her other hand to help. Then she puts the mug down and clears her throat.

'Emma, the way he spoke to you... That wasn't cool.'

Emma nods. 'I know. But it's nothing. Seriously.'

Mike scratches thoughtfully at his stubbly cheek. 'I probably should have barred him, huh?'

'No, Mike,' Emma says. 'You were great. Thank you.'

The argument is replaying in my mind. 'Daryll talked about a note. Has he been bothering you?'

'No, no,' says Emma. 'He just takes pleasure in making people uncomfortable.'

'He's certainly succeeded with you. Do you want me to speak with him?'

'No, Tom. That would only make things worse.'

'Emma,' Mike says, gently. 'We have to do something.'

'No!' Emma says, her voice suddenly thick with panic. 'Please! Please. Don't stir things up, either of you. Things are fine as they are, I promise.'

There are tears in Emma's eyes, so I say nothing more. But I look towards Mike and see that he's thinking the same thing as me: *there'll be trouble before all this is over*.

SEVEN

'WELL,' MY MOTHER SAYS THE NEXT DAY AS I ARRIVE BY HER bedside with a fresh pot of tea. 'What should we do?'

I look at her, puzzled. 'Do?' Until now, I thought we'd spend our time together doing very little, or nothing at all, and that I'd be miserable, although I'd hide it and deny it. I imagined, in other words, that we'd see one another, as we always have, across a divide.

'The rain seems to be holding off for now,' my mother continues, glancing out of her window. 'Perhaps we could take a walk in the garden?'

'You think you can walk?'

'No. But there's a wheelchair on the back porch. Do you feel fit enough to push me around?'

'Well,' I say, brightly. 'That would certainly make a nice change.'

My mother snaps her head around and glowers at me. Confused, I replay the final lines of conversation in my head, then panic. 'No, no,' I say, backtracking. 'I meant a nice change from being holed up in the bedroom.'

My mother continues to regard me with her penetrating stare. 'Of course, you did,' she says, drily.

I start to explain further, but I haven't managed more than five words before she throws her blankets aside and calls downstairs for Emma to come and help her get dressed. Defeated, I skulk off downstairs to grab the wheelchair and a couple of blankets to place across my mother's lap.

When my parents' house was built back in 1906, Alexander Bennett, the Edinburgh physician for whom the house was being constructed, commissioned Rosamund Hyde, the leading landscape designer of the day, to create a garden whose elegance would match that of the towering three-storey building it surrounded. Within three months, the space was transformed from a rocky section of ancient pasture into a veritable Utopia, complete with grass tennis court, a small putting green and an elegant garden whose stone paths were softened by enormous herbaceous borders overflowing with lilies, lupins, delphiniums, and lavender. A pretentious stone fountain depicting Perseus and Andromeda was placed in the centre of the circular driveway to welcome visitors, while foxgloves and roses were planted to clothe the house walls and hug the balustrades of the formal stairs that descended to the grounds. On the day it was unveiled, one hundred and twenty of Edinburgh's most distinguished citizens arrived in the village to celebrate its completion.

After moving into the house, Bennett immediately hired two full-time gardeners, and for the next forty-two years the garden was so carefully maintained that barely a leaf fell out of place. But after Bennett's death in 1958, the gardening staff was laid off by the London financier who bought the property as a holiday retreat for him and his wife, and by the time my parents bought the house in 1981, the garden had long fallen into decline.

My mother was far too proud of her new house to allow this to continue. Within a week of purchasing the property, she wrote to the Kensington Horticultural Society to request copies of Hyde's plans for the garden, and spent the next three years restoring it to its original glory. By the time she was finished, the garden was considered to be the most authentic and perfect restoration of a Hyde creation, and in the thirty years since then, it's played host to a remarkable number of Hyde enthusiasts and horticultural societies who are willing to travel surprising distances to walk our hallowed grounds.

I share none of their enthusiasm as I push my mother's wheelchair across the driveway and onto the lawn. Although my mother's too busy studying her beloved plants to continue our earlier conversation, the silence between us is anything but comfortable. We're building up to something, I can tell, the tension that pervades us deepening with every step I take. Desperate to maintain the peace, I head towards the south edge of the garden, a place to which my mother has long escaped to steal a few moments of quiet contemplation. I understand her choice; this, the garden's highest point, offers a series of incredible vistas that stretch for miles in almost every direction. I'm becoming lost in one of these scenes myself – the Forth estuary, flat and steel-grey today in the overcast October sky – when, to my dismay, I realise I've let my guard down and my mother's broken the silence.

'Sorry, what?' I say, when, finally, I see her looking expectantly up at me.

Glancing back to her lap, my mother gives a weary sigh.

'I said, we haven't always got on as well as we could have, have we?'

Still cursing my carelessness, I search desperately for an answer. I know what's coming and I want to spare her. To spare me. 'None of that matters now,' I say.

My mother doesn't seem to hear this. 'I know I was hard on you,' she continues. 'Some of the things I said... well, they were very unkind. Please, Tom, you must forgive me.'

'Lorraine. There's really nothing to forgive.' It's not true, but I say it.

She seems disappointed, and for a moment I'm worried that she's going to say more. But just then a slight breeze starts up, and she turns away from it in her thick winter coat and her little head with its tea-cosy hat on top of it and says, 'Take me back to the house, Tom, before this wind blows me out of my chair.'

That evening, after dinner, Dad makes his way upstairs to spend time with my mother, leaving Sophie and I to our own devices on the living room sofa. Sophie's device is her laptop, which, from the look of intense concentration on her face, she's using to catch up on important work. I know better than to bother her when she looks like that, so I turn my own attention to the television. It's seven o'clock, so there's not much on, and as I've sickened myself of *Flog It* in the past few days, I settle for an ancient Western, which looks good until I see that it stars a young John Wayne. I can't stand John Wayne. The man makes my blood boil.

'God, would you just look at him,' I tell Sophie. 'He's about as creaky as a moist floorboard.'

'Mmm hmmm,' Sophie says, without looking up from her laptop.

John stares off-camera with all the emotion of an artichoke. 'Howdy, Pilgrim,' he drawls, woodenly. 'We got Cochise cornered up there in that box canyon...'

'Christ, he sounds like he's concussed. How the hell did that man win two Oscars?'

'Tom...'

'Even his greatest speeches sound like a shopping list.'

'Tom!' Sophie barks. 'I'm trying to work.'

'Alright,' I say. 'Sorry.' Taking a deep breath, I switch the telly off and shake my head hard in an attempt to purge all images of Johnny from my mind. 'How's work going, anyway?'

'Oh, fine. Nicola's managing the volunteers from the office, so there's not an awfully great deal for me to do. To be honest, it's nice to get a break from it.'

'It's stressful?'

Sophie looks at me. 'This email here? It's from a woman who woke up in her bed last month and realised she'd been raped. She woke up, evidence everywhere, but with no memory of the thing. The policeman she saw told her that not remembering the rape made it barely reportable. So, there she is. Completely helpless and fucked for life, probably.'

'That's awful,' I say.

'You have no idea. And that's just one of a thousand stories I've heard.'

'I'm sorry.'

Sophie shrugs. 'Not as sorry as those women are.' She stretches her arms above her head, then slams the lid closed on her laptop. 'Still, at least one relationship seems to be improving. You and Mum were very friendly today.'

'You saw us?'

Sophie turns to me, smiling. 'Sure. Watching the two of you pretending to get along is always good for a laugh.' She brings both feet up onto the sofa, narrows her eyes towards me. 'So, are you going to tell me what you were talking about?'

'She asked me to forgive her.'

Sophie looks at me, surprised. 'And...?'

I shrug. 'I told her there was nothing to forgive.'

Sophie shakes her head, half-amused, half-exasperated. 'Oh, Tom. You really are a pussy.'

'No, I'm not,' I say, arguing because I don't want it to be true. I shift uneasily in my seat. Then, with a terrible attempt at indifference: 'What did you say when she asked you?'

'She never *had* to ask,' Sophie says. 'Unlike some members of this family, Mum and I have it in ourselves to discuss our problems, mother to daughter. Mum's more than aware of what a bitch she was to me. And she knows how I feel about it.'

'Which is?'

'That I hated her for a long time. But that, yeah, I've forgiven her. She's okay with it.'

'That's pretty much what I said, when you think about it.'

Sophie rolls her eyes and falls back into the sofa. 'Tom, you're going to have to speak with her. Properly. She needs to find closure on this.'

'So, she can assume she has it. I've told her everything's fine.'

Sophie's expression grows more serious. 'Tom, have you considered that this is your last chance to get to know her, to understand her? Do you honestly think that's going to happen while you're holding this grudge? Just talk to her. Tell her what a shit she was. Tell her how cruel and insensitive she was. Tell her you love her. Because you *do*, you know. You *do* love her. It's just hidden underneath all this resentment you've allowed to build up inside of you. Please, Tom. Please. Promise me you'll talk to her.'

I don't, but I promise that I'll try. Right now, it really is the best I can do.

EIGHT

It's Wednesday evening, around seven o'clock, and I'm taking the recycling bin out onto the street. I've just passed through the main gate when, through the darkness, a figure appears in front of me. Letting out a yelp, I whirl around and fall into a karate pose. I've never taken karate, but I did watch *3 Ninjas* once as a kid and it all feels pretty authentic until my eyes refocus and I look into the face of my potential attacker, who seems entirely oblivious to the danger he's in.

'Jesus, Mike,' I say, grabbing at my chest. 'You scared the shit out of me.'

'Sorry, Tom. I just wondered if you fancied a walk.'

I feel my heart melt just a little. It's as though the clocks have been turned back twenty-five years, to an age when Mike would appear at the house every other day to ask if I was allowed to come out to play. But while it's sweet, I can't help wondering why he didn't just use a phone like everybody else. Which leads me neatly to my next question...

'How long have you been standing there?'

'Oh, not so long,' Mike says, with a shiver.

'You look frozen.'

Mike looks self-consciously at the pavement. 'Ah, well, I suppose I might've been here a while, right enough.'

'But... why didn't you just come in?'

'I tried pressing the Intercom a few times, but there was no answer.'

I look towards the 'Intercom'. 'That's the vehicle sensor, Mike. Dad's not the KGB. If you want to come in, just push the gate open.'

'Oh, right,' Mike says. He tries a laugh, but something's clearly still not sitting right with him. 'It's just... does he still have those geese?'

Ah. Of course. I'm surprised I'd forgotten about Mike's fear of birds. It was a topic much discussed during our days at Cranston Primary, and very much in evidence during class trips to public parks or the zoo. It had all started one Saturday morning, when Mike paid a visit to Sandy the Parrot. Sandy the Parrot was already something of a Myreton legend by the time I was born, having spent the better part of fifty years greeting villagers who passed his cage by the foot of Mrs Gilchrist's garden. We children were particularly fond of him, and would clap our hands in glee as he wished us a good day or told us what pretty boys we were. But we were always careful not to get too close, because, however charming he might have been, he was also a vicious little bugger.

Mike had still to learn of Sandy's temper when he approached his cage that Saturday morning. Usually, his mum accompanied him into the garden, but she'd met a friend by Mrs Gilchrist's gate and left Mike to go on ahead. When he reached the cage, he found Sandy to be in a particularly chatty mood. 'You're a handsome chappie,' he told Mike. 'What a pretty thing you are.' Mike thanked him, and was wondering what else to say when Sandy leaned forward on his perch and said, 'Come on, then. Give's a kiss.' Mike knew he probably shouldn't – not until his mum joined him, at least – but he'd never kissed a parrot before, and was worried Sandy might renege on his offer. Puckering his lips, he closed his eyes and pressed his face against the cage.

Sandy was confused. He'd done his part – made a few of those stupid noises the humans seemed to like so much. But now, instead of thanking him and walking away like they always did, this little boy-thing was attempting to climb inside the cage with him! Sandy tried warning him off with another of those noises – 'Hey good lookin" – and when this failed to discourage his visitor, he turned directly to Plan B. It took the doctor one hour and six stitches to repair the resulting damage to Mike's face.

I grab a coat from the hallway and make my way back outside, where Mike's waiting eagerly for me to return. I look at him, and notice that he's even more careless with his appearance outside of work. His hair is dishevelled and he's made a lopsided job of buttoning his jacket. There's a spare buttonhole at the top and a lack of alignment at the bottom. He looks so delighted to have company that I haven't the heart to point this out to him. Instead, I say, 'Come on, before Christopher breaks through the gate. He can smell fear, you know.'

Mike shudders. 'Ugh, Christopher. Fresh from the burning depths of hell.'

When we step out onto the street, a chill breeze hits me, makes me hunch and hug myself. I remember that it's almost winter. So much lost time. The last time I was out in the world, it was just nearing summer.

'So, what do you want to do?' I ask. 'Fancy a pint?'

'Actually, I thought we might pay a wee visit to Greywalls. For old times' sake.'

I nod, greatly touched by Mike's suggestion. For the entire summer before I began at St Edwards, Mike and I worked tirelessly to build a den in the ruins of Greywalls Castle. The den was never much to look at – even by the end of summer it comprised little more than some rickety old furniture, a few mouldy blankets and a small collection of comics – but the space was quiet and comfortable and completely ours. For while the castle was undoubtedly remarkable in its prime, it was by 1996 just one of those sad old buildings that had been left entirely to nature. Despite my constant worries about moving to Edinburgh, the six weeks we spent at Greywalls were among the happiest of my life, and when the time finally came to leave for St Edwards, I grieved as much for the loss of my best friend as the family I'd been forced to leave behind.

We've reached the bottom of Myreton Hill when Mike turns to me. 'Why Christopher?'

I smile. 'It was Sophie who chose the name. It took me years to decipher it. I doubt my parents ever will.'

'So, what's the secret?'

I look to Mike. 'Well, first you have to shorten his name.'

'To Chris?'

'Mmm hmmm. Then put it together with his second name.'

'Halliday?' Mike asks.

'No, bird-brain,' I say, laughing. 'Peacock. Go on. Put the two together.'

'Chris Peacock?' Mike says. 'I don't get it.'

'Try saying it slower.'

So, he does. 'Chris Peacock. Chris Pea...' He stops talking, and his eyes widen.

'Ey up,' I say, in something approaching a Yorkshire accent. 'I think the penny's about to drop.'

Mike stares at me with a mixture of amusement and disgust. 'Crispy Cock,' he says, tasting the words on his lips. Then he looks to me for confirmation, and I nod, and he bursts into laughter.

'What do you think?' I ask.

But Mike's already bent double on the pavement, fighting to catch his breath. 'Oh dear,' he says, before falling into another convulsion, his hands pressed against his stomach. 'Oh dear. That... that's filthy!'

'That's Sophie.'

Mike's entire body is shaking with laughter. 'Dear me,' he murmurs, wiping a tear from his eye. 'Oh, dear me. It's no wonder he's such an arse.'

When Mike's recovered enough to walk, we set off once more towards Greywalls. Mike asks after my mother, and I fill him in on her crappy condition and her rotten prognosis, and when I'm done talking, he reaches over and gives my shoulder a sympathetic squeeze. I look up and smile and he smiles right back, and in that moment I realise that, somehow, time already seems to have healed itself, for he and I are entirely at ease with one another, and as comfortable as only old friends can be, friends who even after many years may take up an old conversation as if it had been disturbed only a moment ago.

I've no sooner finished this thought than a second one arrives. 'How did you find out about Lorraine?'

Mike shrugs. 'Oh, you know how it is. People talk. More than a few people, too, in this case.'

I'm rendered momentarily speechless by Mike's answer, having forgotten that in Myreton almost every move is made under the village's collective eye and ear. 'Were they polite, at least?' I ask.

'Oh, sure they were, Tom. Honestly, I've heard nothing but good things.' I see Mike glance towards me from the side of his eye. 'You're not offended, are you?'

'It just seems a bit... morbid.'

'Of course, it is. But it's only to be expected. It was the same when my mum died.'

Mike's Mum, Amani, was killed in a hit and run five years ago, while walking home from her evening shift at the golf club. She had walked only a hundred yards from the clubhouse when the vehicle – investigators later confirmed it was a 4X4 – mounted the kerb and crushed her against the wall of the old church. The noise of the collision woke a number of residents who raced from their homes to offer what help they could, but Amani was already dead by the time they reached her side. The investigation that followed was one of the largest in the county's history, with hundreds of people interviewed, but the driver had been quick to escape the scene of their crime and neither they nor the car they were driving were ever found.

'How are you doing after all that? I mean, you're alright?'

'Ah, mostly,' Mike says. 'Though it's still tough. She was an amazing woman. When I think of how much she sacrificed to bring me up on my own, working all the hours she did just to keep food on our table, I just... well, she was my hero, I guess.'

I'm not surprised to hear this. The youngest daughter of an impoverished, alcoholic sugar farmer, Amani sailed from Antigua to London a week after her seventeenth birthday in search of work and a better life. She spent a decade cleaning the homes of middle-class London families, before an abusive ex-boyfriend forced her to flee the city. She ended up, of all places, in Myreton, where she became the village's first black citizen and therefore something of a curiosity. A year later, Mike was born, though she told Mike nothing of his father other than that he was a 'no-good white man'.

I remember Amani well. She had a pretty face and shiny black hair and ripped upper arms from her years of cleaning bathrooms and polishing silver. She was petite and full of energy and worked long hours in various jobs through the village, making just enough money to keep her and Mike's heads above water. Mike's skin was a few shades lighter than hers, but they had the same dark eyes and the same warm smile, which rarely left Amani's face. Whenever I returned home with Mike after school, she was there to greet us with a delicious black cake and regale us with strange and fascinating stories of her Caribbean childhood. My afternoons at Mike's house were among the happiest of my young life, and Amani treated with me such tenderness and affection that I came to love her as much as Mike. 'She was a good person,' I tell Mike.

'She was,' Mike says. 'Which makes it all the worse, in a way. She just deserved so much more from life. I can't understand why she had to go as quickly as she did. Fifty-seven's no age at all, not these days. It pisses me off that she had to die so young when there are so many pricks out there living to a hundred.'

'Doesn't it get any easier?'

'A little. But don't ever let anybody tell you you'll get over it completely. Losing someone you love changes your life forever. You can't get over it because "it" is the person you loved, and how could you ever forget them? Why the hell would you *want* to?'

I look around in time to catch Mike wiping a sleeve across his eyes. 'As for the pain,' he continues, his voice thicker now. 'It might dull over time, but it never leaves you. You just have to find space for it inside yourself, along with all the other pains, and carry it around with you.'

I feel quite close to tears myself, suddenly. 'I'm so sorry.'

'Yeah, well,' Mike says. 'It's not your fault.'

'No, it's not. But I feel terrible that I failed so badly to stay in touch with you after I left for St Edwards. For fuck's sake, I can't believe I didn't even think to call after your mum's funeral. I should have been a better friend to you, Mike.'

'You were always a good friend to me. And you were no more to blame than I was for us growing apart. Believe me, I'm as sorry as you that it happened, but that's life. As for Mum's funeral, it meant the world to me just to see you there. Truly, Tom, I don't hold a thing against you.'

By now, we've reached the old farm steading that marks the southern tip of the village, where the road becomes little more than a muddy track between fields. At the end of this track, we make our way through a rusting iron gate, fixed permanently open against ranks of bramble bushes, and there, ahead of us, is Greywalls Castle. Away from the street-lamps, the darkness of the night steals my breath. There's just enough light for us to make our way to the front of the building. We make our way through the old arched entrance, then climb the crumbling staircase to the castle's one remaining turret, where we take a seat, huddled inside our coats against the cold night.

Mike takes out a pack of cigarettes and holds it out to me. I give him a shame-on-you look, then pluck one from the pack. 'So, have you recovered from your rendezvous with Daryll the other evening?' he asks.

I stare into the darkness, the unlit cigarette hanging

from my hand. 'It just... I just didn't get it. I mean, what the hell's the deal with that guy?'

The deal, according to Mike, is this: after dropping out of school, Daryll ignored his father's offer to join the family's plumbing business and moved instead to Edinburgh to set up his own micro-brewery. However, within three months he was declared bankrupt, and when Cockburn Senior refused to bail him out, he returned to Myreton to become a plumber after all. While he was apparently good at his work, he was far less interested in plumbing than in cementing his burgeoning reputation as a cruel drunk in the village bars. When, five years ago, Cockburn Senior's dicky heart finally gave out, Daryll celebrated by retiring from plumbing completely and hiring in a bunch of apprentices to undertake the work that arrived into his office. Since then, he's been busy pissing away the money they've earned him on ski trips, sports cars and beer.

'Alright,' I say, when Mike finishes his tale. 'So, he's an arse. But that doesn't explain why Emma was so upset by him.'

'That's true,' Mike admits. 'To be honest, I had no idea they had anything to do with each other. But the guy's a dick. And I should know – he's in the pub at least every other night.'

I draw deeply on my cigarette, sparks exploding in all directions. 'It doesn't seem fair, does it, for him to be doing so well. In an ideal world, he'd have ended up in jail years ago.'

Mike nods. 'Yeah. I mean, I was never a great believer in karma, but it stands to reason that at least some of the assholes from school should be struggling, doesn't it? I mean, come on, what's Tony Easton up to these days?'

'He's in Australia, last I heard. Wife, three kids, stinking rich.'

Mike considers this. 'Are you sure?'

'So says Facebook.'

Mike runs his fingers through his hair and rubs the back of his neck, the same way he always did when stressed. 'Okay, then. So, what about Neale Collins? He was always a bit of a tearaway.'

I shrug my shoulders. 'A lawyer, I heard.'

Mike stubs out his cigarette and flicks it angrily at a nearby oak. It lands a few inches from his feet. He sighs.

'And you?' Mike says, after a moment. 'Is it true about Lena?'

'That she dumped my arse? Afraid so.' I take a final puff of my cigarette, then crush it out underfoot. 'What about you?' I ask. 'Do you have anyone special?'

Mike shakes his head and tuts. 'Not since last Christmas. He dumped my arse too.'

'He...?' I smile, shake my head. 'You know, all these years and I never knew.'

It's hard to tell in the darkness, but I think Mike's blushing. 'Well, I don't make a big thing about it,' he says. 'To be honest, you're the first I've really told.'

'But... why? Mike, it's 2019. Nobody's going to judge you.'

Mike shrugs. 'Probably not, but... well, it's just easier this way, you know? I feel better just keeping the whole thing to myself.' He clears his throat and turns to fully face me. 'You won't tell anybody, will you?'

I shake my head. 'Of course not.'

Mike nods. 'I know. Didn't even need to ask, really.' He reaches out and lays a hand gently on my shoulder. 'You were always a good pal, Tom.'

'Yeah, well. Right back atcha.' I give Mike's knee a

friendly squeeze, then turn my head towards him, and he looks so intensely grateful for the compliment I've just paid him that my heart almost breaks. But I'm happy, too – happy beyond measure, really – and as we sit side by side, staring out at the glowing Milky Way, I'm filled with a sense of companionship that's been missing from my life for so long that it feels almost alien to me.

NINE

I WAKE UP THE FOLLOWING MORNING FEELING PRETTY GOOD. Not bright-eyed and bushy-tailed, precisely, but certainly less gloomy and slow-witted than I've been in recent weeks. However, I've no sooner begun to rub the sleep from my eyes than I begin to hear high cries from the floor above. Jumping out of bed, I run upstairs to find Dad sitting on the edge of my mother's bed, a wet flannel in his hand, and my mother yelling out in agony.

'She's in terrible pain,' Dad says, when he sees me standing by the door. 'She says it's her stomach.' Then he turns back to her. 'It's alright, my darling, shh, shh. Emma's just calling the doctor now. Shhhh.'

My mother's body arches, a cry tearing itself from between clenched teeth. 'Oh, Jack,' she says, plaintively. 'Make it go away.'

It's only now, as I turn my head from this dreadful scene, that I notice Sophie standing by the window, her eyes bright with tears. I cross the room and take her in my arms. 'Oh, Tom,' she says, miserably. 'It's just awful.'

'How long has she been like this?'

'She was sound asleep only an hour ago. Then I went downstairs for breakfast and Emma arrived and... Oh, I don't know!'

Just then, Emma arrives back into the room. She walks calmly to the bed and bends down close to my mother. 'It's alright, Lorraine,' she says gently. 'The doctor's leaving the surgery now. And look, I've got you a hot water bottle.'

'There we are, see?' Dad says, forcing a smile. Still perched on my mother's bed, he's trying desperately to remain positive. 'Dr Sullivan will have you right as rain in a few minutes.'

With Dad's help, Emma rolls my mother's duvet down to her waist and places the hot water bottle against her stomach. My mother's wearing only a thin nightgown, so it's distressingly easy to see the toll the disease has taken on her body. The skin on her upper arms hangs down like brittle paper. Her clavicles stand out like the bones of a shipwreck at low tide. Her legs are bruised and as thin as stalks. When Sophie sees this, she throws a hand to her mouth and runs, sobbing, from the room. I want to run after her, say something reassuring, but I'm numb, my mind blunt and slow as though I've just woken from a long sleep. Breathing hard, I turn to face the window, and I stay there, not moving, not really thinking, until I feel the warmth of a hand against my shoulder; I turn around to find Emma smiling gently towards me. 'I know,' she says. 'I know it's tough. But please, try to be strong.'

A few minutes later, Dr Sullivan appears by my mother's bedside. When she sees her, my mother lets out an audible sigh of relief. 'Oh, Catherine,' she says. 'It's my stomach. The pain's unbearable.'

Dr Sullivan nods sympathetically. She takes my mother's pulse, then fills a syringe and injects something into her arm. Almost immediately, my mother relaxes, and her eyes begin to drop. 'Oh, goodness,' she says, sinking back into her pillow. 'Oh, thank goodness.'

Under any other circumstances, I would be happy to see Dr Sullivan again. She's been a doctor in the village since I was a young child, and has helped us through chickenpox, mumps, measles, back pain (Dad's), UTIs (Sophie), and a broken leg (me, following an ill-conceived attempt to skateboard down a paved section of Myreton Hill). I haven't seen her for a few years, but she looks exactly the same as she always did, the same strong, handsome face, the same proud, honest expression. Even her hair is the same dark brown it always was, though she can only be a couple of years from retirement.

Whatever pain medicine Dr Sullivan gave my mother, it's certainly helped. Standing by the foot of the bed, Dad, Emma and I watch with relief as her breathing slows and deepens. When it's clear that she's comfortable, Dr Sullivan rearranges my mother's blankets, then walks over to Dad's side. 'I'm sorry,' she says. 'That can't have been pleasant for you. To be honest, I hadn't anticipated this much pain so soon. I'm afraid the cancer seems to be progressing far more quickly than any of us would have suspected.'

Dad sighs. 'The pain,' he says. 'It will happen again.' This is not a question; his voice is resigned.

Dr Sullivan nods sadly. 'From this point on, one of the most important things is going to be managing the pain. I'll make out a prescription for some morphine pills. You need to give them to her every eight hours to get her through the next part.'

'The next part?' I ask.

Dr Sullivan frowns. 'The pills will keep the pain at bay for the time being. Longer term, however, it's difficult to tell.'

There's a pause while Dr Sullivan weighs her next words. 'Jack, are you sure she won't consider hospice care?'

Dad shakes his head firmly. 'No. And neither will I. You can leave it to me to do all that's necessary to make her comfortable.'

Dr Sullivan reaches over and touches Dad's arm. 'I've no doubt she's in good hands. Just... it's not going to be easy.' She hands Dad the prescription. 'Take care, won't you? And call me whenever you need anything.'

When Dr Sullivan leaves the room, Dad turns to me and Emma. He looks exhausted, his blue eyes ringed with black shadows. 'Why don't you two go out and grab some fresh air. Go on. I'll hold the fort here until you get back.'

Emma reaches towards the paper in Dad's hand. 'Shall we take the prescription to the chemist?'

Dad smiles sadly. 'Dear Emma,' he says. 'Always thinking.'

We step outside to find the sky hanging low and heavy, the wind whistling through the old oaks that line the streets of Myreton Hill. So beautiful during the spring and summer months, they're now readying themselves for another long winter's sleep, and only a few leaves of brown and yellow remain on their otherwise bare limbs.

Emma and I walk down the hill in silence, which is hardly surprising, I suppose, given the events of the past hour. But we're still too haunted by my mother's tortured cries to be alone with our thoughts, so it's not long before we fall into conversation. I begin it by asking how Emma likes working with my parents.

'*For* your parents, you mean,' Emma says, and smiles. 'It's good. It has its moments, of course, like this morning, which was shit, but your mum and dad are really kind. And I've always liked to keep things clean and tidy, so I suppose I do get a sense of achievement from the work I do.'

'Is it what you always wanted to do?'

'What?' Emma asks. 'Housekeeping? No, not really. I suppose… I suppose there was a time when I thought maybe I'd go back to university, train as a counsellor. But it hasn't happened yet. To be honest, I'm not sure it ever will.'

'You don't know that.'

Emma sighs. 'I guess not. But I suspect no. I'm veering towards no.'

Neither of us speak for several moments. Then I say, 'It's horrid, isn't it, that feeling you missed out somewhere.' I look sidelong at Emma. 'If it helps, you're not the only one who feels like that.'

Emma turns to face me, her expression a question. 'You? Are you serious? You already have a successful career under your belt. And a marriage.'

'A failed marriage,' I point out. 'And work was hell, from the first day until the last.'

Emma tilts her head to the side, and her eyes are curious. 'That's something I don't get. If you hated your job so much, why did you ever get involved with it?'

'I never had a choice. Lorraine was determined to see me build a career in finance. When I finished school, she packed me off to Glasgow to study economics. After that, it was straight to the bank with me. She'd have killed me if I'd refused to follow her plan.'

Emma smiles a little, but the smile doesn't spread to her eyes, which are concerned. 'You speak about your mum as though she was some sort of tyrant.'

'She was, though, in her way. I'm not surprised you never knew. No one who met her ever guessed that she isn't the kindest, most generous, most charming person in the world. She's always known exactly what to say to different people, how to match her own mood to theirs. A person might be having the worst day of their life, but then they'll meet my mother, and within ten minutes they'll be laughing and clapping. But there's another side to her. A side they'll never get to see.'

'So, you were never close?'

'Oh, I liked her enough as a child, I suppose, but then I didn't know any better. As far as I was concerned, that's how mums were supposed to act. It was St Edwards that really did the damage. I'd been happy until then, but life was hell after she packed me off to Edinburgh.'

'You were never happy there?'

I shake my head. 'It was just awful. I have literally no positive memories of my time there. And it just… I mean, it *completely* shattered my confidence. I was wretched by the time I finished there, and a complete liability around other people. Truly, I hardly made a single friend at university, and I was a borderline hermit during my first two years at the bank.'

Emma smiles. 'From one hermit to another, two years is pretty impressive.'

'Thank you,' I say, grinning. 'I like to think so, too.'

We laugh, still in step with each other, then let the silence spread and break while we search for something else to say.

'So, your marriage?' Emma says, after a moment. 'Do you really think it's over?'

I shrug. 'I certainly won't be placing any bets on a reunion.'

Emma nods. 'I'm so sorry.'

'Yeah, well. Me too.'

There's another brief silence. Then, very quietly, Emma says, 'Do you... do you think she'll come to the funeral?'

Instantly, I feel my entire body tense. 'What? No. Why? Do you?'

'I don't know. Would you blame her if she did?'

I pause for a moment's reflection. 'Probably not.' Then, after another significant pause, I touch a hand to my stomach. 'Oh god. I feel a bit sick now.'

We're only a stone's throw from the chemist now. Smiling, Emma nods towards the building. 'I'm sure they've got something for that in there.'

Inside the chemist, we hand the prescription to Mr Simpson. When he hands us the medicine, he does so without pleasantries, except to say, 'Give my love to your mother.'

By the time we leave the chemist, I've begun to feel stupid for complaining so much to Emma. 'I'm sorry for the little pity party I threw myself before. Please don't think I'm always such a moan.'

'I don't think that at all. In any case, you're not really moaning, are you? You just have a lot of shit to make sense of right now.'

'Doesn't everybody, though?'

'Yeah, they do. And I'm sure they all need to sound off about it once in a while, too.'

'I haven't heard you complaining.'

'Me?' Emma says, with genuine surprise. 'Christ, Tom, I spend half of every day trying to figure out how to get my life back on track.'

'Oh. No offence, but that's actually kind of reassuring.'

Emma laughs. 'Of course, it is. Don't we all love to bask in a bit of schadenfreude now and again?'

'I just never thought it would be this complicated. I

knew I'd need to have a plan, of course, but I just thought that things would sort of fall into place by themselves once I decided what I wanted to do. Now, here I am, more than twenty years later, and I'm still no closer to the kind of life I imagined for myself as a child. If anything, I'm actually moving further away from it.'

Emma considers this for a moment. 'I never had much of a plan, myself. I just know I was supposed to be somewhere else by now.'

'You're not happy?' I ask.

'I'm not *un*happy. I just feel... lost, I suppose. I mean, how can I be this far along in life and still so unsettled? How can I know so much and still be this confused by everything? It just seems ridiculous.'

I smile. 'Are you having a little party of your own?'

Emma grins. 'I thought I might. How does it compare to yours?'

'It's pretty awful,' I admit. 'But I still think mine was worse.'

We continue to joke about our fears and trepidations the entire way home. It's not so bad, being depressed, when you've got someone to do it with.

TEN

On Friday I wake up early to a quiet house. It's the first time since I returned to Myreton that I've been first out of bed, and I don't like it; after spending so many months alone, it's been nice to finally have some company at the breakfast table. Still, there's no chance of me falling back asleep, so I throw on some clothes and shuffle towards the kitchen.

I'm halfway through filling the kettle when I see a plastic carrier bag by the side of the sink. On closer inspection, it contains a collection of Tupperware, and a note in my mother's hand:

Rose, dear,

Thank you again for all the delicious meals. If it weren't for you, I swear Jack would have spent these last two weeks eating nothing but beans.

L x

I've never been more grateful to read such a boring little note. Smiling, I grab the bag and my coat and skip happily through the front door.

I arrive at Pete's just in time to find Rose wrestling a

pram through the door, looking harassed. Behind her, Crawford is complaining about his coat, which, from the way he's crying and pulling at it, has been fashioned from live fire ants.

'Will you come on, Crawford,' Rose says. 'Please, we can't be late for nursery again.'

'This dacket's making me DIE!' Crawford shouts.

'Oh, don't be so dramatic. Do you want to ride on the buggy board?'

Crawford glares at his mother with barely concealed fury; clearly, this is the most ridiculous suggestion he's ever heard. 'Want my tooter,' he growls.

Rose raises an eyebrow. 'You won't get *anything* asking like that. What's the magic word?'

Crawford throws up his hands, appalled by the injustice of his mother's interrogation. But after considering his options for a few moments, he appears to accept defeat, and mumbles, 'Pees,' in a mournful whisper.

Rose forces a smile, before wandering off to grab the scooter from the garden shed. By the time she returns, Crawford's already been distracted by a football, which he's chasing to the opposite side of the lawn. 'Crawford,' she yells, 'will you... oh, for God's sake.'

I'm only a few feet from Rose now, but she's been so preoccupied with Crawford's antics that she hasn't yet realised I'm there. 'Looks like you're having fun,' I say.

'Jesus, Tom,' she says, touching a hand to her chest. 'You nearly scared the life out of me.' She leans over, kisses my cheek. 'How are you doing?'

'Better than you, by the looks of things.'

The hand at Rose's chest moves to her left temple. 'And this has been one of the easier mornings.'

Just then, Crawford spots me standing by his mother.

'Unco Tom!' he shouts, with obvious delight. 'You be the goal.' After a couple of fresh air shots, he finally makes contact with the ball, which rolls vaguely in our direction. When Crawford arrives to retrieve it, Rose grabs his arm, forces his helmet onto his head, and guides him onto his scooter. For a moment, it looks like he's going to take offence at being forced from his football, but then he decides he's happy enough with the turn of events and speeds off down the path and through the gate.

'You want me to walk with you? Bit of moral support?'

'Lovely,' Rose says, but her momentary smile drops when we reach the gate. 'Oh, no. Crawford?' She has to repeat the name three times at increasing volume to get his attention. 'Nursery's this way, darling, remember?'

Finally, we're headed in the right direction. 'So, how does it feel to be back home?' Rose asks.

'It's surreal. I mean, this sort of thing isn't supposed to happen, is it? It was always strange enough to spend a weekend here with Lena, but to find myself here alone, and indefinitely... it's like I've stumbled back in time.'

'Is it really awful?'

'I'm not sure. But then, I'm not sure how I feel about anything right now. The past half year's been such a horrifying shitstorm that nothing seems normal anymore. If I had to take a guess, though, I'd say that, yeah, it's pretty awful. I might be wrong, but... nah, it's crap.'

Rose smiles. 'Well, if it makes it any easier, we really do appreciate you being here.'

I'm about to ask who she means by 'we' – she can't possibly be referring to Pete – but require all my concentration to avoid tripping over Crawford's scooter, which is lying in the middle of the pavement. Crawford's standing a few yards away, staring longingly at the small playground that sits on the village green. 'Mama?' he says, turning sweetly to Rose. 'We can go to park?'

Rose lets out a long sigh, which is fair enough, given the direction the situation is clearly headed. 'Not just now, Crawford.'

Crawford frowns. 'But my want to go to park.'

'Sweetheart.' Rose speaks calmly, pointing to her watch. 'We don't have time for the park just now. If you're a good boy, maybe we can go *after* nursery.'

Crawford doesn't bother to argue. He just scrunches up his face, clenches his fists and begins to hyperventilate.

Rose turns to me. 'I'm so sorry. He's not usually like this.'

I nod.

'Actually,' Rose says. 'I don't know why I said that. He's like this practically all the time at the moment.'

We turn back to Crawford, who's emitting a series of whimpers that are slowly increasing in volume.

'Crawford,' Rose says. 'Just calm down.'

'No!' Crawford shouts. 'Won't calm down!'

'You're being very silly.'

'*You* silly,' Crawford says, stamping his foot. 'I want the swing.'

'Darling,' Rose warns. 'Nursery's due to start in ten minutes. If we're late again, there'll be no tablet time this evening.'

Crawford folds his arms and glowers at Rose.

'Crawford. Get back on your scooter now.'

'But... I... want... the... park!' Crawford wails.

And with that, the floodgates open; Crawford bursts into piteous tears, bawling so loudly that a dog walker – who's at least a hundred yards away – looks up from his phone to pass judgement on us.

'Oh god,' Rose says. 'Don't do this again.'

'Wait a minute,' I find myself saying. 'Crawford, maybe I could take you to the park this weekend.' The howling continues, but Crawford's eyes move from the ground towards me. Seeing that I have his attention, I look to push home my advantage. 'We could even go and get some sweeties from Mr Taylor's afterwards.'

Crawford stops wailing, sniffs twice. 'Stoberry bom boms?'

'Absolutely,' I say, nodding enthusiastically. I pick up the scooter and hand it to Crawford, whose face breaks into a slightly hysterical smile. Within seconds, we're back on route to the nursery.

'So, is this par for the course right now?' I ask, when I've found my breath again.

'The complaining?' Rose asks, and blows out her cheeks. 'Honestly, it's relentless. Last weekend, he screamed for half the morning because there was a bump in his socks. Yesterday, he had an hour-long tantrum because the sausage kept falling out of his sandwich.'

'It can't always be like this.'

'You'd think so, wouldn't you? Truly, I can understand those mothers who get arrested for throwing their kids against a wall.'

I give her a look.

'I'm not saying I'd do it, but I can understand the impulse. You just want to stop all the noise.'

'I wouldn't share that thought with anyone else if I were you.'

Rose laughs. 'I know, I'm sorry. I'm just thinking out loud.'

'I know it's none of my business,' I say, hesitantly. 'But couldn't Pete take some of the pressure off?'

Now it's Rose's turn to fix *me* with a look. 'Yeah, he could, if he was ever around. But I don't remember the last time we all had dinner together. *Or* breakfast, for that matter.' She reaches into the pram and touches her sleeping daughter softly on the cheek. 'It's just so typical of Pete to spend years badgering me for kids and then increase the number of hours he works as soon as the first one's born. Don't get me wrong, I wanted them just as much as he did, but is it too much to ask for a little help? I gave up my career completely when Crawford came along. The least Pete could do is take a step back from his own job while the kids are so small. Because I don't always feel like I can do it alone.'

'You can, though. You're doing really well.'

Rose shakes her head sadly. 'I'm a shitty mother.'

'You're really not, Rose.'

'Yes, I am. I swear too much and I've failed completely to build up a routine. Most days, I let them eat whatever they want if they make enough of a fuss. And I resent them, too, for tying me down in that enormous fucking mansion of ours.'

'You don't like the house?'

'We've got six bedrooms!' Rose exclaims. 'What the hell do we need with six bedrooms? Pete says he bought the place as a surprise for *me*. But it's me who has to keep the place clean and tidy while he's off working every hour God sends.'

'And you're sure he won't cut his hours at work?'

Rose snorts. 'Yeah, right. He's obsessed with the place. Honestly, it's all he ever talks about. I used to think it was funny, the way he was always on the go, never able to settle down for a second while there was still money to be made. Nowadays, it just pisses me off.'

I nod. 'It can't be easy for you.'

'It's not just me, though,' Rose says. 'It wouldn't be so

bad if it was. But how are the kids ever going to get to know their father when he's always off in Edinburgh chasing the Yankee dollar? Christ, even when he's here in Myreton, it's obvious that his mind's more on his job than his family. It breaks my heart to see it.'

I touch Rose's arm in sympathy. 'I'm so sorry.'

Rose looks at me and her face suddenly twists with pain. 'I've become a single mother, Tom.'

'Is it really that bad?' I ask.

Rose takes a hankie out of her sleeve and dabs at her eyes. 'I'm not even sure he loves me anymore.'

There's a moment's silence as I swallow a sudden lump in my throat. 'He does love you,' I say. 'I'm sure of it. He's just... well, come on, Rose, the guy's always been an arsehole. But he'll listen to you if you talk to him. Tell him how difficult he's making things for you. Tell him how selfish he's being. Tell him what a stupid fucking p–'

Given the torrent of abuse I'm about to unleash, it's probably for the best that Crawford chooses this moment to scoot up to us. 'Mama,' he says, furrowing his little brow. 'Why you crying? Have you hurted yourself?'

Rose turns to him and offers a brittle, unhappy smile. 'No, no. I'm alright, Little Lion.'

Crawford's only partially reassured. 'Get a plaster. That make it better.'

Rose nods, leans over to kiss Crawford's nose, but I can tell what she's thinking. *It'll take much more than a plaster to fix this one.*

And it's true. There's nothing in this world more difficult to mend than the pieces of a broken heart.

ELEVEN

OVER THE NEXT FEW DAYS, A STEADY STREAM OF VISITORS arrives to share tea with my mother in our living room and lie about how well she looks. My father welcomes each of the guests with an unfaltering stoicism, but it's clear that he just wants them to get out of his house and leave him alone to enjoy his final days with his wife.

On Wednesday morning it's the turn of Mrs Bates to pay her respects. I have known Mrs Bates my entire life, which is hardly surprising given that she's another of Myreton's Big Fish. No matter what's going on in Myreton – coffee mornings, council meetings, weddings, house-sales – you will find her among the spectators, her darting eyes taking everything in. Many people resent her sticking her nose into other peoples' business the way she does, but the fact remains that her activities place her at the very heart of life in the village.

I enter the living room to find her lolling in a tub chair in front of the fireplace. Like the rest of my mother's recent visitors, it's clear that the cancer's playing on her mind. She's just a little too jolly, a little too chatty as she sips her tea and pretends to admire the living room furniture. I find myself wondering how it would be if she had the courage to take my mother's hand and ask, 'How's the cancer?' But despite how thin she's grown, how pale her face has become, I know I won't hear the word, not from Mrs Bates or any of our other guests.

I'm only checking on my mother because Dad asked me to. He's always been completely intimidated by Mrs Bates. I hope to get out with a quick 'hello' and a smile, but as soon as I reach her chair, Mrs Bates catches hold of my wrist and pulls me towards her. 'Well, I *heard* you were back!' she says, smiling up at me.

'Yes,' I say. I'm not sure what else to add. I'm quite clearly back.

Mrs Bates is unperturbed. 'And, how *are* you?' The question sounds genuine, but it's apparent from the look she gives me, of mingled sympathy and eager interest, that she's already been apprised of my recent separation. Whether she received this news from my mother or from another of her many sources, I do not know.

'I'm very well,' I say. I'm determined to keep the old busy-body in check, but when I make to leave the room, she tightens her grip on my wrist.

'And your, uh... wife?'

'Still working as hard as ever.'

Mrs Bates smiles. 'Oh, I'm sure. Such an incredible young woman. Tell me, can we expect to see her here in Myreton anytime soon?'

'Well, time will tell.' I look entreatingly to my mother, who takes a final sip of tea before groaning to her feet.

'Norma, dear,' she says, 'it was so kind of you to come, but I really must get some rest now.'

It takes Mrs Bates a moment to realise that she has been

dismissed, and a few moments more to accept the fact. When she stands to leave, she crosses the room and hugs my mother; I see my mother wince and wonder where it hurts. 'Lovely to see you,' Mrs Bates says. 'I do hope we'll see you back at the WI before too long.'

It's a stupid comment, which makes my blood boil. But my mother simply nods her head and continues to smile as Mrs Bates collects her handbag and makes her way from the room. I wait until I hear the front door close before allowing my body to untense. 'Ugh,' I say. 'I should have followed behind and kicked her out the door. The stupid old cow.'

'Thomas!' my mother says, 'that's quite enough.'

'Well, she is,' I say, doggedly.

'I know she is, dear, but you shouldn't say so,' my mother explains. For a moment, she looks tempted to sit back down on the sofa, but then seems to think better of it. 'Tom,' she says, eventually. 'I think I might have meant what I said to Norma. I really am terribly tired. Help me upstairs to my room, will you?'

My mother's fast asleep by the time Sophie creeps into the living room half an hour later. 'Is Bates gone?' she asks. When I nod, she visibly relaxes. 'I hope the nosy old bag got soaked on the walk home.'

'At least then this rain would serve a purpose,' I say, looking towards the heavy, leaden sky outside the window. 'How long will it last?'

'Oh, only till it's over,' Sophie says, as she makes herself comfortable with her laptop on the sofa.

I let out a long, defeated sigh. I haven't left the house since the rain started on Sunday afternoon. It's Wednesday now, and I'm bored almost to tears. 'Fancy a game of Scrabble?' I ask. I hate Scrabble, but it's better than nothing.

'Sorry, Tom. I've got tons to do.'

As Sophie gets to work, I turn on the telly to check if anything good's showing, but it's not, unless you enjoy watching repeats of home improvement shows that nobody enjoyed the first time around, so I turn it off again and grab a book from the shelf. There's no space in my head for words, though, so I throw down the book and pace the floor for a bit instead. But pacing the floor's quite boring, so I pick up a few knick-knacks from the mantelpiece and put them down again before returning to the sofa where, after fluffing the pillows, I grab a pack of cards from the coffee table and...

'Tom,' Sophie says, 'if you don't stop fidgeting, I swear I'm gonna punch you in the throat.'

I laugh, thinking she's joking, but her expression tells me otherwise. I'm tempted to argue back, just for something to do, but Sophie's stronger than she looks and feistier than you'd think, so in the end I simply turn on my heels and leave.

By the time I reach my bedroom, I've already decided I should take the chance to grab some exercise, but then I catch sight of my laptop smiling at me from the top of my desk and it becomes immediately clear where my afternoon is headed. I know I shouldn't – I've steered clear of Facebook since I arrived in Myreton – but I'm upset and lonely and the pull is too strong. Before I can think better of it, I march across the room and throw the laptop open.

I should have thought better of it. Within two minutes, I'm on Lena's profile page and face-to-face with her ghastly new profile picture. It's not Lena that's the problem; she looks as stunning as ever in a red glitter dress and low boots.

The problem is Jeff, who's stuck to her left shoulder like a leech, and smiling the sickening smile of a man whose Christmases have all come at once. I check the date it was uploaded; the 18th October. It's as though she only needed me to find out about her new relationship before making it public. I click on the picture to find it already has over 200 likes. Below the photo there's a long string of comments from her friends – our friends – that I know I should ignore.

In a further act of self-flagellation, I read them all.

Is this the new man? He's gorgeous!

Seeing you two together is like watching a Disney movie IRL

You guys are too cute. I can't deal RN!

You guys should warn people before you're going to post something this cute!

I lean on the desk, my hands planted on either side of the keyboard, my head hanging over it. 'Fuck you,' I say out loud. I slam a clenched fist onto the top of the desk, then send a cup of pens hurtling against my wall. I haven't felt this betrayed since the morning my mother dragged me into her car to begin my terrible new life in Edinburgh. I jump up from my chair, blinking my eyes furiously when I feel them fill with tears. 'Fuck you,' I say again.

Then suddenly the anger leaves, and is replaced by utter exhaustion. I haven't the strength to rage. All struggle is beyond me. I shut the laptop and fall onto my bed, knees to chest, head to knees. My hands claw at my pillow, draw it into me. I want, desperately, somebody to hold, to be held by somebody. I can't remember the last time I felt so alone. Is this to be my life from now on, I wonder. Am I destined to be on my own forever? I press my face into the pillow. Once I've started to weep, I find I cannot stop.

TWELVE

THE FOLLOWING MORNING, I ENTER THE KITCHEN TO FIND THE sun shining, birds singing, and a squirrel scavenging nuts on the lawn. It's a heart-warming scene, and for a second, I feel almost grateful to find myself here in my parents' home. But then I blink, and the squirrel's gone, and I wonder why, until Chris races past the window, a furious purple blur in frantic pursuit of this latest imposter. He reappears a few seconds later, tail feathers spread in celebration of his latest victory against the rest of the world. I flip him the bird, then turn from the window to find my asshole brother drinking coffee with Sophie by the breakfast bar.

'What are *you* doing here?' I ask.

'Visiting Mum before work,' Pete says, without looking up from his coffee. 'That alright?'

'It's a free country,' I say, with a shrug. 'How're your balls?'

Pete sighs loudly and pointedly. 'Like you care.'

I appreciate that he's making no effort to hide his impatience with me. It means that I don't have to hide my irritation with him.

Sophie's been deliberately ignoring my scuffle with Pete; now, she puts her phone down and addresses us for the first time. 'While you're both here, are you all set for the dance in the village hall tonight?'

Pete groans. I look from him to Sophie, cluelessly.

'You didn't tell him?' Sophie says, realising.

'Forgot,' Pete mumbles.

She throws a chunk of granola at him. 'You don't have to come, Tom.'

'Yes, he does,' Pete argues. 'You spent an hour badgering me and Rose into going. If you let him away with it, then I'm not going either.'

'Well, in that case, you're both coming. I promised Norma Bates a week ago that I'd be there, and there's no way in hell I'm spending the night alone with that old boot.'

'Okay, okay,' I tell them. 'Of course, I'll come. You both make it sound so appealing.'

Sophie nods. 'Good. I'm pretty sure that Emma will be there, too, so we're bound to have a wonderful time. Tom, you have ten hours to get your costume ready.'

I gulp, audibly. 'A costume?'

Sophie tilts her head and smiles. 'Well, it *is* Halloween.'

Like many other things, I blame my aversion to Halloween on my mother. My earliest Halloween memories are of my mother locking the front gates and plunging the house into darkness to deter any guisers who were stupid enough to think of calling on us. A few years later, when Sophie and I began guising ourselves, my mother always made the absolute minimum effort required to justify sending us onto the streets in search of sweets.

The results were horrific. Every year, she'd throw a black bin liner over me, colour in my nose with her mascara, and attach a sock she'd stuffed with newspapers to my bottom. Then she'd declare the costume complete and go back to ignoring me completely. Even at age seven, I was aware of how ridiculous I looked. Sometimes I decided to throw on some additional make-up or attach a couple of ears to my head just to avoid confusion, but that was hard work: most years, I just wrote 'CAT!' on a sheet of paper and pinned it to my chest for everyone to see. Sophie had less need to explain her identity to our neighbours, but her *Ghost* disguise – one sheet, two eye-holes – was another classic in the shite costume genre.

Judging from her Facebook posts, Sophie has come to embrace Halloween completely. Every year she appears dressed – barely dressed – as a sexy vampire or slutty nurse or some other variation on the tramp theme. I'm fine with it – she's an adult of relatively sound mind, and she's not hurting anyone – but I'm aware of how standards for makeup and costume have grown in the past couple of decades, and resent being dragged into the big ol' annual pissing contest to see who can waste the most time and money on their outfit.

A quick call to the costume shops in Edinburgh confirms there isn't a thing left to rent or buy at any price, and I realise, to my horror, that I'm going to have to cobble together something from the family wardrobe. I spend the entire morning searching the house for ideas, my panic rising with every uninspired minute that passes. It shouldn't matter, I know, but I'm feeling it – the pressure to come up with an original, inoffensive costume is through the roof.

The solution comes after a full three hours of rummaging, when I find an orange vest and plaid shirt in some old forgotten suitcase near the back of the attic. I look at them with almost tearful gratitude, then carry them down to my room, where I quickly find the denim shirt and trainers to complete the outfit. I fall back onto my bed, breathing an enormous sigh of relief.

At seven o'clock, I'm standing self-consciously in our hallway when I hear the sharp click of heels on the oak floor behind me. Turning around, I see that it's Sophie, and that she's opted once more for the pre-packaged sexy look. Her legs are covered in the world's tightest hot pants, with black boots laced up to her thighs. She has a leather jacket on and it's zipped up half way, showing off an unnerving amount of cleavage. On her head, a tiny pair of sequinned horns offers proof that this is a legitimate costume rather than some middle-aged man's wet dream. However, with so much else on show, I doubt they'll be the source of much attention.

'Hells bells, sis, that's a lot of boobage,' I say, as Sophie reaches my side.

'Thanks.' says Sophie, grinning proudly. 'Who are you supposed to be?'

'Huh? I'm Marty McFly. From *Back to the Future*?'

'The film?'

'No, the Victorian romance novel. Yes, the film.'

Sophie looks again at my costume, a wrinkle forming on the bridge of her nose. 'I mustn't have seen it,' she says, drily. 'Shall we go?'

I watch her walk towards the door in her half layer of clothing. 'Aren't you going to put a coat on?'

Sophie turns to me, disgusted. 'Don't be ridiculous.'

'Ridic...? It's absolutely freezing outside.'

Sophie rolls her eyes. 'Tom, this is the one night of the year where I can dress up however I want without being remotely judged. Just let me have my fun, would you?'

The village hall is already packed by the time we arrive. Myreton's local band, the appropriately-named Unbeerables, is on stage, playing covers of old rock songs, as they have at every party for the past thirty years, to a handful of spectacularly uninterested men in varying stages of intoxication. Right now, they're about half-way through *Bohemian Rhapsody*, and while it's not a song generally associated with Halloween, the way they're murdering the operatic passage really is genuinely shocking, so credit where credit's due, I suppose.

'Oh, Christ,' Sophie shouts, grimacing. 'If there's such a thing as turning in your grave, Freddie Mercury must be getting a lot of exercise right now. Shall we get a drink?'

We make our way across the hall, the previously impassive men becoming noticeably more attentive as Sophie struts by. When we reach the makeshift bar, a trestle table selling wine, beer and not much else, it's Mike who's there to greet us. He's dressed in a fitted black T-shirt over jeans. His upper arms are more muscular than I'd imagined.

'Why aren't you in costume?' Sophie asks.

Mike grins. 'Bar person's privilege.'

'Lucky for us,' Sophie says, with a wink. 'Gives us a chance to see those big strong arms in action.'

'Oh,' Mike says, the colour rising in his cheeks. 'Well...'

'No need to be shy, Big Boy,' Sophie says, touching a hand to Mike's forearm. Then, leaning suggestively towards him, 'Can you tell what I've come as?'

Against his better judgement, Mike sneaks a glance at Sophie's outfit. From where he's standing, it comprises at least sixty per cent cleavage. 'You're a... sexy devil?'

Sophie throws a hand against her chest. 'Oh, Michael, stop!' she squeals, fanning herself with a beer mat. 'You're making me blush!'

Poor Mike looks like he might die on the spot, to Sophie's obvious delight. 'Best just to ignore her,' I tell him. 'And Sophie, I'm no astronomer, but last time I checked, the earth revolved around the sun and not you.'

Sophie narrows her eyes and looks at me for a moment, a spaghetti-western look, before thrusting out a finger and corking a wet willie into my ear. I'm still deciding whether to retaliate when Pete arrives by our side. 'Bloody hell, Sophie,' he says. 'Where'd you hide the other half of your costume?'

Pete's dressed as post-makeover Sandy from *Grease*, complete with five o'clock shadow and a pair of lop-sided boobs. It's impossible to look at him without laughing.

'Hey, how come Mike doesn't have to dress up like a dickhead?' he says, grinning. Then he turns to me and makes a quick inspection of my costume. 'You do know Marty McFly wore Nikes, right?'

I sigh internally, and possibly externally too. 'I'm also pretty sure that Sandy Olsson wasn't seven foot tall, but there you go. Where's Rose, by the way?'

'Rose? Ah, she was ambushed at the door by old Bates and Mrs Higgins.'

'Oh, my god,' Sophie says. 'And you *left* her there with them? Honestly, Pete, you're bloody hopeless.'

We walk back to find Rose still cornered by the two old bags, both tall and angular, both appropriately dressed in home-made witch costumes. I give Rose a nod, and she momentarily makes her eyes go big, an SOS. Norma Bates is in full-flow, and she's saying, '... but in fact the title of Prince or Princess is reserved for Royals who were *born* into the family. Marrying into the family doesn't mean that you'll be a king or a queen, or even a princess.' Sophie and I hover a few feet away, momentarily distracting Rose, who replies, 'Yes, it's fascinating, isn't it?'

I still have no idea how we're going to rescue Rose when Sophie touches my arm. 'It's fine,' she says, with a grin. 'I've got this.' Turning quickly, she cruises over to Rose and smacks her on the arse. The women gape at her. Sophie winks at them. 'Don't worry,' she says, grabbing Rose by the wrist. 'She loves it.' Twirling awkwardly under the force of Sophie's grip, Rose raises a hand in farewell to Mmes Bates and Higgins.

'Oh god, I'm mortified,' Rose says, once she's by our side. She's the Danny Zuko to Pete's Sandy, and looks every bit as ridiculous as her husband in her matching leather and thick black wig.

'Would you rather we sent you back?' Sophie asks.

But Rose isn't listening. 'Oh, Mammy,' she says, her eyes fixed on Sophie's chest. 'Would you look at those hooters, there?'

With the subject of my sister's breasts out of the way, we all take a moment to sip our drinks. I look around the hall and see Daryll by the stage. He's wearing a false Mexican moustache that apparently passes for a costume in itself. He's also staring furiously towards me.

'Is that... Daryll?' Sophie says. I see something pass over her, a brief shudder, before she checks herself and raises a hand in greeting. Daryll's surprised, but a quick look over his shoulders confirms the gesture's meant for him. He begins to wave back, just in time for Sophie to turn her hand and lower all but her middle finger. Daryll's mouth's just begun to fall open when Sophie grabs my arm and spins me back towards Pete and Rose.

'What the hell was that for?' I ask, but she's already found an excuse to ignore me.

'Oh my god! You look amazing!'

I look around and see that Emma has arrived. She's

come dressed as a 1920s flapper girl, complete with silver sequin dress, black jazz shoes and an abundance of Art Deco jewels. Her hair, which is usually pulled back, has been tucked into a faux bob and decorated with a glitzy headband. Sophie's right; she really does look beautiful, though the minutes leading up to her arrival have clearly been stressful, as there's a thin film of sweat on her brow.

'You look hot,' I tell her.

'I *am* hot,' she says, fanning herself.

It's not what I meant, but I let it pass. 'Where did you find the costume?'

'Hmmm?' Emma says, straining to hear me over the noise in the room. 'Oh, everywhere. But charity shops mostly. Thirty-four of them, to be precise.'

'Really?' I say, genuinely impressed. 'How long did *that* take you?'

'Don't ask,' Emma says, raising an eyebrow. 'But it had to be done. Parties are terrifying enough, even without the added worry of being the one person to turn up in a half-arsed costume.'

'A costume like this?' I ask, passing a hand over my own outfit.

Emma frowns, confused. 'No. You're Marty McFly, and Marty McFly rules. Especially at Halloween.'

I beam at Emma, grateful beyond words for her kindness and filled with a new confidence that I look something other than ridiculous.

The Unbeerables announce they're taking a short break from playing, and the room breathes a collective sigh of relief, but almost immediately somebody somewhere flicks a switch, and the Bobby Pickett version of *The Monster Mash* begins to play. I expect a rebellion then, but instead Rose squeals and claps her hands. 'Oh, my god, I *love* this song!'

And with that, she sets off, a one-woman conga line, across the room.

'Oh, shit,' Pete says. 'She's going to ask me to dance with her.' Sure enough, Rose waves from the dancefloor, beckoning him over. Pete turns to Sophie, grabs her wrist. 'Come with me. Please.' Rolling her eyes, she takes his hand and together they weave through the crowd towards Rose.

Emma and I watch as Rose and Sophie dance themselves into a sweat, Pete next to them waving his hands in the air and hopping from foot to foot like a man on hot coals. 'You don't fancy joining them, do you?' I ask.

'Oh, fuck off,' says Emma.

I assume she's talking to me, and am momentarily offended. But then I realise her eyes are fixed on Daryll, who's begun making his way over to us, and I find myself thinking precisely the same thing.

Having stumbled across the dancefloor, Daryll throws his arms open towards Emma. 'Hey Gringo!' he shouts, his voice slurred. Presumably, he's been keeping in character by drinking pints of tequila.

Emma glares at Daryll. 'What do you want?'

The question's not entirely friendly. Daryll's smile drops, his cheer evaporating. 'I just wondered if I could have a word with you.'

Emma hesitates for a moment, then nods.

'You'll be alright?' I ask. 'Do you want me to –'

Daryll cuts across me, mimicking me with an effeminate, high-pitched voice. 'Do you want me to hold off the big nasty man... For Christ's sake, Halliday, I'm asking for a quick chat, not a fucking elopement.'

He leads her over to the stage, just as Sophie arrives back from the dancefloor, her face shining with sweat and excitement. 'Where's Emma?' she asks.

I nod my head towards her and Daryll. We watch as Daryll – who's talking intently to Emma – suddenly reaches forward and takes her hand. Emma snatches it away and says something abrupt to him. Shaking his head angrily, Daryll turns and storms off to the bar, his eyes fixed ahead. Sophie watches after him, shaking her head. 'You know, I think I'd almost feel sorry for him if he wasn't such a motherfucker.'

I look to her, confused. 'Where's all this coming from? You haven't even spoken to the guy in over twenty years. Have you?'

Sophie turns to me. 'Don't want to talk about it,' she says gruffly.

Before long, Emma returns to our little corner, fanning herself as though the room has suddenly grown too hot. Sophie and I look at her but she keeps her eyes on the ground. We all stand in the awkwardness of our silence for a moment, while all around us the place bustles. Then Emma touches a hand to her forehead and says, 'I need some fresh air.'

'I'll come with you,' I say, and before she can think to argue I link my elbow through hers and lead her from the crowded hall.

Outside, the night is cold, chilling the sweat on my face. The crisp scent of autumn leaves wafts through the gentle breeze, and the stars shine with a cold blue light. We sit on a nearby bench, huddling inside our costumes for warmth, and we remain there in silence until I poke my elbow gently into her. 'You don't have to tell me anything, but you need to speak with somebody. Truly, the way Daryll's acting...'

'Is awful,' Emma says, miserably. 'I know.' She groans into her hands, then leans forward, propping her elbows on her knees. 'Oh, Tom, it's just ridiculous. I don't know how it came to this.'

'Came to what?'

'This!' Emma says, wiping a tear from her eye. 'This... fucking *shit*. I mean, I didn't even ask... I didn't want...'

I place a hand on her arm. 'You can tell me.'

Emma takes a deep, stuttering breath, gives her eyes another furious wipe. When she begins to speak, her voice is very soft. 'It happened a few months ago. I was out on one of my walks when I started to feel a little light-headed. I stopped to rest on a bench by the smiddy, and after a minute or two Daryll drove past, and he stopped to offer me a lift home. I wanted to say no, but he looked genuinely worried about me, and he was really insistent, so... yeah, I got in the car.'

'Emma, he didn't...'

'No. But when we reached the house, I realised he'd put the lock on my door. I made a joke about it, and he smiled this weird smile and told me not to worry, he just wanted to talk a while. He told a few stories – these really dumb, boastful stories – and I laughed as much as I could, but he kept stroking my hair and my neck, and when I told him to stop his hand moved to my thigh – my very, very *upper* thigh – and then I got really scared, and I guess he saw that, because suddenly the door was open and he shouted for me to get the fuck out the car.

'He came round the following week to apologise, and he looked so miserable that I forgave him there and then. Ever since then he's hardly left me alone. He follows me around the village and shows up at the house whenever he's had too much to drink, which is a couple of times a week at least. I've made it clear there's no chance of anything, but he's...

well, he's stubborn. It's as though he thinks I belong to him or something.'

'Have you told the police?'

Emma shrugs. 'What could they do? There isn't a shred of evidence against him.'

'What about your parents, then?'

Emma shakes her head. 'They've had enough of my shit to deal with. Besides, Dad's not as strong as he used to be. I don't want to add to his troubles.'

'What if I were to speak with him?'

'No!' Emma says her eyes widening. 'Please, don't do that. I'm fine as things are. I mean, I wish he'd leave me alone, but... I'm okay. I'm not frightened or anything.'

'You sound frightened.'

She touches a hand to my arm. 'Please, Tom. Please just let it go.'

So, I do, and we fall into a silence that's comfortable enough for us to remain side by side on the bench. It's terribly cold, our breath dancing in front of us as we sit hunch-shouldered in our coats, hands buried deep in our pockets, but we remain there until the band stops playing and the guests make their merry way from the hall towards the nearby tennis courts. Sophie's one of the last out of the hall and shivering so furiously that the contents of the wine glass she's holding spill over her boots. 'Yay,' she says, through chattering teeth. 'There's f...f...fireworks.'

'How's it going in there?' I ask, as we all make our way behind the hall.

'G...good,' Sophie says. 'You missed Rose busting some moves to Gh...Gh...*Ghostbusters*.'

I can't help laughing then. She sounds ridiculous. 'S... sorry I missed it.'

Sophie rolls her eyes. 'Very f...f...funny,' she says. 'Now, shut up and g...gimme your jacket. I'm f...freezing my f... fucking tits off here.'

The light's still on in my mother's room when Sophie and I arrive home. We walk upstairs to find Dad sitting on the edge of the bed with the novel he's been reading to her for the past few nights. When he sees us, he places the book on his lap. 'How was your evening?'

'Lovely,' I say. 'The fireworks were good this year.'

'We noticed.'

'You saw them?'

'We watched the whole thing from the window,' my mother says, beaming. She lays her hand on my father's. 'It was beautiful.'

'Yes, it was,' he says, and smiles back at her.

And right then, right in that moment, my heart rips open as I realise for the first time how completely my father will miss my mother when she's gone. I mumble goodnight and turn from the room before anyone can see the tears that have sprung to my eyes.

THIRTEEN

THE FOLLOWING WEEK, I ARRANGE TO MEET MIKE FOR A DRINK at the Myreton Inn. It's a Monday evening, so the bar's empty, save for three of the Myreton greybeards who adopted the place as their permanent haunt when the County closed a few years back. Mike and I find them all at least three sheets to the wind and holding court by the bar, giggling like a bunch of schoolboys.

'Hey, Merv,' says one. 'Should you no' be getting back to that wife of yours? You know how she gets when you're out past curfew, eh? The old ball and chain!'

Merv punches his friend in agreement. 'Aye, you're no' wrong, Gary. Eight ball and chain gang. You'd better watch out yourself before Maggie's here to drag you home by the ears.'

'Oh, dinnae,' says Norrie, the final member of the old-time trio. 'I've sat through a thousand silly horror films in my time, but the thought of my wife walkin' through that door scares the shite out of me.'

They've been talking like this for years. They love to pretend they're afraid of their wives, almost as much as they love pretending to flirt with the barmaids, Sharon and Amy, who will spend their evening serving drinks and wearily smiling at invitations to throw off their aprons and run away to lives of unbridled passion.

Mike and I have barely settled onto our stools before Norrie grabs hold of Sharon's hand. 'Hey, darlin', here's a question for you. I always thought happiness started with an H. Why does mine start with U?'

Sharon, the older of the two women, picks a piece of lint from the sleeve of her shirt and flicks it onto the floor of the bar. 'I don't know, Norrie,' she says speculatively. 'Maybe it's like some subset of dyslexia. In any case, I'd probably see a doctor if I were you.'

All the men laugh. Although she's not quite as attractive as Amy, Sharon's more popular with these old-timers, because Amy makes them nervous. She never joins in with their banter or calls them by name, only smiles, and sometimes doesn't even do that. But Sharon's been waitressing in Myreton for as long as I can remember, first in the County and now here, and knows exactly how to deal with all manner of customers. The old-timers love her, and greet her retorts – particularly the insulting ones – with delight.

Having received his marching orders from Sharon, Norrie shakes his head and turns his attention to Amy. 'How about you, sweetheart? Do you fancy the washing machine experience?'

I watch Amy resisting the urge to roll her eyes as she pretends to polish the bar with the sleeve of her shirt. 'No, Norrie, I do not want your dirty load.'

'Oh.' Norrie looks at Amy, disappointed. 'I didn't expect you to know that one. Alright then, how do you like whales?'

'I don't want to humpback at your place, either,' Amy says, without missing a beat.

Norrie grins. 'You hear this, Mike?' he shouts from across the bar. 'Bet you never get knocked back like this, good looking laddie like you. Probably chasing the girls off wi' a stick, eh?'

I look up just in time to see Sharon and Amy shoot sideways glances towards Mike, and realise I'm perhaps not the only one who's aware of his leanings. Mike, though, is unfazed by the comment. 'You've seen yourself how difficult it is, Norrie. If you can't get them, I don't see what chance I've got.'

Norrie chuckles appreciatively. 'What about your pal, there? Is he married?'

All eyes turn to me. I scratch at my chin, uncertain how best to answer the question. In the absence of any better ideas, I go with the truth. 'Sort of.'

'What do you mean by that?' Merv asks. 'You're either married or you're no'.'

'Well, in that case, I suppose I am. For now.'

Gary, who's sitting at the far end of the bar, leans back in his stool to look past his friends and towards me. 'Here,' he says, scrunching up his eyes for a closer look. 'Here, that's never Lorraine Halliday's youngest laddie, is it?'

Again, all eyes are on me, but the answer's simpler this time. When I offer it, the heads of all three men drop solemnly to their drinks. Some time passes before Merv clears his throat and asks, 'How *is* your mother, son?'

'She's... resting. At home.'

Gary brushes back his hair, which he wears with a deep careful side part to cover his bald spot. 'I heard she was a wee bit... Well, I heard, if you don't mind me saying, I heard, uh...'

Norrie bats Gary irritably on the shoulder. 'Word's going around that she's dying, Tommy. Is that right?'

'I'm afraid so,' I say.

The men stare down at their pints once more. After a moment, Merv clicks his tongue sadly. 'I remember when your mother arrived in the village,' he says, a far-off look in his eyes. 'We were all stinking jealous that your father had found himself a woman like her. Gorgeous, she was. You've got her eyes, you know.'

I'm disturbingly flattered by this comment. I think the drink might be getting to me. I shouldn't have left the house on an empty stomach.

Norrie sighs. 'First time I ever saw your mother, she was standing outside the old Queen's Hotel,' His manner is surprisingly emotional; his voice has a cough waiting in it. 'She looked so fancy that I thought she was maybe some film star who'd come here on holiday.'

'Here, do you mind the time she played the Little Mermaid in the village hall?' Merv asks. 'It could only have been a year or two after she arrived here.'

'I mind it,' Gary says. 'Maggie played Cinderella in that same performance. Bloody awful, she was, as was everybody else, until your mother swept onto the stage wearin' nothing but this tiny wee dress and singin' like an angel. I ended up buying tickets for every single show after that.'

'She was quite somethin',' Merv says, with a far-off look in his eyes.

'Aye,' Gary says. 'She was that.'

~

Last orders come a lot earlier in the country than back in London, and I'm not nearly ready to leave when Sharon begins to usher us out of the pub.

'You don't fancy a lock in, do you?' Mike asks hopefully.

Sharon touches a hand to her forehead. 'Mike, I've been here since two o'clock this afternoon. I would rather shit in my hands and clap than stay here a second longer than I have to.'

'Quite right,' Norrie says. 'In any case, this one's comin' home wi' me tonight.'

Sharon turns to Norrie. 'It's quarter to eleven. Why would you want me to follow you home at quarter to eleven?'

'Why would you think?'

'I don't know. So you can murder me?'

Norrie chuckles. 'See what I'm up against?' he asks, turning to his friends. While they pretend to comfort him, Mike turns to me. 'Hey, Tom,' he whispers. 'I've got a half bottle of whisky back at the house. You fancy taking this party elsewhere?'

I nod enthusiastically. Mike picks up his glass of beer and drains it in one sustained quaff. Then he steadies himself with a hand planted on the bar and climbs down from his stool. I make an attempt to finish off my own drink, but I've had more than my fill of beer for one evening. I place my half-finished glass on the bar and rise unsteadily to join him.

'G'night, ladies,' Mike says, staggering ahead of me towards the exit. Then, 'C'mon, Tom'. Stifling a hiccup, I wave a hand to Sharon and Amy and follow Mike in his zigzag retreat to the car park.

When we arrive at Mike's house, I wait in the garden while

Mike stumbles inside for the bottle of whisky. In the driveway there's an old, rust-covered Vauxhall with an alarming amount of gaffer tape holding it together. On the filthy side-panel, with a finger, someone has written, 'I wish my wife was as dirty as this.' I'm admiring this when Mike arrives back by my side.

'I see you've met Bessie,' he says. 'Beautiful, huh?'

'Mmm. I bet the chicks go crazy for her.'

'You know it,' Mike says, grinning. 'Fancy a spin?'

'Let's leave it for another day,' I say. 'Perhaps when I'm dead.'

When we reach Greywalls, we sit down on our turret and pass the bottle between us. The more we drink, the more we laugh until, at a certain point of drunkenness, a switch is flicked and the conversation turns confessional.

'Thomas?' Mike says.

'Michael?'

'You know Emma?'

I nod. 'I'm familiar with her work.'

'Ha!' Mike says. 'That's funny. But, yeah... how do you think she is?'

I shrug. 'Good,' I say. 'Well.'

It's obviously the answer Mike was hoping for. Something inside him immediately relaxes. 'It's so nice to have got to know her again after all these years. And you, obviously.'

I toast him with the bottle, take a sip of the whisky.

'We make a pretty good team,' Mike says, leaning back unsteadily on his elbows. 'We're like that old John Huston movie. You know the one, with the horses? Marilyn Monroe was in it, and that guy with the moustache. Clark What-shisname.'

'You're talking about *The Misfits*, right?' When Mike nods, I have to laugh. 'Jesus, that hardly says much for us. The characters in that film are a bunch of total losers.'

'Well, yeah, they are,' Mike admits. 'To start with. But when fate brings them together in that little town, they become... stronger, I guess. They become something so much better than the sum of their parts. That's like us, don't you think?'

For the second time tonight, I'm incredibly flattered. 'Well, if you say so.'

'I do,' Mike says. 'And, also, I need a pee.' He rises unsteadily to his feet, then stumbles sideways towards the edge of the turret. I make a grab for his leg, but just in time he rights himself and sets off down the uneven stairs. I listen as he pees noisily against the front wall of the castle while humming a few lines of an old ABBA song. When he arrives back to the top of the turret, he falls back onto his elbows. He says, 'Tom?'

I look over to find him grinning at me through the darkness. 'You should move back here, marry Emma. Then I could be your house boy or something, and we could all live happily ever after.'

'Ha! You'd be bored of me in a week.'

Mike shakes his head. 'Nope,' he says. 'Nope, nope, nope, nope, nope. Because the thing is...' He takes a deep breath, places a hand on my shoulder and puts his lips close to my ear. He hiccups once, solemnly, and begins to speak in a conspiratorial whisper. 'The thing is, it gets very lonely here in the village sometimes. There's times when weeks go by and just... nothing happens.'

'That's... I'm not sure that's really much of a secret, Mike.'

Mike throws an arm around my shoulder and rests his cheek against mine. 'What I mean is, I'm happy you're home. I missed you, Tom.'

Before too long, the bottle of whisky lies empty on the

grass in front of us and Mike appears to have talked himself out. In the silence that follows, Mike begins hiccupping with the most intense seriousness and mental concentration, and I realise that he's thoroughly, disgracefully drunk. 'Come on,' I say, helping him to his feet. 'I think we've had enough excitement for one evening.'

I manage to get him up, but then he sways up against the castle wall, and does not seem keen to move. 'D'you think, perchance, we could call a taxi?'

'We're half a mile from any road, Mike. Come on. Get moving.'

'A horse!' Mike shouts. 'My kingdom for a horse.'

'Yes, yes,' I say. 'Come along now. Here's my arm. Got my arm? Got it?'

'Or a donkey,' Mike says. 'My kingdom for a donkey.'

'Oh, come on,' I say. 'Grab my *arm*.'

'Arm of the law!' Mike shouts. 'Quite right, Colonel. Hup. two three four. And March!'

But Mike, in spite of saying this, does not himself march.

'D'you think February can March?' he asks, turning to me. 'I don't know, but I think April May.' He follows this with a snort of laughter so violent that it propels him away from the wall. I catch him and, taking advantage of the forward momentum, begin the journey homewards.

'My kingdom,' Mike says, returning to his earlier point. 'Wouldn't get much for it now, state the country's in.'

'Yes,' I say. 'Good point.'

'Tories,' Mike says. 'String 'em up.'

'Yes, yes,' I say, soothingly. 'Tories.'

'Bunch of crim'nals,' Mike says, misanthropically. 'String 'em all up.' And with that, he drops his head and is silent for the remainder of the journey.

Mike seems to have dozed off by the time I open his door

and lead him inside. I help him out of his coat and then, lifting him once more by the armpit, lead him towards his bedroom. 'You were always a good man,' Mike says, looking up at me. As he speaks, gusts of boozy breath hit my face.

'Yes, yes.' We've reached the room now, so I drop Mike onto his bed and throw his duvet over him, then make my way to the kitchen to pour him a glass of water.

The house, I'm shocked to realise, is more like a monk's cell, as though Mike took a vow of poverty earlier in life. An ancient TV sits in the far corner of the main room on a cheap fibreboard stand that also contains a DVD player and a couple of tatty paperbacks. Forming an L in front of the TV is a sofa and a small coffee table, while in the centre of the room, a rickety desk appears to double as a dining space. Outside of this small living area and Mike's bedroom, the house contains nothing more than a tiny kitchenette and an even smaller bathroom. Unlike Bessie, however, the entire place is immaculately clean.

I walk back through to Mike's room and place the glass of water on his bedside table. 'Want me to stay with you tonight?'

He stares up at me from his pillow. 'No offence, bub, but you ain't my type.' But when I make to leave a moment later, he reaches across the bed and says, 'Actually, would you mind? I feel a little preculiar...'

'A little *what*?'

'Perooc... Prelook... Aaw, I feel shite, Tom.'

'Okay, okay,' I say. 'I'll take the sofa.'

He's asleep before I even turn off the lights.

∾

In the morning – the very late morning – I wake and make a tentative assessment of my physical and mental condition. Incredibly, I don't feel too bad. My mouth's a little fuzzy, my stomach a little unsettled, but generally I seem to have got away with it. Relieved, I drag my body from the sofa, scribble a hurried note to Mike, who's snoring noisily in his bed, and start off towards home.

I've managed to steer clear of Chris for the past few days, but when I reach the house he's there by the gate, almost as if he's been waiting for me. I try to round him, but he thrusts his long neck forward and snaps his beak painfully around my thumb. When I raise my hands above my head to prevent further attack, he turns his attention to my crotch, his beak digging terrifyingly into the fabric of my trousers. I begin to weave in the direction of the house, Chris' wings flapping madly as he attempts to maintain his hold on me. I finally manage to shake him off as I reach the front steps, but losing hold of my trousers has made Chris frantically angry, and he begins to shake his tail and beat his wings with renewed vigour. I sprint up the steps, trying to get through the front door so quickly that I bounce off it, my shaking hand unable to get the key in the lock first time.

I must have made quite a rumpus as I fell through the door. I haven't even caught my breath before my mother appears at the top of the stairs. Dressed in a thin nightdress and walking with her cane, the ravages of her disease are clear to see. I try not to wince at the sight of her.

'Tom,' she says, her voice unbearably small. 'I thought it might be you. Would you be a darling and bring me a cup of tea?'

When I make my way upstairs a few minutes later, my mother is sitting back in bed with a mountain of blankets piled around her. Her pale, waiflike features are sharp, and her hair is an unwashed, tangled mess. She turns towards me and pats her duvet, inviting me to sit beside her. I cross the room and, after placing the cup of tea on her nightstand, perch awkwardly on the edge of her bed. 'I'm sorry if I woke you.'

She shakes her head wearily. 'I've been awake for hours.'

'You should get some rest. You look tired.'

My mother looks at me, dark circles under her eyes. 'Tom, the way I look has nothing to do with lack of sleep. I look like this because I'm dying.'

'Oh, come on,' I say. 'There's plenty of life left in you.'

My mother smiles. 'Poor Tom,' she says. 'It's awful, isn't it, having to watch your words all the time, act all nice around me.'

'What do you mean?'

'It's not so easy to hate me now, is it, what with everything that's going on.'

'For goodness' sake, Lorraine. You're talking nonsense.'

'No,' she says, softly. 'No, I'm not.' She looks out of the window a while, then turns back to me and smiles and pats my hand. 'You needn't look so offended, darling. I've known for long enough the things you hold against me.'

'Mother...' I say, but she cuts me off with a little shake of her head.

'Another time,' she says. 'Let's do this another time.' She moves a hand to her temple and holds it there. A gold bracelet slides down away from her wrist. Tiny diamonds catching the light.

I swallow the lump that's caught in my throat and walk silently from the room.

FOURTEEN

On Friday, Rose invites Sophie and I around to the house. We arrive at eight, armed with some fancy wine Dad handed us from his cellar. Unsurprisingly, it's Rose who answers the door. Crawford's there, too, talking like he's done ten lines of cocaine. 'Unco Tom, you missed what happened today because I was at the table with the naked sand and I was making a big cake and then I gave it to Mummy and I said "eat a bit of this cake" and she did, she ate a bit, but it was really yucky because it was made of the naked sand!'

'*Kinetic* sand,' Rose says, 'It's called *kinetic* sand.'

But Crawford's way too wired to listen. 'And then after lunch Mummy was changing Ellie's nappy and we took Ellie's nappy off and Ellie farted and a poo fell out and went on the floor!'

'Darling,' Rose interrupts, 'I'm not sure everyone likes that story as much as you do.'

Perhaps not, but it's absolutely slayed Crawford, who's laughing so hard that he's having to gasp between phrases.

'And... and it was... so smelly... Mummy had to... open the window!'

Rose rolls her eyes, then leans in to give me and Sophie a hug. As she's doing this, Crawford gives his eyes a final wipe and says, 'Unco Tom, when are you going to play ball with me? Because today me and Mummy was throwing a ball and Mummy keeped throwing the ball in the wrong erection. I told her she was doing really good, but atchly I just didn't want to make her sad.'

'Oh,' I say. 'Well, that was kind of you to consider Mummy's feelings. But why don't you ask Daddy to play football?'

Crawford giggles. 'Daddy works inna bank, silly.'

'Well, yes, but it's the weekend. You could ask him to play tomorrow.'

'Unco Tom,' Crawford says, his expression turning serious. 'Daddy works inna bank. He's too tall to play football.'

We've reached the lounge now, where Pete's sitting with a bottle of beer, watching the news. 'Pete doesn't do football,' Rose says, with a meaningful glance towards her husband.

Crawford reappears with a glass paperweight he's grabbed from the mantelpiece. 'Hey, Unco Tom, do you want to play cats?' he asks, and I actually whimper, my hand rising involuntarily to my face.

'No,' Rose says, plucking the paperweight from Crawford's hands. 'No. We agreed you could stay up for our guests. Now it's definitely time for bed.'

'Aaw,' Crawford groans. 'Just another hour.' But Rose stands firm, so he gives each of us a kiss, and then walks this Charlie Brown walk, head down, like a rain cloud's following him, all the way up the stairs. 'You don't fancy doing the bedtime tonight, Pete?' Rose asks. 'No? No? No. Thought not.'

With Rose gone, Sophie and I turn our attention to Pete, whose attention, in turn, remains firmly on the television. We join him on the sofa just in time to catch the end of a local weather report and the start of an advert for kitchen cleaner.

'So, how was your day?' Sophie asks.

Pete sniffs. 'Yeah. Alright.'

'Work going well?'

'Mmm hmmm.'

'And the kids?'

'Yeah. Fine.'

Sophie narrows her eyes at Pete in disgust. 'Oh, my fucking god,' she says, punching him hard on the arm. 'Could you be any more of a douche?'

Pete doesn't answer, just takes the remote from his lap and switches channels. We all sit in silence as the Channel 4 News begins to play.

By the time Rose comes back downstairs her eyes are heavy, and I suspect she nodded off herself while putting Crawford to bed. 'Oh, Pete,' she says, when she sees Sophie and I twiddling our thumbs on the sofa. 'You might at least have got some drinks.'

Pete's been lost in the telly, but Rose's mention of 'drink' somehow filters through to his consciousness. Turning to Rose, he smiles and nods, then gulps down the remainder of his beer and waggles the empty bottle at her. Rose throws him a look, which he fails to notice, before grabbing the bottle and heading through to the kitchen.

'Jesus, Pete,' Sophie says. 'What did your last slave die of?'

'What?' Pete says. 'I'm tired.'

'From what? Another day fucking over your clients?'

Pete makes a pfft sound. 'Oh, spare me all the "evil banker" shit, Sophie. That stuff's ancient history. Yes, we all know there were plenty of bad apples back in the day, but bankers nowadays are a different breed from the bastards who brought the country down. My colleagues and I care about each and every one of our clients...'

And he's off, waxing lyrical about this new generation of bankers, about how much less greedy, how much more ethical and informed they are than their predecessors. It's bollocks, of course, but Sophie and I remain silent; maybe Pete will stop talking if he thinks we're in agreement. It doesn't work, though – Pete's still going strong when Rose reappears with the tray of drinks. I roll my eyes at her and make a blah-blah hand puppet. Sophie mimes putting a gun to her head and pulls the trigger.

Rose sits down next to Pete and lays a hand on his arm. 'Darling, do you think we could talk about something other than work?'

'What?' Pete looks at her, offended. 'You say that like I'm obsessed.'

'Aaw, you're not *obsessed*, Pete,' Sophie says, flashing him a patronising smile because she feels like winding him up. It has the intended effect; Pete turns his head to the window and sips his beer huffily. Sophie turns to Rose. 'So, how are things here at home?'

Rose has taken a sip of wine and takes her time swallowing. She glances at Pete before she answers. 'Good.'

'Hmmm.' Sophie says. 'And the kids are well?'

'Oh, you know,' says Rose. But I don't, and I won't, because Sophie suddenly turns her body towards Rose, effectively cutting me off from their conversation. Left alone with me, Pete passes the time listing, in intricate detail, the terms and conditions of a recent investment he made with a construction firm in Dundee. I pass it quietly contemplating the various ways I could kill Pete.

Half an hour later, Pete's completed his trade deal and moved onto a long story about an awards dinner to which he was recently invited, a story with a few well-known names but no context or narrative, as far as I can tell. Somehow, like a ventriloquist drinking a glass of water, he's managed to consume another three bottles of beer without pausing for breath. I sip my drink and occasionally nod or smile when I feel it's appropriate. I'm starting to feel slightly tipsy by the time Rose finally glances over Sophie's shoulder and notices the glazed look in my eyes. 'Pete,' she says, gently. 'You're doing it again.'

Pete turns to Rose, confused. 'Huh? No, I was just telling him about the party last month, when Sir David and his – oh, yes, yes, very amusing,' he mutters, as Sophie drops her head onto Rose's shoulder, feigning narcolepsy. 'Actually, Tom was perfectly interested. You were interested, weren't you, Tom?'

'He's wasn't, Pete,' Sophie says, dryly. 'The poor boy's bored to tears.'

Pete folds his arms across his chest. 'Well, I'm sorry if you find my life so depressingly dull.'

'Nuh-uh,' Sophie says, shaking her head. 'Not your life. Just your work. Your kids are awesome, and so is Rose, but trust me, nobody gives the first fuck what you get up to with your wee wanky-banky pals.'

Pete sniffs. 'Not a very intelligent remark when you've been badgering us all year for a donation to your charity.'

Sophie snorts. 'For all the good *that's* done. I'd have more luck drawing blood from a stone.'

Pete and Sophie glare at one another. The atmosphere's becoming rather strained. It's nothing new – my brother and sister have always sparred like this – but I've never quite got used to it, and neither has Rose.

'So, you're saying money's not important?' Pete continues.

Sophie nods. 'That's right.'

'And you haven't given any thought to the money you're about to inherit.'

'Thought about it, yes. But I don't care a damn.'

Pete's nostrils flare, not so much in anger as in a kind of exasperated amusement.

'Right,' Sophie says. 'So, *I'm* the freak here, because I'm not counting the days until Mum's money drops into my account?'

'Hey,' Pete says, defensively. 'I'm not counting anything. I'm just saying it's normal to think about it. I find it strange that you haven't shown more of an interest.'

Sophie turns to me. 'What about you? Have thoughts of a second home been keeping *you* awake at night?'

I shake my head. 'To be honest, the whole subject makes me pretty uncomfortable.'

Sophie nods. 'And you?' she says, turning to Rose.

'Oh, Rose doesn't count,' Pete interrupts. 'It's not *her* mother we're talking about.'

'Right,' Sophie says. 'Because why would Rose ever dream that she should have a say in how *your* money's spent?'

Pete blanches. 'You're making me sound like an arse,' he grumbles.

'No,' Sophie says. 'You're doing that all by yourself.'

And with that, the four of us hunch a little further into the sofa, our wine glasses held in front of us like shields, and we remain there, staring awkwardly at the carpet, for a very long time.

FIFTEEN

My mother's condition begins to deteriorate rapidly over the next few days. Her hand starts to tremble whenever she lifts her cup of tea. It becomes so difficult for her to swallow that she's forced to swap her beloved shortbread for yoghurts and pureed fruit. She begins to rub, almost unconsciously, at her temple as though she has a pain there.

And the rages begin. As the pain intensifies, her temper continues to weaken, transforming her from time to time into a person I've never seen before. She rages when Dad tries to help her on with her coat. She rages when the novel she's reading gets splashed with tea. She rages when Mrs Hendrie pats her arm during a visit to the house ('Like a rabbit in a petting zoo').

It's shocking to watch. While my mother has never been a patient woman, neither has she ever been prone to losing her temper. When these bouts of anger come, she seems so different from the mother I know that it's almost as though the cancer itself has found a voice. That, or it's the voice of her medication.

I manage to avoid my mother's anger until Tuesday

morning, when I'm sent up to her room with a pot of tea. Emma's already up there and greets me with a smile, but my mother's clearly out of sorts. 'Tom,' she says, as I reach her side. 'I need one of my pills.'

'Your pills?' I say. 'But you're not due one until after lunch.'

My mother hardly pauses, but I hear the edge come into her voice. 'Get me a pill, Tom.'

'But Dr Sullivan said –'

'I don't *care* what Dr Sullivan said,' my mother shouts. 'Just get me one of my fucking pills.' There's something wild in her eyes, something so desperate it borders on rabid. Stunned, I turn and walk in silence to the medicine cabinet. When I return with the pill, my mother grabs it out of my hand and throws it into her mouth, then washes it down with a sip of water. 'I can't see why it matters to you in any case,' she mumbles. 'After all, an overdose would suit you perfectly.'

'What are you talking about?'

My mother laughs. 'Oh, come on, Tom! You want me dead! You want me to die so you can go and get on with your pathetic little life.'

I look at her with my jaw hung. It takes a while to get it up where it belongs so I can talk. 'That's... That's not true.' I glance over at Emma, who's been watching us from the corner of the room. She looks away self-consciously and wipes a duster around the edges of the window.

I look back to my mother. 'I should go,' I say. She doesn't respond, just stares, fierce and determined, at the sunlit square on the wall ahead of her. I remain by her side, frozen in disbelief, a moment longer, before turning and walking from the room.

I'm not more than ten feet along the corridor when I

hear the patter of footsteps behind me. I turn to find Emma already by my side. 'Please don't worry about what your mum said. She didn't mean it.'

'It certainly sounded like she did.'

'She didn't. She's just in pain. And she's scared.'

I look at Emma, doubtfully.

'I know what I'm talking about, Tom. I said some terrible things to my own family back in the day.'

'Really?'

Emma nods. 'They did everything they could to help but almost all of it annoyed me. The anger just built up. It needed to be released, and I never cared a jot who caught the brunt of it. Looking back now, I'm shocked the words even left my mouth. But fear and exhaustion will do that to you.'

'So, what should I do?'

Emma shrugs. 'Just... be nice. I know it might be difficult, but she'll appreciate it. She might not show it, but she'll be grateful.'

It seems worth a try. And so, for the next three days I play the doting son, doing everything I can to make my mother comfortable and wearing an elaborately faked smile that leaves my jawline sore to the touch. In an ideal world, I'd have continued this charade for the remainder of my visit, but by Thursday evening I'm starting to suspect I'm going actual bat-shit crazy, so I pick up my phone and arrange to meet Emma and Mike at the Myreton Inn. An hour later, I'm gathering my coat from the hallway when Sophie's head appears from around the living room door. She's wearing the same haunted expression I've begun to recognise in myself over the past few days.

'Room for one more?' she whispers.

'You don't even know where I'm going.'

Sophie tiptoes quickly across the hallway. 'Unless you're planning an actual trip to Hell, I can't imagine it could be any worse than this.'

I look around to the stairs and cast my mind back over the last 72 hours. Fair point well made.

I start to tell Sophie to hurry up and get ready, but when I turn back, she's already by the door and struggling into her shoes. I'm startled by how fast she's moved; if she were a cartoon sketch, there'd be a puff of smoke and ZOOM! written in large letters where her form should be. I have to hurry to catch up with her.

We arrive at the pub to find Mike and Emma already seated at a table with Amy. I turn to Sophie, who's gazing around the place with the same astonished expression I wore here a fortnight ago. 'Whoa,' she says. 'Time warp.'

I smile, take a step closer to the bar. 'What are you drinking?'

Sophie looks to me. 'It doesn't matter. It'll be going down too fast to taste.'

A couple of hours later, I have a pretty good buzz going and the atmosphere in the room has become almost festive. Sophie's holding court at the table, telling funny stories to me and Emma and Sharon, who, in the absence of any other customers, has made herself comfortable on a stool and left us to fetch our own drinks. Mike's standing by the jukebox, putting together a playlist of old-time classics that's already too long for us to get through before closing time. A few feet away, a decidedly wobbly Amy is standing in the middle of the floor with a pint-glass of wine and belting out the Bonnie Tyler classic *Total Eclipse of the Heart*. She's getting the words wrong but singing it with gusto nonetheless.

Sophie's started telling us about a trip she took to Paris

with Bill a few years back. I've heard it before, but it's a good story and always worth a listen.

'So,' she says, 'It's our last night in the city, and Bill books us a table at this really fancy little restaurant. He hopes I'll see it as a big treat, but I've been eating nothing but bread all week, and, honestly, I'm stuffed to the gills. I haven't taken a shit in days, and there's just no room left inside me for anything. So, when we get the restaurant, I order a plate of the French onion soup, which I manage to force down, then spend the rest of the meal sipping water while Bill makes his way through three huge courses of this delicious food. Man, it looked so good, and I was so jealous, but, you know, hey ho...

'Anyway, I sleep okay that night, but the next morning I start to get these awful pains in my guts. I know it's the shit knocking on my insides, pleading to get out – desperate to get out – but I haven't even reached the toilet when the taxi arrives to take us to Charles de Gaulle. And I think, *Fuck.*

'As usual, Paris is chock-full of traffic, so when we get to the airport there's no time to do anything but check in and run to the gate. By now I'm freaking the fuck out. It's genuinely 50/50 whether I'm going to get to a toilet on time. Then we arrive at the passport check and, obviously, there's a massive queue. By the time the passport guy invites us up to his booth, I'm barely holding my arse together and there's sweat pouring down my face. But then there's movement somewhere inside me and I think, *oh, sweet Jesus, there might be room for a fart.* So, with infinite care, I unclench my cheeks, and yes, oh, thank God, this huge, silent fart releases, and finally I can breathe again. But my relief's short-lived. On the third inhale, I become aware of this French, oniony smell. By the fifth inhale, it's impossible to ignore. Bill takes a couple of steps back from me, tries to throw me an accusing look, but it's not easy because his eyelids have started to flicker. A few seconds later, the passport guy notices it; I know because at this point, he ACTUALLY FUCKING GAGS. The smell – honestly, the smell. It's just unbearable. I can't even look at the poor guy as he hands us the passports back. He's clearly wishing to be anywhere else right then, but where can he go? I leave him there with actual tears running down his cheeks.'

'Oh... you poor... cow!' Sharon's laughing so hard that she has to gasp for breath between phrases. 'That's just... mortifying!'

Sophie grins. 'So, the next time someone tells you that only *raw* onions make you cry? Don't believe them.'

Our laughter appears to have broken the spell that was keeping Mike by the jukebox. He walks back to the table, followed closely by Amy, who groans as she falls clumsily into an empty seat. Some of her hair has come loose from her ponytail, and it cups her face. Her mouth is screwed into a pout of serious contemplation, and I wonder what she's thinking until it becomes clear that she's simply trying to decide which of the tables in front of her is actually real. We watch with bated breath as she lowers her glass towards a coaster, then breathe a collective sigh of relief when she touches down with the majority of her drink still intact. Amy nods, satisfied, and then, with a final, serene smile, drops her hands to her knees, hiccups and promptly falls asleep.

We stare at Amy with a kind of horrid fascination, trying to comprehend the sheer scale of the hangover she'll wake up to in the morning. Finally, Sharon turns to Sophie. 'So, uh... Bill's in Australia?'

Sophie reluctantly peels her eyes away from Amy. 'Mm

hmm. For at least another fortnight. Which, let's face it, is hardly perfect timing.'

Sharon touches Sophie's hand in sympathy. 'I'd heard about your mum. How *are* things?'

Sophie shakes her head, slouches down into her chair. 'Cancer sucks,' she says. 'It really does. Honestly, when my time comes, I hope it's quick. I hope a bus will just appear from nowhere and – bam – dead.' The words are no sooner out of her mouth than she swings her head around to Mike. 'Oh god,' she says, horrified. 'Mike, I'm so sorry.'

Mike waves his hand dismissively. 'Don't be silly. It's just one of those things people say. To be honest, I used to think the same thing. I never imagined myself with a lingering illness, subjecting myself to the doctors and nurses and the pain of it all. But then, after Mum... There was no time to prepare, to say goodbye. So maybe a little warning wouldn't be too bad after all.'

'That's what I'd choose,' Sharon says. 'A nice long death, so I can get my affairs in order, maybe tick a few things off my bucket list. I heard kidney failure was a good way to go – that you just kind of fade out and then... that's it. You're gone.'

'Perfect!' Mike says, slapping the table. 'Put me down for one of those.'

Sophie considers it for a moment. 'Nah, screw that. I'm sticking with quick. The quicker the better.'

Mike smiles, then turns to me. 'What about you, Tom?'

I shrug. 'I have no answer. I figure it'll be whatever's appropriate for me.'

Sophie rolls her eyes. 'Oh, don't be so boring.'

Emma clears her throat. 'I know what you mean, though, Tom,' she says, shyly. 'I've come close enough a few times to know there's no *good* way to go. Some ways are better than others, of course, but however it happens, the end result will always be the same. I guess all you can do is try to be happy and make the most of your days, so when the time comes, the people you leave behind can rest happy knowing you lived your best life.'

I look to Sophie, convinced she'll have something to say to this, but her gaze has fallen to the table. She's the strongest person I know, my sister, but Emma, it seems, has punctured through a layer of her near-impenetrable defences. It's some time before she raises her eyes again, and when she does, they're brimming with tears. 'What do you think, Tom?' she asks, quietly. 'Do you think Mum's lived her best life?'

I close my eyes, suddenly exhausted. 'I don't know.'

Emma clears her throat. When I turn to her, I find her eyes are on me and that they're seeking permission to speak. She doesn't need it, of course, but I nod in any case, inviting her to continue. She takes a deep breath. 'I don't know Lorraine like you do, obviously, but I know there's a lot she's grateful for. A loving husband, three amazing children, two beautiful grandchildren; these aren't things to be sniffed at, and she knows it. She loves you all so much.'

We fall silent then, listen thoughtfully to the jukebox. Gloria Gaynor's playing, which is fun, but very soon she makes way for *Everybody Hurts* by REM, which only serves to intensify the maudlin mood. I look to Sophie, who's staring sadly at her drink. She does this all through the first verse, Michael Stipe's haunting vocals filling the room. Then, quite suddenly, she pushes her glass aside, places her head down on the table, and begins to cry. And because of all the beer I've drunk, or because I miss Lena, or because of all my mother's pain and suffering, I start to cry right along with her.

~

By closing time, Amy's snoring peacefully in her chair. Nobody wants to wake her, so Sophie and Mike each grab an arm and sleepwalk her into the back seat of Sharon's car. It proves rather a struggle in the end, so Sophie offers to ride with Sharon to Amy's flat and help get her back out of the car. I watch with Mike and Emma as Sharon's taillights fade into the mist that's settled over the village.

Mike lives only a few yards from the inn, so when he sets off for home, Emma and I join him on his journey. After bidding him goodnight, Emma says goodnight to me in turn, then sets off towards home. But I'm not keen to let her walk by herself, so I jog to her side and fall into step with her, keeping my eyes down to avoid any possible attempts at protest. But Emma only smiles. 'You do realise you're not in London anymore, don't you?'

I shrug. 'You can't be too careful these days.'

Emma laughs. 'Oh god, you sound exactly like my parents – who, incidentally, will be in their living room right now, waiting to see that I get home safe.'

'That's nice.'

'Well, yes. But then again, I *am* 35.'

'You'll always be their baby.'

Emma considers. 'Yes. There's that. But also, I think they've just forgotten how to relax around me. I really did give them a hell of a time back in the day.'

'They must be so proud of you for fighting the illness like you have.'

Emma shrugs. 'They're certainly relieved. They were so happy when I told them I was going out tonight. A year ago, I really struggled to go out socialising at all. Now I've been out three times in a fortnight, and to the local *bar*, no less.'

She clears her throat. 'I have you and Mike to thank for that, you know. It's been a long time since I had such good friends around, friends I could trust to accept my peculiarities and keep me safe. I really am so lucky to have met you again.'

I turn to Emma in surprise. The timescales might be different, but she's just described precisely how I've been feeling over the past couple of weeks. For a long moment, I search for something meaningful to say, but nothing comes. In the end, I only nod my head in recognition of her words.

We continue the journey in contented silence. The mist is growing thicker now, diffusing the yellow lamplight, creating an eerie glow on the streets below. As we walk, the village begins to vanish around us. In the absence of sight or sound, I suddenly become aware that Emma and I are holding hands. Quite possibly we have been for some time.

Conditions on Myreton Hill are even worse than they were at sea level. By the time I'm halfway to the top, I can barely see more than a few feet in front of me. The whole thing's just a little bit too reminiscent of an '80s horror movie for my liking, so I start whistling a tune to distract myself from the uneasy feeling that's building in me. It works, too, until a shadow appears by my parents' gate and I almost shit my pants.

'Alright, dickhead?' it says.

I squint towards the face. 'Daryll? What are you doing here?'

'I'm here to offer a friendly warning.'

'Oh?'

Daryll nods. 'You stay the fuck away from Emma Barnes or I'll cave your head in.'

'That's your idea of a friendly warning?'

Daryll takes a pack of cigarettes from his pocket, lights one, and takes a long, deep drag. 'I never fuckin' liked you, Halliday, but these past two weeks, I've liked you even less. I've gone easy on you out of respect for your mother, but I'm done with all that now. I swear, you're fucking dead if I see you talking to her again.'

'I'm not even allowed to speak with my mother now?'

'I'm not talking about your mother,' Daryll says. 'I'm talking...' He falls silent, shakes his head wearily. 'You think you're so fucking clever, don't you? Well, we'll see how clever you look when you're walking round town with a broken neck.'

'I thought you were going to kill me.'

'Yeah,' Daryll says. 'I am.'

'But first you're going to break my neck.'

Daryll nods.

'I don't know, Daryll. It all just seems a touch haphazard, as plans go.'

Daryll takes a step forward. We're standing so close now that our chests are touching. I can smell the harsh whisky on his breath and feel the spittle as he speaks. 'Just stay away from her, Halliday. I'm not kidding. Do you hear me?' He stands for a few seconds, waiting for an answer. When I give none, he storms off back into the darkness with his shoulders heaving like a bull's.

I stand motionless for some minutes, waiting for the fury to drain out of me. Then, when I can breathe again, I push open the gate and traipse towards the house, where I throw off my coat and stalk through the hall past my father, who looks at me with a discreet question in his eyes that I ignore.

SIXTEEN

THE FOLLOWING MORNING, I'M SHUFFLING ZOMBIE-LIKE towards the coffee machine when I find Dad pacing back and forth across the hallway. His shoulders are slumped and his face wears a pale, beaten look, his eyes fixed ahead of him with an expression of fear. I call his name but he doesn't hear me, so I cross the room, place a hand on his shoulder. He stops pacing and then, very slowly, turns to me. 'Dad?' I ask. 'What's wrong?'

Dad stares at me for a moment, bewildered and shell-shocked. 'Your mother had a difficult night. I've called Dr Sullivan. She'll be here soon. Let's hope... I mean, I'm sure... Oh, god...' He's exhausted, and on the verge of tears, and I have no idea how to help, but then, thank goodness, the doorbell rings, and relief that is almost tidal in scale washes over him like a wave.

I've gone to elaborate lengths over the past couple of weeks to avoid Dr Sullivan's visits to the house; the last call I attended left me reeling for days, and I'm not keen to go through the same trauma a second time. But Dad's clearly carrying a huge weight on his shoulders, and I don't want to add to this by staging yet another ill-timed disappearing act. So, when he and Dr Sullivan head upstairs to my mother's room, I force myself to follow.

When we reach the room, the signs of my mother's recent struggle are painfully clear. Her bedsheets lie tangled around her, and the room, as large and airy as it is, holds the distinct odour of sweat. My mother lies prone on the bed, looking pale and exhausted, her blue eyes ringed with dark shadows. When she sees Dr Sullivan, she raises herself from her pillow, but it's clearly an effort. To save her further discomfort, Dr Sullivan paces quickly to the side of the bed. 'How are you feeling?' she asks.

My mother's lips quiver as she replies. 'Not so good.'

Dr Sullivan takes my mother's hand. 'I'm sorry, Lorraine. I know this is all very difficult.'

My mother's head drops, and a moment later, tears begin to fall onto their joined hands. 'I'm sorry,' she says, pulling a tissue from her sleeve and dabbing at her eyes. 'I'm usually better than this.'

'There's no need to apologise for expressing your feelings, Lorraine.' My mother considers this for a moment, then nods her agreement. 'Right, then,' Dr Sullivan says, patting her hand. 'Let's have a look at you.'

I watch, dazed, as Dr Sullivan moves around my mother, flashing lights in her eyes, taking her pulse. Part of me is frightened – for what's just happened, and what's still to come – but for the most part, I'm ashamed to say, I'm simply relieved I managed to sleep through the nightmare that played out here overnight. But then Dr Sullivan brings my mother up into a seated position on the bed and her nightgown slips down over her shoulders and, for the first time, I see how fully the cancer has taken hold. The skin on her upper arms hangs loose as though it has lost interest in life, and the basins of her collarbones are deep enough to collect water. I hold my hand to my mouth and turn away, my head against the cold oak jamb of the door.

I spend the next few minutes staring at the floorboards of my mother's bedroom, trying desperately to ignore the pounding in my skull. I'm aware of nothing until, finally, mercifully, Dad and Dr Sullivan brush past me and into the hallway. I follow behind, still reeling.

'You'll be back soon, won't you?' Dad asks, when we reach the front door.

'Yes,' Dr Sullivan says, buttoning her coat. 'She'll be needing me more often now.'

'Dr Sullivan?' I say, my voice cracking a little. 'I just... It's just...' I clear my throat. 'How long?'

Dr Sullivan turns to me, her eyes gentle. 'It's impossible to say for sure. At this stage, it's more important to make the best of the time you have than worry about how much time there is.'

And that's precisely what we do. Over the next few days, we take her out in the car, wrapped in coats and blankets against the cold, to the beach, and the county museum, and for lunch at a couple of little restaurants she never got round to visiting. She gets tired very easily, and sleeps through the afternoons, but in the evenings we all huddle together on the living room sofa to watch one of her old favourite films.

Old friends and acquaintances continue to approach my mother each time we step outdoors, crowding around her wheelchair with compassionate smiles. I can't remember how people used to greet her before she was ill, but now they seem to make a special point of it, and I wonder if talking with her makes them feel virtuous, like they've done a good deed.

On the sixth day, we're taking a walk around Cranston harbour when we meet Janet Patterson, a small, jovial-looking woman with wiry grey hair who served on the tennis club with my mother, and who, following my mother's first diagnosis, set up a rotation with a group of fellow Myreton housewives to ensure that neither of my parents would go hungry during her illness. 'Lorraine!' she cries, grabbing my mother's hands. 'It's so good to see you out and about.'

'Well, I wouldn't get too used to it,' my mother says.

'You look well,' Mrs Patterson says, her eyes crinkling up with sympathy.

My mother sighs. 'Oh, come on, Janet, I look bloody awful.'

Mrs Patterson's face drops. 'Oh. Well... I mean to say...'

Dad lays a hand on her arm, smiles sympathetically. 'How's Mr Patterson?' he asks.

That brings the smile back to Mrs Patterson's face. 'Oh, you know David. I thought he might settle a bit once he retired, but if anything, he's more restless now than he ever was. I tried buying him some things for the garden, then some watercolours, but nothing seems to suit him, so he just sits in front of the telly all day, complaining that he's nothing to do. Still, he's a stubborn old bugger, so I doubt I'll ever find a way to change him now.'

'You could threaten to leave him,' my mother suggests.

Mrs Patterson laughs. 'Oh, you're terrible,' she says, then looks at me. 'She was always the terrible one.'

I can believe it, I think, but I only smile.

～

Through all these adventures, my mother has been busily planning our first family dinner in more than a decade. At least once every day, I've found her leafing through cookbooks and worrying what to serve, what wine to serve with it, which dishes to use, which clothes she and Dad should wear. Finally, on Friday morning, a delivery van arrives with all the ingredients for the evening's meal. I'm in the kitchen unpacking them when my mother appears by the door.

'Right, then,' she says, taking a seat at the breakfast bar. 'I thought it best to keep things simple. We'll make some potatoes and green salads, and I've bought some nice steaks to go alongside. Rose told me the little ones will be happy with a pasta Bolognese.'

'Sounds lovely,' I say.

'Indeed. So, shall we get started?'

I gulp, audibly. 'Pardon?'

My mother rolls her eyes. 'Well, Tom, I'm not exactly bursting with energy these days. Your father will take care of the dinner itself later this evening, but there's still a good bit of prep to do. You can spare an hour of your time to help, can't you?'

So, I do, peeling the potatoes ready for boiling and putting together a bowl of horseradish sauce ('You know I've always hated cutting corners,' my mother says, when I ask her why she didn't just buy it in a jar). By late morning, we're as well-prepared as it's possible to be.

'You know, it's a shame we never did more of this together back in the day,' my mother says, as I begin to stack the dishwasher.

'Really? I only ever remember being shooed from the kitchen whenever I tried to offer any sort of help.'

My mother considers this, and sighs. 'I suppose I *was*

always a little more impatient than I should have been. But I did love you, you know.'

I look to my mother. 'You were dutiful,' I tell her. 'Maybe you considered duty to be the same thing as love.'

My mother gasps. 'Oh darling,' she says, tears springing to her eyes. 'Oh, darling, I think that might be the cruellest thing you've ever said to me.'

'Lorraine, I'm sorry. I –'

My mother shakes her head. 'No, no,' she says, waving a hand dismissively. 'There's no need to apologise.' She studies the selection of food, then nods to herself. 'Well,' she says, struggling up from her chair. 'That's everything ready for your father this evening. Thank you for your help.'

'I really am sorry.'

My mother smiles, touches a hand to my shoulder. 'I'll be in my bedroom.' I watch her as she leaves, the floorboards creaking on the off-beat in time with her failing balance.

I arrive into the living room promptly at six. I've done my best to spruce up for the occasion, but an unfortunate decision to include my two best outfits in last night's wash has left me with only an ancient pair of chinos and a slightly tattered shirt. My poor choice of wardrobe is laid even more bare by Dad, who greets me in a sharp charcoal-grey suit with a white soft-collared shirt. Fortunately, he's too polite to comment.

Dad pours me a measure of whisky, hands me the glass with something resembling a smile. 'Well, here's to you,' he says. He's trying to make his voice bright and cheerful but failing miserably. It's heart-breaking, but at the same time

I'm glad I'm not the only one who's nervous about the evening ahead.

After a few minutes, Sophie arrives, dressed in a short black skirt and red sweater, her hair pinned up off her face. She kisses Dad's cheek, then turns to look at me. 'Love the costume, Tom.'

'Thanks,' I say. 'It's hobo chic.'

Sophie nods. 'Shame you didn't have a straw hat to go with it. We could have put you in the garden to scare the pigeons.'

Pete and Rose arrive a few minutes later. Rose is carrying Ellie, who's chewing on a Peppa Pig toy and watching us all with her alert blue eyes. They're followed by Crawford, wearing a black cloak and waving a wand.

'Hey, buddy,' I say. 'How are you doing?'

'Good,' he says. 'I'm going to turn you into frog.' He mumbles an incantation and I bounce around on all fours croaking until he turns me back into his uncle.

'That's a good spell,' I say. 'Where did you learn it?'

'Harry Potter,' Crawford says. He taps the wand against the corner of the coffee table and looks slyly at me. 'He's my friend.'

'Well, I hope he won't come over here and turn me invisible.'

Crawford grins. 'He won't if you be nice to me.'

Dad pours Pete and Rose both a dram of whisky and Rose puts Ellie on the floor, where she and Crawford immediately fall into a spirited tug of war over his wand.

Pete turns to Dad. 'When's Mum getting here?'

'Ask her yourself,' Sophie says, as the door from the hallway opens and my mother comes into the room. She's dressed in her crimson shift, which has grown too large for her frail body. Dad's eyes are fixed on her as she makes her way slowly towards the armchair; his lips are held tightly, one to the other, but when she looks over, he smiles brightly.

'Well,' my mother says, once she's caught her breath. 'Isn't this wonderful. Goodness, I don't remember the last time we all had dinner together.'

'It was at The Cellar,' Rose says. 'When Tom and Lena announced their engagement.'

Sophie's eyes widen. 'Hey, wasn't that the night Tom high-fived that twelve-year-old waitress?'

'Oh, I'd forgotten about that!' Rose says, laughing. 'We'd just heard the news when she came over to the table all shy like and held her hand out and... Ah, Tom, what was it you said again?'

'Hoo yeah, gimme some skin!' Sophie yells, in a goofy American accent. 'And then, SLAM!'

'That's right!' Rose says, clapping her hands in delight. 'And the poor girl was like, "Actually, if I could just take your menu".'

I shrug my shoulders, smiling goofily. 'I thought she wanted to congratulate me on my news.'

Sophie shakes her head, still chuckling. 'You're such a fucking idiot, you know.'

'Language, Sophie,' my mother warns, indicating the children on the floor.

'Anyway,' I say, looking at Sophie. 'You're hardly one to talk. Didn't you once set fire to a menu as you made goo-goo eyes at old Brian Carty from across the table?'

Sophie laughs. 'Singed my eyebrow, too. Honestly, those little candles are dangerous.'

'Wait a minute,' my mother says. 'Brian Carty? Wasn't he the Head of English at Mary Stewart?'

Sophie nods. 'But I'd left by then, so you needn't worry.'

My mother shakes her head. 'Dirty old man.'

Sophie grins. 'We only had the one date, anyway. I ended up so full of wine that apparently, at some point in the evening, I raised my hand to ask if I could use the toilet.'

My mother rolls her eyes, but smiles despite herself. 'Honestly, I don't know where I got you from.'

'Could have been worse,' Sophie says. 'I could have done what Pete did at last year's work Christmas party.'

For the past few minutes, Pete's been sipping his whisky in silence on the sofa. Now he sits up straight. 'Hey.'

My mother looks from him to Sophie, her eyes twinkling. 'Why? What happened?'

'They were out at The Tower – so, you know, *very* posh. Halfway through the meal, Pete needed to use the loo and pushed his chair straight back into a table that was being used to display all the restaurant's fanciest wines. The table went over and about fifteen bottles smashed everywhere.' She turns to Pete. 'How much was that spillage worth, again?'

Pete throws out his bottom lip. 'I don't remember.'

'Two thousand pounds, wasn't it?'

Pete folds his arms over his chest, huffily. 'I don't see why you always have to drag me into your stupid little games.'

'Because it's such tremendous fun, Petey,' Sophie says.

Pete shakes his head, stands up to pour himself another drink. He's glaring so hard at Sophie that he fails to notice Ellie, who's coasting towards him along the edge of the sofa. When his leg brushes against her, she loses her balance, her nappy hitting the carpet with a soft thump. Pete glances down at her for only a second before continuing towards the decanter.

'Jesus, Pete,' Rose says angrily. 'Will you not at least pick her up?'

'What?' Pete says. 'I didn't hurt her.'

Rose sighs. 'That's hardly the point, though, is it?'

Sophie and I look to one another. The tension in the room has ramped up from zero to sixty in a matter of seconds, and everyone seems at a loss for words. But rescue appears in the unlikely form of Crawford, who stands and points an angry finger at Pete. 'Daddy, I swear you a atchel bawhair away from the naughty step'.

All heads turn to Crawford. Rose, who's just taken a sip of whisky, chokes. It takes several moments of coughing before she can gasp out, 'Where on earth did you hear that?' She turns to Pete. 'Did you teach him that?'

Pete turns to her, then to Crawford, who places his hands on his hips. 'It was Henry teached me,' he says proudly.

'Do you even know what that word means?' Rose asks.

Crawford furrows his little brow. 'Sumfin about farties?'

And just like that the evening's back on track. Rose shakes her head indulgently, Pete walks over to ruffle Crawford's hair, and the rest of the room breathes a collective sigh of relief that the pressure's been lifted. The conversation resumes just in time for Dad to check his watch and announce that it's time for him to make dinner. He kisses my mother's cheek, then disappears off into the kitchen.

My mother watches him leave before turning to us. 'While we're confessing to one another, I have a story of my own my tell. This happened in the mid-seventies, so long before any of you lot were born; a year, I think, before I even met your father. I was working at an Italian restaurant in Edinburgh at the time, and had got into the habit of pulling toppings from pizzas before serving them to the customers. I know that sounds disgusting, but you must remember I was as poor as a church mouse back in those days and didn't always have the money to buy food for myself.

'Anyway, one evening I grabbed a pizza for my table and, when nobody was watching, pulled a meatball from the cheese and gobbled it down. When I brought the pizza to my table, the entire table fell silent and began staring at me. I was all ready to profess my innocence, but then looked down and there it was; a long string of cheese running from the pizza to my mouth.'

There's a moment of stunned silence, before we all fall into laughing. 'Oh my...' Rose gasps. 'Oh god, that's...'

'Filthy?' my mother suggests.

'Mortifying!' She goes into another convulsion, which lasts some time. 'Oh god,' she says, wiping a hand across her eyes. 'You poor thing.'

My mother chuckles. 'Stupid cow, more like.'

'And?' Pete asks. 'Did they sack you?'

My mother shakes her head, smiling. 'The restaurant manager had a huge crush on me. I think I could have spat on every meal I served and still got away with it.'

Crawford and I are enjoying a hotly-contested game of tiddlywinks when Dad arrives to announce that dinner is ready. We make our way through to the dining room and take our seats at the old mahogany table, which is full of food. We all spend the obligatory few seconds *oohing* and *aahing* over the wonderful job Dad's done, before tucking in.

Within five minutes, the room is alive with conversation. To my left, Sophie is trying to decide which fictional world she would most like to live in, while at the other end of the table, Pete is holding forth to my parents about something that appears to involve salt, pepper, and both his forks. Across from me, Crawford is complaining loudly that the sauce on his pasta's the wrong colour, and Rose is rattling off the impressive list of things that'll be taken away from him if he doesn't eat it. Ellie, bless her, is oblivious. She's planted in her booster seat beside Rose, and most of her pasta is on her face or in her lap.

When the main courses have been set in front of us, Rose asks Sophie how Bill's faring in Australia.

'Good,' Sophie says. 'The job's close to finished now, so he's finally managing to catch up on some sleep and see a bit of the country.'

'Sleeping in. Day trips out,' Rose says. 'I think I remember what that was like.'

'Ah, but you've got something far more special,' Sophie says, smiling towards Crawford and Ellie.

'It's certainly special,' Rose says. 'Especially with this little mischief-maker around.' She ruffles Crawford's hair affectionately.

'Did he manage to get over that little scuffle he had at school last week?' my mother asks.

'Ah, you know how it is,' Rose says. 'Boys will be boys. To be honest, I imagine he probably gave as good as he got.'

Pete laughs. 'He'll need to learn to look after himself if he's going to make good at St Edwards.'

Rose snorts. 'Yeah, right,' she says, more to herself than anybody else. 'Like there's any chance I'd ever pack my kids off to some hideous fucking boarding school.'

The table, immediately, falls silent. For a few minutes the only sound is cutlery against plates and the ticking of the old grandfather clock. Then, placing her cutlery down, Rose clears her throat and turns awkwardly towards Sophie and I. 'No offence,' she says, quietly.

'None taken,' Sophie and I say in perfect unison.

'Sorry, Lorraine.'

My mother gives a tiny shake of her head, a little tightening of her lips to indicate, *don't be silly*. 'There's no need to apologise, dear. I realise these schools aren't for everyone.' I look up when she says this and realise that her eyes are on me.

The rest of the dinner passes surprisingly peacefully as we make our way through several bottles of wine and a hundred old stories. My mother doesn't eat much, though this surprises nobody, as the bulk of her calories now comes from fortified drinks and powders. When the main course is finished, she tells Dad that she might just pass on dessert for now. We make a point of looking away as her plate's taken from the table.

By the time we've finished coffee, Ellie's fallen asleep in her seat and Crawford's head is nodding dangerously close to his half-finished bowl of ice cream. 'I think we'll take this as our signal to leave,' Rose says, plucking Crawford from his chair and into her arms.

'I'm not even tired yet,' Crawford mumbles, without opening his eyes.

'Well, I know someone who is,' says my mother, laying down her napkin. 'So, I hope you won't mind if I take this chance to disappear. Thank you all, though, for a wonderful evening. It meant a very great deal to have you all here together.' Leaning heavily against the table, she groans to her feet, before teetering slightly. 'Oh,' she says, touching a hand to her forehead. 'Oh, dear me. Jack, would you mind?'

She needn't have asked; Dad's by her side before she's even finished talking. He takes her elbow, and together they begin the arduous journey back upstairs. I fall back into my seat and close my eyes tightly against a sudden prickling of tears.

It takes more than an hour to tidy away the dishes from dinner. By the time I'm finished, the house is enveloped in silence, though when I leave the kitchen, I see that a light's still on upstairs. I follow the light to Dad's office, where I find Dad slumped over his desk, his face in his hands. I think at first that he's crying, but when he hears me by the door, he looks up at me through dry eyes.

'Have a seat, Son,' he says, pointing to the dark green velvet armchair to the front of his desk. 'Will you take a drink?' When I nod, he pours us each a double measure of whisky, his with water, mine without, and, smiling gently, hands me the glass.

I sink back into my chair, breathe in the room's warm, leathery smell. I'm not a religious man, but if I were to imagine Paradise, it would look a lot like Dad's study. Two floor-to-ceiling walls of bookshelves, left side and right. Hundreds of hardback books with old bindings and gold lettering. Antique rugs on gleaming hardwood floor. The place has an overpowering presence of history, and has long provided a welcome retreat from the stresses of life.

Dad, having folded his long body into the dark leather chair behind his desk, sips at his whisky. 'So, what do you say?' he asks. 'Was tonight a success?'

'It was lovely.'

Dad nods. 'It's a long time since I saw your mother looking as content as she did this evening.'

I smile. 'We should do it again soon.'

Dad sighs. 'I don't think so, Tom. The past few days have taken a lot out of your mother. She's ready now just to take things easy. We'll be taking things one day at a time from now on.'

In the silence that follows, Dad's gaze falls to the framed photo of him and my mother, which has lain on his desk for longer than I can remember. The photograph, taken the year after they first met, shows them posing in front of the New Town flat my grandfather bought for Dad when he began his studies in Edinburgh. My mother, dressed in a pink satin dress and platform sandals, is holding my father's arm with both of her own, an incandescent smile lighting her face, as though life knows no greater happiness than this. Dad is leaning dandyishly against the bonnet of his orange Citroen, a cigarette dangling from his right hand, his head full of hopes and dreams for the future.

This image of wealth and health and happiness stands in sharp contrast to the pain and sickness we've lived with for the past month, and as I look from the photograph back to Dad, it's impossible to reconcile the carefree youth in the picture with the old man sitting across from me. 'It's all just so unfair,' I hear myself say.

Dad turns to me. Clears his throat. 'It can be,' he says. 'But every life has its bad patches. The thing is not to be overwhelmed by them, let them defeat you. It's the hardest thing, but you learn to get through it. We'll get through it, Tom.'

We fall into silence then. I sip tentatively at my whisky, though I'm sure by now I've had enough for one evening. Across from me, Dad holds the fingers of his left hand tight with the fingers of his right hand and rolls the ball of his thumb over and back across the smooth golden curve of his wedding ring, his eyes fixed on an old glass paperweight that sits atop his desk. A long moment passes before he speaks again. 'How are, uh... the marriage? How's the marriage? Have you heard from Lena since you got here?'

'No. But it wouldn't have been good news if I had.'

'Do you really think it's as bad as all that?'

'It's far from perfect.'

'Couldn't you find someone to speak to? A couple's therapist, maybe?'

'It's gone beyond all that, Dad.'

'But surely you're not headed towards… divorce?' He only mouths the word *divorce*, doesn't say it out loud, to shield me from the horror.

I'm not surprised to find Dad and I tiptoeing around the edge of conversation. After all, we've never spent a great deal of time discussing affairs of the heart. I had classmates at school who had startlingly candid exchanges with their fathers, frequently settling down on their living room sofa to confer on relationships, sex, drugs and mental health. The nearest my own father ever came to opening up about relationships came a few weeks before my twelfth birthday, when I awoke to find a copy of 'The Joy of Sex' by my bedside. Inside, Dad had written *Any questions, just ask!* in a jaunty script, but I think we both sensed that at least one of us would die of embarrassment if we were ever to have the conversation, so I never followed up on the offer and, mercifully, neither did Dad.

'I suppose divorce is a possibility,' I say now, in answer to Dad's question. Immediately, I understand why Dad chose to avoid the 'D' word – it tastes like poison on my lips.

'I just don't like to think of you being alone,' Dad says.

'No. Neither do I, but it is what it is.'

Dad raises his eyes to me. 'You'll be alright?'

'I've managed well enough up to now,' I say. It's not entirely true, but still.

Dad opens his mouth to speak and then closes it again. To my horror, I realise our conversation might be headed into even deeper territory, and stare hastily at my own feet. In the end, Dad only sighs and says, 'It's a terrible shame. You were good together. And I'm sorry for you.'

'It's okay,' I say, with a shrug.

There's another silence, longer this time. Then Dad clears his throat and says, 'Tom?'

I clear my throat, too. 'Yes?'

'You do know I love you, don't you?'

I swallow nervously. 'Of course.'

Dad nods. 'Okay. I just didn't want you forgetting, that's all.'

I nod, look shyly to my knees, and for a while the only noise in the room is the soft crackling of logs on the fire. Then Dad takes a final sip of his whisky and says, 'Well...' and stands. Places his hand on my shoulder as he passes me, and continues on to my mother's room.

SEVENTEEN

ON SUNDAY, I KEEP MY PROMISE TO TAKE CRAWFORD TO THE park. Rose was delighted when I called to arrange, told me he'd been talking about the trip for the past two weeks. I imagined she was exaggerating, but he's there to greet me the moment I open the front door to Pete's house, the cannonball of his head crashing into my stomach. 'Unco Tom!' he says, pushing a sheet of paper towards me. 'I drawed you a picture.'

I look at the drawing. A few red lines, a black squiggle and a little green tornado. Crawford points to the tornado. 'That's your hair. And that's the rest of you over here.'

'Wow.' I point to the squiggle. 'And what's this?'

Crawford giggles. 'That's the playpark, silly.'

It's a disturbing image, but not nearly as disturbing as the one I see as I hand the drawing back to Crawford; Pete, at the end of the hallway, wearing his coat.

'What are you doing?' I ask.

Pete steps forward, ruffles Crawford's hair. 'Rose thought it would be nice if we spent more time together.'

I look to Crawford. 'You see him every day.'

'She was talking about me and you.'

'Oh. And you're sure you don't want –'

'Let's just get away to the park, shall we?'

When we reach the playground, Crawford throws off his hat and scarf and makes a beeline for the slide. I used to have calluses from the monkey bars and the tricks I performed for hours, showing off for my mother. She was never as impressed as I hoped she might be.

With Crawford away, neither Pete nor I quite know what to do. Pete asks a few questions about my future plans, and I answer with my face becoming hot. 'I'm sure something will come up,' I tell him. 'I just need to be patient.' Pete forces a smile, but I can sense his disapproval; he hasn't missed a day of work in years.

'Anyway,' I say, desperate to change the subject. 'How are you?'

'*I'm* alright,' Pete says. 'But I need to make twelve of my staff redundant tomorrow. I'm sort of dreading that.'

'I'm not surprised. Those poor people.'

Pete nods. 'Three of them are really great at the job as well. Still, at least I'll have hit my target for the quarter.'

'You're targeted on redundancies?'

Pete shrugs. 'Got to get rid of the deadwood.'

'Deadwood? You just told me that some of these people are great at their jobs.'

'Well, sure, yeah they are, some of them. Hell, I don't know, Tom. I just do what they tell me.'

'But... Couldn't you have refused? Couldn't you at least have tried to save their jobs?'

Pete shakes his head. 'At the end of the day, it's their job or mine. I have to consider Rose and the kids.'

'Right,' I say. Then snicker.

'What is it?'

I shake my head. 'Doesn't matter.' I snicker again.

'Oh, Tom, don't be a dick,' Pete says. 'Tell me why you're laughing.'

'Two weeks ago, you told me the banks were friendlier now. You said the bad guys didn't exist anymore. Apparently, that wasn't true. And apparently, you're one of them.'

Pete shakes his head crossly. 'Don't be so fucking naïve, Tom. How else do you think a business survives? When we need people, we hire them. When we don't, we let them go. Yes, it sucks, but that's the world we live in. Maybe you'll realise that, if you ever get your act together.'

'Get my act together? You mean work myself to the bone, like you're doing?'

Pete narrows his eyes to me. 'I'm only providing for my family, the way any man should.'

I can't help it; I laugh. 'Your family? You're doing it for your...? Your family's miserable as *shit*, Pete. Rose is sick of being by herself every night. Your kids hardly know you. Not that I should be surprised. After all, you were always a shitty brother. Why shouldn't you be a shitty parent, too.'

'*I'm* the shitty brother?' Pete says. He's angry now, talking through his teeth. 'Jesus Christ, you're a self-centred little fuck. Sure, I might be rotten, but believe me, Tom, you're far from perfect yourself.'

I stare at Pete in disbelief. 'What?'

Pete lets out a sound somewhere between a scoff and a cough. 'Oh my god, you haven't a clue, have you? You genuinely haven't a clue what I'm talking about.' He squeezes his eyes shut, digging the heels of his hands into his forehead. 'Tom,' he says. 'The last five years have been hell. Mum's been struggling so badly since her first treatment. There've been times – entire months – where she's been too sick to leave the house. Last summer, Dad was so busy caring for her that he literally ran out of food in the kitchen.'

I stare at him, speechless.

'Why else do you think he hired Emma Barnes, you asshole?' Pete asks.

I shake my head. 'I had no idea.'

'Well, you wouldn't, would you? You've been too busy messing up your own life to give the first fuck about anyone else's. I mean, for Christ's sake, Tom, I know you and Mum have had your differences in the past, but would it have killed you to offer a bit of support?'

'Hey!' I shout, my hackles up. 'That's not fair. I'm as much a part of this family as you are.'

Pete bites his lip, tears welling in his eyes. 'Do you know how many times you've visited Myreton since Mum first got sick?'

'I don't know. Eight?'

Pete holds up three fingers. 'Three times, Tom. You've been here three times. That's all.'

'That can't be right.'

'It's not right,' Pete says. 'But it's the truth.'

I stand in silence for a moment, trying to absorb this. 'Okay,' I say, at last. 'Fine. But I'm here now. Right here.' I spread my arms, not to embrace my brother, but to show how wide I am, how much of me is here. Pete, however, is barely listening. 'Make sure Crawford's home by four,' he says, turning back towards the hill. 'And don't feed him too much shit.'

I should shout out to him, I know, beg him to come back, now that we're finally talking. But we've never found it easy to communicate. It's taken thirty years of suppressed bitterness just to get to this point. And so, I stand, speechless, watching him leave.

When I come to my senses again, Crawford's standing by my side. 'Oh, buddy,' I say, wrapping an arm around his little shoulder. 'I'm so sorry you had to see that. I know it's never easy for little people to see grownups argue. But you know, just because it happens, it doesn't mean, er –'

'Can you tie my shoelace?'

'What?'

Crawford points to his unknotted shoelace. 'It needs done up.'

'Oh,' I say. 'Alright.'

As I tie Crawford's lace, I wonder how best to explain what just happened between me and Pete. I made a muck of the first attempt – I'm worried I sowed the seeds of some future trauma or something.

Crawford looks on thoughtfully as I fumble about with his filthy shoes. 'What colour was those swings when the world was black and white?'

'What?' I turn around and look to the playground. 'Oh, right. Well, actually, the real world was always in colour. The only thing that was black and white were the films and photographs people took, because the technology for colour film came later than the technology for cameras themselves. The world looked like this even when Nana and Papa were little.'

Crawford muses on this for a while.

'My face is hurting,' he says, finally. 'I fink I better put my scarf back on.'

～

Half an hour later, Crawford and I are standing outside the Myreton Inn, each with a bag of strawberry bonbons from Mr Taylor's shop, when Emma arrives in her car. 'I'm glad you called,' she says, smiling. 'I was going stir crazy back at home.'

'I'm glad you came,' I tell her. 'You wouldn't believe the energy this little guy has. He makes me feel like I've been living on one lung.'

Emma chuckles sympathetically. 'Sounds like you had a good time.'

'We did!' Crawford yells, triumphantly. 'I goed all the way across the monkey bars. And Unco Tom's bum was so big, he got stuck on the slide.'

I nod. 'That actually happened.'

Inside, the inn is packed with weekend visitors. The table by the fireplace – my table, as I've come to see it in the past few weeks – is taken, so we sit down in one of the booths by the front window.

'So, how was your afternoon?' Emma asks Crawford.

'Good,' he says. 'We went to the park and Dada and Unco Tom had a big fight. Dada said a naughty word.'

'Oh dear,' Emma says, looking to me with a smile. 'That's not good.'

Crawford shakes his head. 'It was funny. Dad said lots of bad words. I'm not apposed to say them, but if you want, I can tell you what –'

'How about we order some hot chocolate?' I say.

Crawford gives a little cheer, then points excitedly towards Sharon behind the bar. 'That's the one what works here. You tell her what you want and then she'll give it to you.'

Emma and I nod. We understand how it works.

'And at the end you give her the money,' Crawford adds.

I let Crawford place our order. Then he tells me and Emma about a boy in his class called Ethan. 'He's a naughty one,' he says. 'Once, he putted his fingy in my ear.'

'His thingy?' I ask, appalled.

'Not his *fingy*,' Crawford says, rolling his eyes. He holds up his hand and points to his index finger. 'His *fingy*.'

He talks about pizza and his favourite toppings and all the playparks he's visited in his life and the time he hurt his foot somewhere in a place that began with an *e* where he saw the Lego he wanted for Christmas. Then Sharon arrives with our order; hot chocolates for me and Crawford, a cup of tea for Emma. 'Why you not having hot chocolate?' Crawford asks her.

'Oh, I prefer a nice cup of tea.'

'My nana likes tea,' Crawford says. 'She *always* drinks tea. But she's going to go to heaven soon.'

'You know, they have tea in heaven, too.'

Crawford sits up a little straighter in his chair. 'Really? Do they have the grey tea?'

'They do indeed. And red tea, and turquoise tea, and rainbow tea, and a hundred others you can't even get here on Earth.'

'Oh my gosh,' Crawford says, with a smile so wide that I feel something squeeze inside my chest. 'Nana is going to *love* that!'

'I know she is,' Emma says. 'She'll have a wonderful time.'

Crawford brings a hand up to his mouth and bounces his fingers absently against his lips. 'I'm going to be sad when she goes away.'

'I know you are,' Emma says.

He gnaws a little on his pinky. 'I love her a awful lot,' he whispers into his knuckle.

Emma smiles gently. 'And she loves you. Very, very much. So, remember that, when you miss her. And remember that that love will always, always be inside you.'

Outside the inn, Crawford leads Emma through the semi-darkness to the children's golf course, where he wants to show off a few of the moves he's been learning from old Power Rangers episodes. I'm getting ready to join them when I see a black van parked in the far corner of the car park, and for a second my blood turns icy. It's Daryll. He's slumped in the driver's seat, staring directly at me. His unshaven face, silhouetted in the gloom, looks tense and furious. After a few seconds, he leans forwards, and I think for a second he's planning to get out and confront me, but in fact he's just reaching for the key in his ignition. The car starts and he drives away slowly, his furious eyes never moving from mine in the reflection of his wing mirror.

EIGHTEEN

On Monday evening, I meet up with Mike at the Myreton Inn. We buy a pint of beer and sit down at a table by the open fireplace, where we spend some time clapping our hands together and making 'brrrrr' noises. Winter truly is on the horizon. The sun begins to set at four now, going full dark by five. There's snow forecast for later this evening.

'Cheers,' Mike says, lifting his pint from the table. We drink in unison, then let out a collective sigh and wipe the froth from our upper lips.

It's as quiet in here as you'd expect for a midweek night in November. The six other customers are all men, all past retirement, and all laughing about the Brexit fiasco and the upcoming general election. 'We just need to go ahead and get the bloody thing done,' says the fat one with sideburns from his bar stool. 'Christ, we've had three years already to cut our ties with those arseholes over in Europe.'

'I'm no' so sure, Frank,' says Merv, from the opposite table. Of the six men, he and Norrie are the only ones I recognise. 'After all, we're hardly the great empire we used to be. If anyone decided tae attack us –'

'If anyone decided to attack us, *we'd* get to choose when to press the buttons,' Frank says, defiantly. 'That's the whole point. Finally, we're ready to take back control.'

'The trouble with people like you,' a voice says angrily to Frank, 'is that you never even think to question the words of people like Boris Johnson. All this ridiculous talk of taking back control. We never bloody *lost* control in the first place. The EU's never had any influence over Britain's policies, in defence or in health, housing, pensions and welfare. You've been fed nothing but lies for the past three years, and you've fallen for them all, hook, line and sinker.'

There's silence. Everyone seems a bit shocked by the voice. I'm especially shocked, because the voice appears to be mine. And it's not finished yet.

'You describe Brexit as the "will of the people". Have you even bothered to consider that almost half the people voted the other way, or that the people who'll be most affected by Brexit never even had the chance to vote? Would those who voted to leave have done so if they'd known the "easiest" deal in history would prove impossible, or that the "short-term" hit to their living standards would last for 50 years? Personally, I really fucking doubt it.'

More silence, but deeper this time. When the red mist clears from my eyes, I find everybody in the room is staring at me uneasily. 'Uh, Tom?' Mike asks. 'Are you okay?'

I place a hand to my forehead. 'I'm... so sorry,' I say. 'I don't know what came over me.'

Mike laughs nervously. 'Ah, well, nothing to worry about,' he says, touching me gently on the arm. Then, turning to the others, he mouths: 'He's got a lot going on at home.'

I look to Mike, offended, but say nothing more. This is partly because I'm tired, but mostly because, despite everything, I think he probably has a point. I'm not even all that bothered about Brexit.

Fortunately for me, the conversation soon turns from politics to legends of local brawlers and womanisers. Mike and I move closer to the six men and listen to their stories over pints of beer, and whisky chasers, and one for the road, and another one for the road, and a final one for the road. At closing time, I struggle tipsily into my winter coat and, holding myself steady against Mike's shoulder, wish my new friends a very happy evening. When we step out into the darkness, I turn to Mike. 'So, what do you think? Fancy a little walk to Greywalls?'

Mike shakes his head. 'I need to hit the hay, Tom. You should really do the same.'

'I would,' I tell him. 'But I'm not tired.'

'You're exhausted,' Mike says. 'You should see yourself.'

'I may be exhausted,' I concede. 'But I'm not tired.

I make my way alone to Greywalls, where I lay down on the turret and look upwards into a night slashed and grazed with shooting stars. Billions and billions of stars. Billions and billions of worlds. We little humans all believe ourselves to be the very centre of this universe, but in the grand scheme of things, our problems, our lives – they mean nothing. Aching hearts, broken marriages, cancer – they all mean nothing. It's time I started getting used to the whole benign indifference of the world.

I'm trying to shake off this horrible thought when I hear grunting sounds behind me. Thinking Mike's had second thoughts about coming here, I stand up, ready to greet him. But the figure who materialises out of the darkness is altogether bigger and more frightening than I expected.

'Alright, Halliday?'

'Daryll,' I say. I can't tell if it's fear or anger that I'm feeling, but whatever it is, I swallow it back. 'What brings you here?'

'I decided to take a little walk.'

'You decided to take a little walk,' I repeat sceptically.

Daryll nods. 'Couldn't sleep. Too busy picturing the things I wanted to do to your face.'

'And here we are,' I say.

'Alone at last,' Daryll adds.

I sigh wearily. 'Daryll, have you been following me?'

Daryll smiles. 'Maybe.'

I nod. 'Well, you win, I guess.' I take a step towards him, but he makes no attempt to move out of the way. I clear my throat, not quite able to make eye contact. 'Daryll, would you please move? I don't have the energy for stupid games right now.'

'Except this isn't a game, is it.'

'I don't know. You tell me.'

'I already did,' Daryll says. 'I told you exactly what would happen if you didn't listen to me. This whole thing could have been avoided completely if you'd only –'

'She hates you, Daryll.'

The words hit Daryll like a fist. He stares at me through wide eyes.

'It's the truth,' I tell him. 'She's terrified of you. She can hardly bear to leave her house these days for fear of running into you.'

Daryll takes a step forward, glaring at me. 'Take that back.'

But I won't. 'If you think there's even the hint of a spark

between you, you're completely crazy.'

'I said take it back,' Daryll growls. He steps closer and prods me in the chest, pushing me even closer to the edge of the castle wall.

'Daryll,' I warn. 'Don't do anything silly.'

'But you *know* what I'm going to do. I *told* you what I was going to do ten days ago.'

I look over my shoulder towards the ground, ten feet below.

'Scared, aren't you?' Daryll says, baring his teeth in a lethal grin. 'Probably starting to wish you'd listened to me now, eh?'

I'd hoped to walk unscathed from this skirmish, but in the past few moments Daryll's expression has taken on a manic quality, and I understand, with perfect clarity, that it's too late now to change my fate. And so, I decide to go out with a bang. 'Fuck you, Daryll.'

Daryll looks at me and sighs. 'No, no, Tommy. You're the one who's fucked.' And with that, he raises a hand and casually pushes me off the turret.

When I come to, I find myself on a small ledge a few feet from the ground. I daub at my head and face with tentative fingertips. There's no blood, I think, and nothing's missing, but there's a mushiness there that doesn't feel quite right. I slide off the ledge slowly, using the side of the wall for assistance, and let out a yelp of pain when my right foot hits the grass.

I roll up my trouser leg and inspect the damage. My ankle's horribly swollen, and there's a gash running down my calf with enough blood seeping from it to send a wave of nausea rolling through me. Swallowing sickly, I grab a stick from the ground and, using it as a crutch, begin to take some tentative steps across the frosty ground. After a few seconds, my ankle starts to hurt a little less.

My panic's just starting to fade when I'm seized by a sudden thought; what if Daryll, having seen me off at the castle, decided to continue on to Emma's house? Panicking all over again, I grab my phone from my pocket, desperate to call her, but the screen's covered in a spiderweb of cracks. Disoriented and weak, I half walk, half stagger towards Emma's as fast as my leg will carry me.

The journey's a struggle. The rain has started falling, and seems to be getting heavier with every passing minute. I'm incredibly cold – I can see my breath steaming out in front of me, and my fingers have frozen inside my gloves. By the time I reach Emma's street, I'm so drenched that even the jumper I'm wearing under my overcoat is clinging to my every contour.

Emma's house has changed a great deal in the twenty years since I last saw it. The old red garage has been swept away, replaced by a small, two-story annexe that sits to the left of the main building. The old property is shrouded in darkness, but a light is glowing in the new extension, so I make a beeline for that and knock impatiently on the door. Moments later Emma opens it, hugging a dressing gown around herself. 'Tom? What are you –'

'Where's Daryll?' I interrupt, my voice shaky with panic.

Emma stares at me, confused. 'What?'

'Where's Daryll?' I say, again. 'Where is he?'

Emma laughs nervously. 'Tom, I've no idea what you're talking about.'

'Really?' I say, and Emma nods. Closing my eyes, I take a breath, and it becomes so deep that I realise I haven't taken one for a while. 'Okay,' I say, raking a hand through my hair. 'Okay. Thank goodness.'

Emma looks at me anxiously. 'I think you'd better come inside.'

As I move past her and into the light, Emma notices the stick I'm leaning on. 'Tom, what on earth happened?' she says. 'Oh my god, you're bleeding! There's a cut on your head!'

'What?' I touch a hand to my forehead, study it distractedly. 'Oh, yes. That's right. Erm, can I use your bathroom?'

In the quiet of the bathroom, I examine my face in the mirror. Emma's right; I have a gash on my right temple, and the skin around it is swollen and turning purple. There's another bruise forming on my collar bone, and a disturbing clicking sound whenever I move my left shoulder.

By the time I rejoin Emma I feel calmer and ready for her questions. I tell her about my walk to the castle, my encounter with Daryll, my one-legged race to her house.

'Why on earth were you walking alone at this time of night?'

I wrinkle my nose to cover a laugh. 'Emma, this is Myreton, not Caracas. It's not the sort of place you expect to be attacked.'

Emma shakes her head and sighs. 'Well, you'd best let me see.' She grabs a small first-aid kit from a drawer, then ushers me onto her sofa, where she takes a look at the cut in my temple, wiping away the crusted blood from the side of my face. She looks at my collar bone, which is only slightly bruised, and the gash in my leg, which she wraps in a bandage. Then she removes the sock from my left foot and tests the range of movement in my ankle. It hurts like hell, but I force myself not to wince. 'It's not broken, is it?' I ask, sounding more pathetic than I meant to.

Emma bites her lip to keep from laughing. 'You'd have done well to walk all the way here on a broken ankle, Tom. No, it's just a bad twist, I think.'

'Oh.' I'm almost disappointed. My brush with death was way more convincing when it came with the possibility of a broken bone or two.

Emma tears open another antiseptic wipe with her teeth and begins scrubbing at my bloodied hands. 'I can't believe he did this,' she says. 'I knew he was bad, but I never imagined...' Bringing the back of her hand to her mouth, she stops talking. Shaking her head again, she slowly lowers her hand. 'Tom?' she says, her voice small. 'I'm frightened.'

'It's okay,' I tell her. 'We'll fix it.'

'How?'

'I don't know. But we will.'

With my wounds all cleaned and bandaged, my attention drifts towards Emma's house. It can't measure more than a few square metres, but it has everything; a kitchen, living room, dining area and, upstairs, a bathroom and double bed. It shouldn't be possible, but she seems to have used every trick in the book to save space. Interior walls have been replaced with shelving units, a narrow staircase doubles as a series of bookshelves, and there's one of those cool kitchen tables that fold up to close off a spice rack on the wall. The entire space is also impeccably tidy, which makes me ashamed of the glorified bombsite I call home back in London.

'I can't believe the change in this place. Wasn't this your dad's old workshop?'

Emma nods. 'Right up until he retired five years ago.'

'Then it became yours?'

'Mm-hmm. I'd been in Edinburgh for a decade by then, and desperate for years to move back here, but there was no question of ever living with my parents again, and the house prices here were astronomical, so I'd all but given up hope of it happening. Then Mum and Dad offered me this space and... well, it was just the perfect place to set up home. I feel so lucky to be here.'

'You *are* lucky. Truly, this place is amazing.'

Emma laughs. 'I meant I was lucky to be here in Myreton. But, yes, it's not a bad spot for an old maid to end her days.'

She makes the statement so casually it takes a second to process what she's said. 'What?' I say, letting out a startled laugh. 'You're not an old maid.'

'Oh, but I think I am,' Emma says, shrugging one lean shoulder. 'I don't think I'll ever end up with somebody. I'm not sure I ever want to. I'm happy here. I like being alone. Besides, I'd make a terrible partner. I have a hard enough time managing my own life without being responsible for someone else's.'

'I think you're being a bit hard on yourself.'

Emma smiles. 'Perhaps. I've always had a bit of a thing for gallows humour. But I am serious, in a way. I'm pretty sure I'm going to be one of those lifelong singletons you read about sometimes.'

'Doesn't it make you a bit... sad?

Emma shakes her head. 'There are far worse fates, Tom. When I think back to my darker days, and to how things might have been... well, I just feel so lucky. Truly, I have so much to be grateful for.'

'And you're happy?'

'I am. I really am. I have my parents and James, and Holly and the kids. I have my job, and my questionable health, and now I even have you and Mike.'

It makes me so happy to hear this. 'Why did we ever stop being friends? It's so nice to be friends, don't you think?'

Emma nods. 'It is. Let's not lose touch again. After all, it's not hard to keep in touch these days. It's far easier than it used to be, what with the Internet and texting.'

'Oh, let's be text friends,' I say. 'Let's text each other every day with pointless memes and photos of our meals.'

Emma smiles. 'I'm guessing your photos will be a lot more interesting than mine.'

'Oh. Well, yeah. Sorry. We can iron out the details later on. In the meantime,' I say, rising painfully to my feet. 'I should get going.'

Emma immediately stiffens. 'No!' she says, her voice pitched with panic. 'You can't go home now.'

'I'm alright. I'm not as sore as I was.'

'Yes, but... Oh, Tom, he might be out there! Please, I don't want you walking home alone. Not tonight. Stay here, won't you? I can drive you home in the morning.'

I hesitate for only a second before agreeing. Emma heaves a sigh of relief, before disappearing upstairs for some blankets and a pillow. When she returns, we lay them down on the sofa, and I climb under the duvet.

'So,' Emma says. There's an endearing nervousness in her voice. 'Sleep well. I'm sure you will. It's very comfortable, apparently. Actually, I sleep here myself sometimes, when there's a film on the telly and –'

'Emma,' I say. I take her hand and pull her gently towards me. A small, nervous laugh bursts from her throat. 'It's very late,' she says, her cheeks flushing. 'I should... But, well...' She rolls her eyes. 'Alright.' She slides down onto the sofa next to me.

'It's okay,' I reassure her. 'I know nothing's to happen.'

Emma nods shyly, and we lie side by side, her head

against my chest, her arm around my waist. 'Is this okay?' I ask.

'Yes,' Emma says. She swallows, clears her throat. Then, hoarsely, she says, 'I never did this before. Just... lie with someone. That's completely pathetic, isn't it?'

I shake my head. 'I don't think you're pathetic at all.'

Emma peers up at me. 'You don't?'

'No. To be honest, I think you're about the bravest person I ever met.'

Emma blows air out of her nose, an involuntary snort. 'Yeah, right.'

'I mean it. When I think of everything you've been through, and of how you are now, and how, despite everything, you remain... *there*, for so many people, I just... well, you're pretty special.'

Emma shakes her head against my chest. 'You're such an idiot.' But I can tell from her voice that she's smiling.

I lie still, wondering whether Emma will remain with me or head back up to her room. After a few minutes, something in her begins to relax and it becomes clear that she's going to stay. I'm glad. It feels so good to be held.

'Well,' I say. 'I guess I'll see you in the morning.'

'Mmm hmm,' Emma says. She's fading, her voice growing smaller as sleep begins to take hold.

'Goodnight.'

'G'night.'

I plant a chaste kiss on her forehead, then sink back into my pillow. And as I lie staring into the darkness of this unfamiliar room, I feel more at peace than I have in months. I try desperately to stay awake, prolong the feeling for as long as possible. But it's been a long day, and tiredness has already begun to rear its ugly head. Pretty soon, it takes hold of me completely and I'm forced into a deep, dreamless sleep.

NINETEEN

I HEAR VOICES COMING FROM UPSTAIRS THE MOMENT I ARRIVE home the following morning. The voices are female, so I guess my mother has a friend around, or that Dr Sullivan's come to check up on her. I pause for a moment to collect my thoughts, then walk towards her room and am ready to greet them, but I stop dead, my mouth agape.

'Hello darling,' says my mother.

'Hello Tom,' says Lena.

Lena. I stand looking at her for several moments, feeling that old heart-lurch, the weakening spine-shudder. She's wearing a cashmere sweater, soft blue-grey, and her green eyes have a luminous emerald tint. She's ridiculously beautiful, I think. Too beautiful, really – it's something of a joke.

Lena smiles warmly and starts towards me with her arms open, but I step back like she's contagious. She lowers her hands and nods sadly.

'I thought you were out with Michael last night,' my mother says.

'I was.'

'You look as though you were off fighting a war.'

'What do you mean?' I ask defensively. When I woke half an hour ago, it felt like my ankle was on fire, but since then my muscles have warmed, my injuries cooled, and I'm moving pretty normally again. Or, at least, I thought I was.

'You have a plaster on your head,' my mother says.

'Oh!' I say, flushed with relief. 'Yes. I walked into a table.'

'With your head?'

Ah. Good point. 'Actually, it was a door.'

My mother smiles thinly. 'Of course, it was.'

Thankfully, she has nothing more to say on the matter, so I turn my attention to Lena. 'I didn't expect to see you here.'

Lena looks to my mother, and then back to me. 'I had some holidays to take, and I was overdue a trip to Myreton, so...'

I stare at her, letting the anger and frustration surge through me. 'Are you staying long?'

Lena shakes her head. 'I'm flying back in a few hours.'

'Right,' I say. 'Well, it was good to see you.'

I turn to leave then, but my mother has other ideas. 'Goodness, Tom,' she says, 'you can't go now. Lena's flown the length of the country to see us.'

I forgot how frustrating it is to be with Lena around my mother, the way she automatically takes Lena's side on every one of our disagreements. During our last visit to Myreton – a ferocious, ear-splitting three days of wrangles and recriminations – my mother continued to rally around Lena with such determination that I eventually stormed from the house to spend a full seven hours stamping wrathfully through the streets of Edinburgh. Maybe she does it just to protect Lena's feelings – that's how Lena's always seen it –

but I can't take her lightly, not with everything that's gone before.

'I'm only going downstairs,' I tell my mother, testily. Then, turning to Lena, 'I'll see you before you leave, yeah?'

By the time I hear Lena's footsteps on the staircase half an hour later, I'm ready to launch into the furious argument I've been preparing for her in my head. But when she arrives in the kitchen, she's changed completely from the smiling woman who so surprised me in my mother's room; her face is pale now, and there are tears in her eyes. However angry I feel, I can't quite bring myself to raise my voice to her. 'Are you alright?' I ask.

Lena doesn't answer, just shakes her head and dabs at her eyes with a soggy tissue.

'Well, she'll be glad you came,' I say.

Lena nods miserably. 'I'm sorry, Tom. I know it must have been a bit of a shock to find me here this morning.'

I feel my jaw clench. 'Yes, well... I do wonder why you didn't think to call me ahead of the visit.'

Lena swallows. 'I was worried you'd try to put me off.'

I stare at her, my expression wry. 'Really?' I say, the familiar anger returning to my voice. 'What could possibly have made you think I'd do that?'

Lena's eyes fall to the ground. 'Tom,' she says, her voice small. 'Can't we just be nice to each other? Please?'

I lean back heavily against the countertop. 'Fine,' I say, raising my hands in surrender. 'I suppose we could try.'

Lena closes her eyes, lets out a jagged breath. 'Okay.' For a moment all is silent. Then, cocking her head slightly, and with the barest hint of a smile, she says, 'So, while we're being nice, will you let me buy you a coffee?'

Lena and I climb into her rental car and drive the short distance to the Village Coffee Shop. I'd hoped to find a few moments' privacy here, but as soon as we enter, I'm dismayed to find Mrs Bates seated at one of the tables with my old piano teacher, Mrs James. Old Bates spots us immediately, freezing in place, her cup of tea steaming an inch from her mouth, her eyes fixed triumphantly on Lena.

Lena forces her eyes to the ground and slinks past Mrs Bates into an empty table by the corner of the room. I try to do the same, but I'm too slow to prevent Mrs Bates from grabbing my arm. 'Well,' she says, swinging me round to face her. 'There's a young lady I'm just de*lighted* to see.'

There's nothing I can really say to that, so I just stand there, silently, cursing my luck.

Mrs Bates swoops her laser-like gaze over Lena. 'Just here for the day?'

'Possibly,' I say.

She pinches her lips together. She wants to know precisely how long Lena will stay. 'And how's your mother?' she asks.

'She's not too bad.'

Mrs Bates smiles with half her face in wretched pity. 'It must be so hard for you right now,' she says, glancing meaningfully towards Lena. 'Change is hard. I always say that.'

'It is.' I purse my lips to keep them from talking. Mrs Bates is going to lose this particular game of chicken. After a moment, she seems to understand that she's lost and releases me from her grasp.

I place our order by the counter, then take a seat at the table, where I sit in silence, watching as Lena bites her lip, fiddles with her shirtsleeves and looks in every direction but mine. I feel hopelessly uncomfortable, and filled with an imbalance of desires – one to leave, the other desperate to prevent departure. I have absolutely no idea what to say.

It's Lena who finally breaks the silence. 'So, you've been here for five weeks already?'

I nod. 'For my sins.'

'And how do you feel?'

'As little as possible.'

Lena eyes are sad and full of sympathy. 'I can understand that. I'm sorry.'

'It's alright. I've had a good bit of practice these past few months.'

Lena pretends not to hear this. 'And what do you do with all your time?'

I never do anything, of course, my days blending together into a sameness that I might find comforting if they weren't so traumatic to boot. I guess Lena already knows this, so I don't bother answering.

'I just don't get it,' Lena continues. 'I don't get why you quit your job. All those years of hard work completely wasted.'

'Because it was bullshit. The whole industry's bullshit.'

'But you were doing so well.'

'But I hated it. I was fucking miserable.'

Lena gives a deep sigh. 'And now?' she asks, fixing her eyes on me. 'Are you any happier?'

'Well, right now I'm back living with my parents while my mother dies a slow, agonising death two rooms away. So, no, I'd say I've been better.'

'That's not what I meant.'

I know it, but I'm too angry to be reasonable. 'Plus,' I continue, 'there's the small matter of you having walked out on me six months ago. I can't say that's helped matters much, either.'

Lena tilts her head to one side, searching my face. 'Did I really make you happy? I'm not sure I did, towards the end.'

I sit back in my chair, trying to take this in. 'Of course, you did. Why would you have to ask?'

Lena says nothing. A tear forms at the corner of her eye.

'Didn't I make you happy?' I ask.

Her words come out thickly. 'Not during those final months. No.'

I look at her aghast. 'But we were happy. Before I quit work –'

'For Christ's sake.' Lena pinches a tear off the bridge of her nose and shakes her head. 'Do you really still think it was just you quitting work? Do you really think I'm that shallow? After all the years we've known one another?'

I don't know. I don't seem to know anything anymore. 'What was it then?'

'It was *you*,' Lena says. 'You changed, in so many ways. And maybe your work contributed to those changes, but it was more than that. When I look back to when I met you, you were so smart and kind and funny – even your bitterness was sweet and manageable. And you were honest – not just with me, but with yourself. You understood your issues. But you *changed*, Tom. You became a different person, and that person was far more difficult to love.'

I feel the blow travel through me. 'You could have tried harder, to support me, to make things work.'

'You don't think... You don't think I supported you? All those months you spent complaining, all the weeks you lay on that fucking sofa, either drunk or comatose. Do you know how much strength it took for me to work all day and then come home to you, knowing how you'd be? You don't think it was hard for me, too? I loved you, Tom. Christ, I loved you. But it was fucking hard, and in the end, I just didn't have anything left to give you.'

I can't believe what I'm hearing. 'But... Jeff. What about him?'

'What the hell does Jeff matter, Tom? Jeff's nothing to do with this. He wasn't the reason I left you. For god's sake, aren't you listening to me at all?'

I fall back against my seat. 'Wow. It's worse than I thought.'

Lena wipes away tears as she nods. 'It wasn't pretty.'

'And you're absolutely sure the whole thing wasn't entirely your fault?' I ask, forcing a smile.

Lena rolls her eyes. 'You're such an idiot,' she says, with a little laugh. Lena's laugh is one of the greatest sounds I've ever encountered, but hearing it now, for the first time in months, fills me with sadness, a reminder of how happy we used to be.

Mrs Bates has already left by the time we settle our bill, so our departure from the café is less dramatic than our arrival. When we reach her car, Lena offers me a lift home, but I need to walk and clear my head. For a long moment we stand facing one another, neither of us sure what to say. Then Lena pulls me into her and embraces me so tightly I can feel her heartbeat racing in her chest. 'Oh, Tom,' she says, her voice catching in her throat. She kisses my cheek, then takes her keys out of her pocket and walks around to the driver's side. 'Take care.' She climbs into the car and rolls down the windows. 'And, for what it's worth, I miss you.'

I nod, tears choking my eyes.

Lena puts the car into first gear. 'Take care,' she says again.

'I miss you too,' I call, desperate at the sound of the revving engine.

Lena's mouth curves, like she's going to smile or cry, her face, somehow, caught in between. 'Goodbye, Tom.'

She turns onto the road and disappears into traffic, and it takes me a long time to walk away from that spot on the kerbside.

~

When I arrive home, I find Sophie perched on the edge of my mother's bed, tapping away on her work computer. My mother, tucked beneath her duvet, is snoring quietly.

'You alright?' I ask.

Sophie nods. 'Just enjoying a bit of Mummy/daughter time with Rip Van Winkle here.'

'How long's she been asleep?'

'She hasn't,' my mother interrupts, her eyes still closed. 'She's just resting her eyes.'

'Oh?' Sophie says. 'Just enjoying a bit of quiet wakefulness, I suppose. A little nappetiser before lunch.'

My mother nods. 'That's right...'

Sophie laughs. 'Mum, that's such a lie! You've been out cold for over an hour.'

'Nonsense,' my mother says, struggling to a seated position. She takes a moment to catch her breath before turning her attention to me. 'Well?' she asks. 'How did it go with Lena?'

Sophie stops laughing and turns wide-eyed to me. 'Wait, what? Lena was here? In Myreton? Shut up. No, she wasn't. Was she?'

'It's true,' I say.

'Oh my god!' Sophie says, throwing up her hands. 'Why did nobody tell me?'

'It was a fleeting visit,' I say. 'She just wanted to check on Lorraine.'

'Oh, don't be so naïve, Tom,' my mother says. 'It wasn't me she came to see.'

'I'm pretty sure it was, actually.'

'I saw the way her eyes lit up when you walked into the room.'

'I think you might've been going a little heavy on the old meds, Lorraine.'

My mother raises an eyebrow. 'I'm just saying. Things may not be as finished as you think.' She yawns, before groaning back down onto her pillows. 'Now, if you don't mind, I'm going to grab another few hours of quiet wakefulness. So, off you pop.'

As we make our way from the room, I see from the corner of my eye that Sophie's watching me with increasing interest. I know from experience that no good will come of the resulting conversation, so I quicken my pace, hoping to avoid it completely. But it's not to be; the moment we reach the foot of the stairs, she plants herself in front of me and points to my leg. 'What's with the limp?' she demands.

'I, uh, walked into a table,' I stammer, like a panellist on *Question Time*, fumbling around for the correct answer, not sure whether to tell the truth or avoid the question completely.

Sophie holds my gaze for a while, a snake hypnotizing a small mouse. 'Tom, you're talking bollocks, aren't you?'

'Yes,' I tell her. 'Yes, I am.'

'So? Tell me. What happened?'

When I answer her question, the blood drains from Sophie's face. 'Why did he do that?'

I want to tell her everything, but I've been sworn to secrecy by Emma. 'Because he hates me,' I say.

Sophie gives no reply. She looks beyond my right shoulder. I turn around to see what she's seen there. Nothing. I look back at her. She seems close to tears. 'What's wrong?' I ask. 'You look like you've seen a ghost.'

Apparently, I'm not the only one with secrets. Sophie turns and walks from me without a word.

TWENTY

MY MOTHER IS SLEEPING MORE AND MORE NOW, GOING TO BED early and rising late, napping throughout the day. Dr Sullivan told us to expect this, that she'd be harder to wake as she got closer to the end. Nevertheless, Dad remains by her side for all but a few hours every day. The entire time, he holds her hand in his, and I imagine it's all he can do not to constantly bring her out of sleep and buy a few more precious moments of her company.

In these new, spare hours, Sophie and I have taken to rediscovering Myreton, walking along roads and passing houses that trigger all kinds of memories, things we thought we'd forgotten years ago. We wave to people as we pass them – Mr Johnstone, our old gym coach; Pauline Glass, who owned the best sweet shop Myreton's ever had; Reverend Faulkner, who had such a crush on my mother for so many years. I glance back and look at Reverend Faulkner again. An old man now. It makes me smile to think of the way he used to fawn over my mother after church every Sunday.

We continue to meet old friends of my mother. They ask, 'How *is* she?' and they ask, 'How are *you*?' But they don't want to hear that she's tired all the time, that her appetite has gone, that her system's shutting down. They want to hear that she's at peace, that she's led a great life, that she's happy her children have returned – and for the most part, that's what we give them.

A few days after Lena's visit to Myreton, Sophie and I find ourselves by The Dairy Shed, a rather dilapidated steel-framed barn on the eastern edge of the village, long abandoned and which has long acted as a snogging-ground for the older Myreton kids. My mother had another bad night last night, so neither of us is feeling particularly chirpy.

'I can't believe we've already been here five weeks,' I say, the first words we've shared in nearly an hour.

'Me neither,' Sophie says, gloomily. 'I never imagined it would last this long... I'm grateful, of course, but it's difficult, all this uncertainty. I wish I knew when it was going to end.'

'When's Bill due home?'

'Next Friday.'

'What are you going to do?'

'I know what I *want* to do,' Sophie says. 'More than anything, I just want to go home, back to my boring, monotonous old life. But I'd never forgive myself if something happened while I was away. The problem is, I'm not sure how much longer I can stand all this.'

I know what she means. When I first arrived in Myreton, the thought of a few weeks with my family seemed almost manageable. But now those weeks are over, and in the past few days I've even begun to imagine that my mother will reach Christmas, three and a half weeks away. I can picture it clearly, in fact; my mother, wrapped in a tartan blanket, smiling bravely while the children open their presents, sad to think there will be no more Christmases but soothed by the joy and continuity around her. Goodness knows, she might even still be alive three months from now. Dr Sullivan's dismissed the possibility of her making it much past New Year, but on the rollercoaster of terminal illness, it's difficult to be sure of anything.

'I know it's not easy,' I say. 'I'm struggling, too. I feel ridiculous sitting around the house all day. Being depressed and unemployed is difficult enough when you're on your own. Doing it in the company of your family's almost unbearable.'

Sophie glances at me, then to the pavement. 'I know it's awful,' she says thickly, 'but there's this little part of me that resents her tenacity, her ability to go on and on, day after day. I keep hearing this voice inside my head, whispering to me beneath all the small talk and fake cheer, willing her just to hurry up and die.'

'It's natural, to wish for an end to all this.'

Sophie nods. 'I know. I just... Fuck, I just *hate* it, Tom.'

I place an arm around her shoulder and we continue in silence along the street, past a row of Edwardian villas and towards the clubhouse of Myreton's most prestigious golf course. We've reached the second from last of these mini-mansions when Sophie stops dead in her tracks. 'Look!' she says, pointing to a black van that's parked a little further down the road. 'That's Daryll's, isn't it?' Before I can answer, she leaps into a nearby hedge, pulling me with her. 'Tom?' she whispers. 'I need you to watch out for anybody coming.'

I look at her suspiciously. 'Why?'

'Because I said so,' Sophie tells me. When I don't answer, she rolls her eyes impatiently. 'Oh, Tom, don't be such a drip. Just keep an eye on the street, okay? And if you see anyone coming, give a little whistle.'

I cross my arms across my chest. 'What are you going to do?'

But Sophie barely hears me. She's peering over the top of the hedge, her head darting between Daryll's van and the empty street.

'Sophie?' I say, shaking her shoulder. 'What are you going to do?'

'Nothing,' Sophie says, with an impish grin. She pats my head before returning to her lookout post.

'Come on, Sophie. Let's go home. We can grab some biscuits and watch a film together.'

'Uh huh,' Sophie says, plucking a twig from her hair. 'Okay, Grandma.'

'Stop it. I don't like this.'

'Give me your keys.'

'What?'

'Your keys!' Sophie says, impatiently. 'Quickly!'

I take the keys out of my pocket, hold them stupidly in front of me. Sophie grabs them, then jumps the hedge and sprints, knees bent, head low, across the road.

'Sophie, what the hell are you doing?' I say from behind the hedge. I'm trying to scream and whisper at the same time. 'Get back here this minute,' I holler.

Sophie doesn't seem to hear. When she reaches Daryll's van, she takes the keys and carves a series of deep scratches into the paintwork. She's a good thirty yards away, but even from this distance I can read what she's written; a single word, in foot-high letters.

PERVE

When she's done, Sophie turns on her heels and runs. I wait for her to join me back in my bush, but instead she darts right past me, yelling 'Scarper!' as she goes. I thrash my way back out onto the street and set off after her.

We've been running for more than two minutes when Sophie finally decides we've put enough distance between ourselves and the scene of her crime. She slows to a crawl, then begins walking in a tight circle, shaking her hands as if she's just washed them and there's no towel. 'Oh my god,' she says, breathlessly. 'Oh my god oh my god oh my god. I can't believe I did that.'

'What the fuck, Sophie?' I gasp, falling into a crouch on the pavement. I haven't moved so fast for so long in years. My chest feels like it's going to explode. 'You could have had us arrested.'

Sophie considers this for a second, then lets out a burst of laughter. 'That's true,' she says. 'But wasn't it fun?'

'Fun?' I ask, incredulous. 'What were you thinking?'

'He's an arsehole, Tom. He pushed you off a castle *wall*.'

'No,' I say. 'It's more than that. There's something you're not telling me.'

Sophie shakes her head. 'Shut up.'

'Why did you write that word on his van?'

'Shut *up*, Tom!' Sophie yells.

'No, I won't. Tell me what's going on.'

And just like that, Sophie starts to cry. It takes her a full minute to find her voice, but when she does the words begin to pour from her mouth. 'It was during my second year at university,' she says. 'I was back home for the Christmas holidays. Daryll's parents were off skiing in France, so he'd arranged a party. I didn't like him, but everyone was there. The party was one of those generic house parties with some stupid drinking game and the Killers blasting from the stereo.

'I didn't drink beer, so I'd brought my own bottle of cheap vodka, which I drank mixed with some orange juice I found in Daryll's fridge. I circled around for a while, talking to one group of people, then another, before my head started spinning and I thought I was going to be sick. The last thing I remember is lying down on the sofa. Just to close my eyes, I told myself, just for a minute, but...' She drops her head. She puts her fists in her eyes, presses down hard like you press down on a cut to stop it bleeding.

'It's okay,' I tell her. 'Go on, if you want to.'

Sophie rakes the fingers of both hands through her hair. 'When I woke up, I found myself stretched out on Daryll's bed, well away from the main party, and... Oh Christ, Tom, he was playing around inside my knickers.'

'He didn't do anything more?'

'He never got the chance. I screamed blue murder as soon as I woke up and he ran off.' She pulls a crumpled hankie from her pocket and swipes her nose.

'Did you go to the police?'

'No. I was too ashamed, for drinking so much, for not being able to stop it from happening. Plus, at the time I didn't recognise the experience as rape.'

'But it did fit the definition, right?'

Sophie sighs. 'Yeah,' she says, her voice barely a whisper. 'Yeah, it did.'

'Christ Sophie. How did you cope?'

'I didn't,' Sophie says. 'I fell apart. That winter, the winter of 2004, I had sex with more men in three months than in all the years before and all the years after combined. I convinced myself that if I gave my body away, over and over, I could prove to myself that intimacy was my choice.'

I feel like I've been punched in the stomach. Pressing a hand to my abdomen, I close my eyes for a couple of seconds and then open them again. I can think of absolutely nothing to say.

'You know the saddest part?' Sophie asks. 'I actually

considered myself lucky. Sure, Daryll might have left me damaged, but at least he didn't kill me. He didn't put a bullet through my head or a blade through my chest. I survived. I taught myself to be grateful for that, even if survival no longer looked like much.'

I shake my head; a small, almost imperceptible movement. 'It's just awful,' I say. 'So... is this why you started your charity?'

Sophie nods. 'After it happened, I began volunteering at a local sexual assault support organisation, staffing the crisis line. Honestly, Tom, the stories I heard in that office were just awful. And there were so *many*. Until then, I'd always dreamed of making it big in finance, but the attack changed everything. By the start of spring, I knew completely where my career was headed. So, I got my degree, and a loan from the Bank of Dad, and voila – the charity was born.'

'Do Mum and Dad know?'

'No. Only Bill. And now you.'

'And you? You're...?'

'I'm alright.'

I tip my head to the side, a look of doubt.

'No,' Sophie says. 'I really am. I'm not saying I'm over it – I doubt that'll ever be possible – but I've fared better than most.'

I shake my head angrily. 'I could fucking kill him.'

Sophie smiles sadly. 'You've no idea how many hours I've spent dreaming of sticking a knife in that wanker's crotch. But there are better ways to deal with it.'

I reach out, lay a hand on her shoulder. 'I wish you'd told me. We could have talked about it. You know I wouldn't have judged you.'

Sophie sighs and looks down to her hands, which are involuntarily picking lint balls from her coat. 'I couldn't. I didn't know how; not at first, anyway. And by the time I *was* able to talk about it, I was already coming to terms with what had happened and it seemed selfish to bother you.'

'It wouldn't have bothered me,' I tell her. Then, on reflection: 'I mean, it *would* have bothered me, but I'd have been glad to help.'

Sophie smiles, then lifts her arm and gathers me into a gentle embrace. 'I know that. And thank you. But don't worry – I really am okay.' The hand that rests on my back rubs it a bit, comfortingly. Then it gives my shoulder a little squeeze. 'You do know you said "Mum" before, don't you?'

I take a step back. 'What?'

'Lorraine. You called her "Mum".'

'Did I?' I cast my mind back over our conversation. Crap, she's right. I say: 'Ugh,' and give a shudder for comic effect before adding: 'Sorry. It won't happen again.'

Sophie shakes her head, rolls her eyes, and we stand, grinning, at one another for a few seconds. Then we remember the writing on Daryll's van, and that Daryll himself is close by. We hurry off for home through the back streets of Myreton as fast as our legs will carry us.

TWENTY-ONE

I WAKE THE FOLLOWING MORNING TO A HOUSE STEEPED IN silence. It's far too early for breakfast, so with nothing else to do, I walk upstairs to check on my mother, who is snoring softly. She's incredibly thin, thinner than ever, as if her wrists might snap from the weight of the books she attempts to read in her more spirited moments. With every day that passes she grows a little weaker. The skin on her cheeks has turned as thin and sheer as a veil.

The room feels way too stuffy. I slide the window open, and as I do, I nearly knock a card off the windowsill. It's a hand-made one, featuring a smiling, waving plaster who's wishing her a speedy recovery. My mother never showed the slightest interest in her own children's artwork during my years at school, but she was delighted when Crawford handed her this last week. I don't know; perhaps she's growing sentimental in her final days.

When I turn around to look at her again, her eyes are wide open and I fight back what would have come out as a frightened yell. 'Oh my god, Lorraine. You scared the shit out of me.'

My mother clears her throat, then swallows – painfully, it seems. 'Come here a moment, won't you?' she asks, and I'm struck again by how old she sounds. How papery, somehow.

I walk to her bedside. 'Shouldn't you get some sleep?'

She moves her head on the pillow and smiles at me, her face worn almost to the bone. 'I'll sleep when I'm dead.' Her breath stutters, and I realise it's a laugh. A weak laugh.

Her voice trails off, and she's quiet for so long that I think she might have fallen asleep after all, but then she opens her eyes again and takes a deep breath. 'It wasn't fair, was it,' she says. 'My being so offhanded with you. Sending you off to that school.'

'You shouldn't worry about it,' I whisper.

'Yes, I should,' my mother says.

'It's in the past.'

'Tom!' my mother cries. 'For God's sake, we *need* to talk. We need to! All the things we've never said, all the words we've swallowed, they've caused us nothing but trouble. I need to talk before I die. I want to leave knowing I did everything I could to make peace with my family.'

'Alright.' This is hard. Everything in me starts quivering.

My mother turns onto her side to better face me. 'I hope you know that I only ever wanted to give you the best chance in life. I know I might always have seemed a little cold, but I placed great value in teaching you children to be independent. I'd seen so many children grow up to be feeble, whining creatures who were going to need their hands held their whole lives – I wasn't going to let that happen to you.'

'Couldn't you have settled for a happy medium?'

'Possibly. But I felt convinced I was doing the best thing

for you. And I was, in a way. You grew up strong, all of you, because I allowed you to.'

'We grew up *hard*,' I say, a little too loudly. 'Because you *forced* us to.'

My mother smiles weakly. 'Perhaps a little of my cynicism has rubbed off on you, after all.'

I blow my breath out irritably. It pisses me off, being compared to my mother like that.

'How are you about... everything?' I ask. 'Are you frightened?'

'No,' she says, wistfully. 'Not frightened. Just sad. Sad that I won't get to see my grandchildren grow up. Sad that I won't get to grow old with your father. There was so much I still wanted to do.'

'I'm sorry,' I say. 'Truly, I am.'

'Really?' my mother says, with a smile. 'I'd have thought you felt it was the least I deserved for sending you to St Edwards.'

I click my tongue. 'Don't be silly.'

My mother laughs quietly, then sighs and becomes serious. 'I know it's hard to believe,' she says, touching my hand, 'but I really did think I was doing the best thing for you.'

'Even when I came home battered and bruised that first Christmas?'

My mother winces. 'That *was* unfortunate. I hope you know how angry I was when I saw you that afternoon. Any other child would have been expelled for what that horrible Acker boy did to you.'

'And yet you sent me back in the new year for more of the same.'

'No,' my mother says. I see her swallow, her neck moving with effort. 'I knew you'd be alright. I knew the school would do everything they needed to do to keep that little terror away from you. They knew what would happen if they didn't.'

'It wasn't just the fight, Lorraine,' I say irritably. 'I was miserable for the entire time I was at the school. That's a long time to be miserable.'

'You were never in any danger.'

'You sound awfully certain. How did you know I wasn't going to hang myself?'

My mother laughs. 'Oh, darling, you were never *that* badly off.'

I cross my arms over my chest. 'You couldn't possibly have known that.'

'Tom, I used to call St Edwards every week just to make sure you were alright.'

I stare at her, mouth agape. 'What?'

My mother nods. 'Every week for six years.'

'Oh.' It takes a force of will for me to hold onto my anger. 'But... if you'd spoken to me. If you'd only spoken to me. Then you'd have known – I wasn't alright at all. I was depressed, Lorraine. The whole time I was there I was really, really depressed.'

'And yet you pushed through.'

'Barely.'

'But you *did*. And look at you now.'

'Look at...?' I stammer, incredulous. 'What are you talking about? What is it that's so attractive? The failed marriage?'

'You don't know that it's failed.'

'Alright – the failed career, then.'

'You're between jobs,' my mother insists. 'You'll find work soon enough.'

'Right,' I say, with a snort. 'You wish.'

In a consoling tone, my mother says, 'I have every faith in you, Tom. You're a good boy. You'll find your feet again.'

I say nothing, just glare at her in irritation.

'For goodness' sake, please stop sulking,' my mother says. 'I'm trying to pay you a compliment.'

No wonder I'm so uncomfortable. 'Sorry,' I say. Then, after a long silence; 'Thank you.'

My mother nods. 'Yes, well,' she says, clearing her throat. 'You're welcome.'

More silence. I shift self-consciously from one foot to the other. 'Did you really check up on me while I was at the school?'

She rolls her eyes and coughs. 'What kind of mother do you think I am?'

The conversation with my mother has left me completely exhausted. It's the most we've said to one another in years, and the closest we've come to connecting in longer than I can remember. I eat breakfast in a sort of daze, then shuffle back through to my room, and when I catch sight of myself in the mirror, I can hardly believe it's me. I look beaten up, like Daryll caught up with me for another one-sided round of fisticuffs. I look into my eyes, but they aren't really mine, not the ones I used to have. They're the eyes of someone very tired and very sad.

I climb back into bed and spend the next few hours staring at my ceiling and half-listening to Peter Gabriel's greatest hits on repeat. At some point I must fall asleep, for when I reawaken, the bedroom is in darkness. I grab my phone, and gasp when I realise it's half past seven, a full eight hours after I last checked the time. But the screen holds a second, more pleasant, surprise; a message from Mike, inviting me and Emma round to his house for the evening. With a smile, I send a text to let him know I'll be there. Then, realising I've only half an hour to reach his door, I gasp again and spring towards the shower.

I arrive at Mike's to find Emma already waiting for me under the street light by his house, the collar of her winter coat turned up against the rain. We give Mike's door a knock and a moment later he's there to help us shrug off our jackets. He takes them away somewhere and then returns, smiling, and as we all stand there together in his hallway, I'm overwhelmed by how happy I am to see them – that this is always how I feel when we meet up with one another.

When we're all done grinning, I hand Mike the bottle of wine I grabbed from the cellar on my way out of the house. 'Whoa,' he says, staring reverently at the label. 'This is certainly better than the cheap plonk I usually grab from the Co-op.'

'A good wine for the best of friends,' I say.

Mike smiles. 'Aaw, shucks,' he says, pretending to be embarrassed. Or maybe he actually is – it's difficult to tell sometimes.

Emma and I make ourselves comfortable while Mike heads off to the kitchen for a cup of tea and a couple of wine glasses. When he joins us in the living room, he lays the tray down on the coffee table, then plucks the bottle of wine from the tray, holding it before him like a sacred offering. 'I feel a tad guilty about drinking this,' he says.

'Oh, Mike,' I say, with a frivolous wave. 'It was made for drinking.'

'Yes, but it's older than we are.'

Oh. 'Is it?' I ask, but I can see the label from where I'm sitting, and there it is – a Chateau Margaux, 1978. 'Uh...' I say, raising a finger, but the effort's drowned out by the popping of the cork. Cringing, I wait for Mike to hand me my glass, then take a tentative sip. Oh dear; it's like manna from heaven. I hope Dad won't be too upset when I tell him what I've done.

Mike takes a sip of wine, then leans forward in his chair. 'So, how are things at home?'

I sigh and let my head fall back against his sofa. 'It's horrible,' I say. 'Really, it's all just so sad. Even in the best moments, my heart's just a second from breaking. I can hardly bear to watch my parents together any more – it's just too awful to know they'll soon be lost to one another.'

Mike's smile is sad and full of sympathy. 'I'm so sorry, Tom.'

I nod, distracted, rubbing the back of my neck. 'There's something else,' I say. 'She's become almost... kind.'

'Your mum?' Mike asks.

I nod. 'I think she's trying to make amends.'

'Well, that's great,' Mike says. But when I say nothing, his smile falters. 'Tom?'

I think I'm going to cry. I wait until my throat unclenches and I can be sure the timbre of my voice won't give me away before I answer. 'It *is* great. But it's sad, too. It breaks my heart that we failed to reach this place sooner. I can't believe it's taken her death for us to get here.'

'I doubt the timing's a coincidence,' Mike says. 'It's natural your mum should use this time to reflect on the mistakes she might have made in life.'

'I guess,' I say. 'I just... I just...'

'Wish it happened years ago?' Mike says. Then, when I nod: 'I suppose it would have, in a perfect world. But at least you've been given the chance to work things out before it's too late. It's a chance a lot of people don't get.'

I nod uncertainly.

'And, honestly?' Mike continues. 'I'd make the most of this time. Because, however you might feel now, you're going to miss her when she's gone.'

I let out a quiet sigh. 'Yeah,' I say, my voice barely more than a whisper. 'Probably.'

We fall silent, and for some time the only sound in the room is the steady patter of rain against the window. Then Emma pulls a packet of tissues from her pocket and offers it to me. I stare stupidly at the packet, and then at her. Then I touch my face, only to discover I've begun to cry. Wordlessly, I take a tissue from the packet and wipe my face.

'Do you know yet what you're going to do when all this is over?' Mike asks.

'I guess I'll go back to London.'

Mike shoots Emma a look. 'Alright,' he says, nodding slowly. 'And, uh... why?'

'Because I live there,' I say, simply.

'Sure,' Mike says, continuing his slow nod. 'Sure. But... you don't have a job, right?'

'That's right.'

'And, I mean, you're only renting your flat.'

'Mm hmm.'

Mike and Emma glance quickly to one another, then back to me. They open their mouths as though about to say something, but then they shake their heads and close their mouths once more. I'm pretty sure I know what they were going to say, but far less certain that I'm ready to hear it. I hold my glass out to Mike, inviting him to pour a little more of Dad's wine. The room, once more, falls silent.

TWENTY-TWO

The following afternoon, Dad walks through to the living room looking even more than usually dishevelled. He has bruise-coloured bags beneath his eyes and it looks as if he's been crying, or not sleeping, or both. A sparse frost of white beard shows on his normally clean-shaven cheeks. For once, he looks every one of his sixty-seven years.

'Are you alright?' I ask, as he falls into the chair opposite.

He absentmindedly massages the muscles of his jaw with the heel of his hand. 'Your mother and I took a walk in the garden.'

'She was able to walk?' I ask.

Dad shakes his head sadly. 'To think, she wouldn't even look at that wheelchair three months ago. She hated it beyond words. But those days are well and truly over now. Now she lets me put her feet on the paddles. She says thank you.'

I look at Dad, confused. 'But... she didn't even *have* the wheelchair three months ago.'

'Hmmm?' Dad's so lost in thought, he hardly seems to have heard me.

'Why would she have needed the wheelchair three months ago? You told me she was fine until October.'

This time, the words get through. Dad's eyes, which have been staring into space, dart to mine, and he throws a hand to his mouth.

'Oh my god,' I say, my face pulled together in disbelief. 'Have you been lying to us?'

Dad leans forward in his chair and lets out a long, sad sigh. 'Tom, your mother knew what was happening a long time ago. Long before you, long before the doctors.'

'And you?'

He nods. 'Yes, I knew. As soon as she knew for sure what was causing the pain, she told me.'

'But there might still have been time. Why didn't you get help?'

'She's tired, Tom. The last treatment exhausted her. She couldn't bear to go through it all again.'

'I can't believe this,' I say, eyes shut, shaking my head. Already I can hear the panic colouring my own voice.

'I know,' Dad says. 'I'm sorry.'

I open my eyes, turn them to Dad. 'You should have told us.'

Dad bows his head as in prayer. 'She swore me to secrecy. She didn't want to worry you. And I agreed with her. After all, what good would it have done any of you to know? You had enough to worry about already.'

'But she's my mother.'

'Children shouldn't become responsible for their parents, Tom. It's against the natural order of things.'

'That's not true, Dad.'

Dad sighs again. 'Well, what's most important is that you're here now. I hope you know how glad we are to have you.'

I let out a one-note laugh with my nose. 'For all the good I'm doing.'

Dad frowns and looks at me. 'That's a silly thing to say. We're grateful to you, Tom. For your help. For being here. And I can't tell you how relieved your mother was after your conversation yesterday.'

I give him a look. 'I'm surprised she bothered to tell you.'

'Of course, she did,' Dad says. He stares at me for a moment, then clicks his tongue impatiently. 'You can be very hard on your mother sometimes. She's only ever wanted what was best for you.'

'That's true, but the *best* is however she defines it.'

Dad shakes his head. 'You can't blame her for everything.'

'I think I can,' I say.

'You don't think I'm to blame at all?' Dad asks.

'What?' I say, with genuine surprise. 'No.'

'I could have put an end to your time at that awful school. I know it wasn't my decision to send you there, but I still used to see how unhappy you were when you came home for the holidays. And yes, I spoke more than once to your mother about transferring you to Cranston during those years, but never forcefully enough to convince her it was really necessary. I wonder now why I didn't fight harder, why I didn't *insist* on bringing you home. Was it because I trusted your mother's judgement so fully? Or was it just easier to stay quiet, to keep the peace? I still don't know the answer to that one, Tom. But I *do* know I should have done more to make life easier for you.'

'Perhaps you weren't perfect, but you loved us, at least. That's more than she ever did.'

Dad looks at me, his mouth ajar. 'You don't really believe that, do you?'

I shake my head, fighting back tears. 'I don't know what I believe anymore. I just... god, I *hated* her.'

'I know,' he says. He puts his hand on my shoulder and squeezes it. 'But she loves you very much.'

I try to say something, but I'm too busy choking back sobs. 'Oh, Tom,' Dad says. 'I'm sorry. I'm so, so sorry.' He puts his arm around me and pulls me against his chest. He smells the way he did the last time I hugged him, way back in my third or second year at St Edwards.

It's late in the afternoon by the time I finally force myself into my coat and out of the door for my daily walk through Myreton. It's achingly cold, the wind coming east off the Forth bringing tears to my eyes, but as always it feels good to breathe the fresh air, and to have escaped the stuffiness of my parents' home.

This sense of contentment lasts until I'm about halfway from home; then, in half a second, it's shattered completely, turning first to confusion when I hear the screeching of car tyres on the road behind me, and then to terror as I look around to see Daryll clambering out of his van.

'You!' he shouts, pointing towards me, as though I might wonder which person he's addressing on this otherwise deserted street. 'I want a word with you!'

Fair enough, I think, *but you'll have to catch me first.* Then, without warning, I set off down the high street and into Hopetoun Terrace, where I leap over a small wall into Mrs Shaw's front garden and cower down behind a rhododendron bush. I settle just in time to hear Daryll's heavy footsteps appear at the street corner.

Daryll takes a quick look around him, then shakes his

head, smiling. 'You might as well come out,' he says. 'I can see you hiding there.'

He's bluffing. It's already too dark for him to have picked me out so easily from my hiding spot. Plus, I can see his back, and it's pointed away from me.

'For fuck's sake, Halliday, I can hear you breathing, too.'

Another bluff. Still, I hold my breath a little more tightly than before.

The standoff's no doubt unspectacular by spaghetti-Western standards, but as games of hide-and-seek go, it's absolutely terrifying. I crouch, heart in mouth, as Daryll continues his search. A couple of times his eyes settle briefly on my hidey-hole, but the sky, apparently, is just dark enough to keep me hidden. After a few minutes of this, I'm desperately uncomfortable, and my legs are starting to cramp. But then, just as surrender's beginning to look like a very real possibility, Daryll drops his shoulders and heaves a sigh towards the ground.

'Alright, Tommy,' he says, with a shake of his head. 'Have it your way. But you're only making this worse for yourself. You *know* this isn't over.'

It's true, I know; this *is* far from over. Nevertheless, when Daryll finally trudges away and I hear the engine of his van roaring to life, I breathe a sigh of relief so deep that it seems to come all the way from my feet.

I return to the house just as Sophie and Dad are sliding a couple of ready meals into the oven. They invite me to join them but I'm barely hungry, despite having not eaten since breakfast. I grab an apple from the fruit bowl. 'How's Lorraine?' I ask them.

It's Dad who answers. 'Frustrated. She's having trouble putting her words together and her whole body seems to ache.'

'Have you called Dr Sullivan?'

Sophie shakes her head. 'Mum's determined to leave it till morning.'

'Shall I go check on her?'

Dad and Sophie both turn to me. 'Um, yes,' Dad says, trying vainly to hide his surprise. 'She's been sleeping most of the afternoon, but... yes. Go ahead.'

I reach my mother's room to find her snoring softly against a mountain of pillows, her mouth open, her eyelids fluttering as though she's being chased through her dreams. Feeling I should do something, I step forward to straighten her tangled bedsheets. Almost immediately, her eyes open, startled, as though she expected to see someone else, in a different room.

'Jesus, Lorraine,' I say, clutching a hand to my chest.

She looks up at me, frowning. 'Wasn't Mother just here?'

I shake my head.

She sighs. 'I was with her just now in my dreams.' She gives a shudder, then pulls the blanket higher over her shoulders.

'Are you cold?'

She shakes her head. 'Thirsty.'

I take the glass of water from her table and hold it to her lips while she sucks a few times on the straw, her cheeks hollowing. When she's finished, she gives a little sigh of relief, then lays back against her pillows, propped up but not quite sitting up, looking at me.

'What were you dreaming?' I ask.

My mother draws in a deep breath and lets it out gently. 'I was thinking back to the afternoon Mother caught your

Uncle Davy reading the Dandy in his bedroom. He'd got a bad mark in school the week before and was supposed to be using the hours before dinner for extra study but... well, I suppose he'd just had enough. My god, she was livid when she found him. And that evening, she made him stand and watch as she placed the comics one by one into the living room fire.'

I'm surprised to hear her speak like this. It's rare for her to talk about her childhood. 'Was she always so strict?' I ask.

My mother nods. 'She was a harsh woman, your grandmother. Tell the truth, I was always a little frightened of her.'

'Why? What else would she do?'

'She'd lock me in the privy.'

'What?'

'She'd lock me in the privy and leave me there for hours.'

I give her a look. 'Come on, Lorraine.'

'In the middle of winter, too.'

'Oh my god, that's dreadful.'

She laughs at the word. 'She was dreadful all right. Not that I turned out much better myself.'

'Don't talk like that,' I say. Not because I disagree, but because the conversation's making me uncomfortable.

My mother looks at me for a long moment. Her smile is gentle and sad. 'It wasn't all bad, though, was it?' she says softly. 'We had *some* good times, didn't we?'

'Of course.'

'Do you remember that holiday we took to Cambridge? That was the summer you fell in love for the first time, with the hotel owner's little daughter.'

I don't think I remember, but then I see myself playing by the little stream at the foot of the hotel's garden. Sophie's standing to my left, searching for fish in the shallow water, and to my right is Clara, with her raven hair and ice-blue eyes, who calls me Tommy and who I'll marry just as soon as we're old enough.

'That was the same holiday we took you to see Jurassic Park in the local picture house and you upended a carton of popcorn over yourself when you started screaming at the raptors. I had to carry you out of the cinema and into the brightness of the afternoon before you'd calm down again.'

'I'd almost forgotten about that.'

My mother smiles. 'You had some awful nightmares after watching that film. I lost count of the number of nights I woke to find you clambering into bed with your father and I. Dad always said I should send you back to your own room, but it seemed so cruel. Plus, if I'm honest, I enjoyed the cuddles.'

I open my mouth to say something, but find myself too surprised to speak.

'You were my sensitive one,' she says. 'You weren't like Peter and Sophie. They always seemed so... indestructible. But you cared about things. You always felt things more than they did. I think that's what I loved most about you.'

'You called me The Wimp,' I say.

'I know,' my mother says, sadly. 'But I only wanted to toughen you up. Stupid, of course, but then I made so many mistakes. It's no wonder you resented me the way you did.'

I start to say something, but then she takes my hand, and she sets it flat between her two light hands, and looks up at me. 'I am so, so sorry, Tom. Truly I am.'

'Lorraine –'

'Please, Tom,' she says hoarsely. 'Please understand. I've never been more sorry. If I could turn the clocks back, I swear... I'd do things so differently.'

A tear curves down my mother's cheek; with my free

hand, I wipe it away. Then, touching the hand to my mother's face, I say, 'It's alright.'

This takes her by surprise. She shakes her head, quite unable to find a response.

I smile reassuringly towards her. 'It's alright,' I say again. 'It's all in the past.' Then I add, awkwardly, it's been so very long: 'I love you, Mum.'

My mother's eyes go wide. I feel her small body tense, then let go, the breath leaving like a low soft wind. 'My darling child,' she says, as another tear creeps down her cheek. 'My darling, darling boy.'

They are the final words I will ever hear her say.

TWENTY-THREE

THE FOLLOWING MORNING I'M IN THE BATHROOM SCRAPING A razor over my face when Dad barges in so suddenly that I cut my cheek. 'Tom,' he says, in a shaky, breathless whisper. 'Things have progressed.'

I touch my face and look at the blood on my fingertips, then glance at him, confused.

'It's your mother,' he says. 'You'd best come upstairs. Quickly, now.'

When we reach the upstairs corridor, I find Sophie already by my mother's door, her face ghostly white between dark hair and dark pyjamas. Dad makes his way into the room ahead of her; before I can follow, Sophie grabs my shoulder and pulls me into her. 'Oh, Tom,' she says, in a trembling voice.

'What's going on?'

'I don't know. Dr Sullivan's with her now.'

'Is she... still here?'

'Yes. But not conscious.' She rakes a hand through her tousled hair. 'It was Dad who found her when he came up from breakfast. It couldn't have happened more than an hour before, as he'd been with her until six, but I... I just don't know.' She starts to say something else but it gets caught and she leans into me.

We watch anxiously as Dr Sullivan runs a series of checks on Mother. When she's done, she walks with Dad to our side, her expression grim. 'Tom,' she says. 'Sophie. I'm afraid your mother has had a stroke.'

'A stroke?' Sophie says. 'But –'

'I know. But it's quite common with this sort of cancer. Normally, I'd have her taken to hospital for an operation to repair the blood vessels, but in her condition...' We know what she means, and nod understandingly. Dr Sullivan continues. 'I'm afraid it's only a matter of time before we see a second bleed, which is likely to be fatal. I'm sorry, but the best we can do is make her comfortable.'

'She couldn't get better?' I ask.

Dr Sullivan shakes her head. 'I'm sorry. I've given her something to keep her comfortable, and I'll be back to check on her again in a couple of hours. In the meantime, just try to enjoy these final hours with her.'

Dad returns to Mother's bedside as Sophie and I lead Dr Sullivan downstairs. We're a yard from the door when Pete burst through it. 'What's happened?' he asks, breathlessly. 'Dad said to come straight away. Is she alright?' Then he notices our mournful expressions, and Dr Sullivan, and he drops his head, sighing deeply.

After Dr Sullivan leaves, Sophie and I lead Pete upstairs. We find Dad with his lips pressed to Mother's ear, and although his song is too quiet to hear, I know already that it's 'The Air that I Breathe', the Albert Hammond version, my mother's all-time favourite song, and the first my parents slow danced to as a couple. I wonder for a moment if it's even possible that my mother can hear, until a tear forms in the corner of her eye and slips sideways towards the pillow. Falling silent, Dad picks a handkerchief from his pocket and presses it gently against her pale, bony face, and to our surprise her eyes slide open at the touch. She looks at us, her husband, her three children, one by one, before closing her eyes once more.

After that, there's nothing more until lunchtime, when Rose arrives with Crawford and Ellie. Crawford looks confused as he's led to Mother's bedside. 'Why does Nana look like that?' he asks, looking to Rose.

'Nana's getting ready to go to heaven, my darling.'

'Is she dead?'

'No,' Rose says. 'But she'll be leaving us soon.'

Crawford's chin starts to wobble. 'I wanted to show her my pitcher.'

'We can leave your picture by your bedside. Then Nana will see it when she visits you from heaven.'

Crawford considers this for a second, then nods.

'Alright then,' Rose says. 'Now, give Nana a kiss before we go.' She gently pushes Crawford towards Mother. Crawford leans against her palm, afraid to venture beyond its reach. 'Go on, sweetheart,' Rose says, softly. 'It's alright.'

Crawford takes a deep, steadying breath and steps forward to kiss Mother's cheek. When he steps back again, Rose lifts Ellie from her sling and presses her little face against Mother's.

'Right,' Rose says, wiping a tear from her cheek. 'That's us away. Goodbye, Lorraine. You take care, now, you hear?'

With the children gone, the room falls quiet again. Time slows to a crawl, the hours punctuated by small-talk, toilet breaks, and trips to the kitchen for fresh rounds of coffee. At some point Dr Sullivan arrives back to check on Mother, but little's changed since the morning and she's soon gone once more.

It's early evening, just before sunset, when Mother briefly comes to consciousness. She turns her head on the damp pillow and looks at us with an expression of wide-eyed startlement. 'Lorraine?' Dad says, a hopeful tone to his voice, but she shows no hint of having heard him. By now, I suppose, she's got near to a place so far away that what's happening to her here barely seems to register. Within seconds, she's asleep once more.

When Dr Sullivan calls Dad for an update on Mother's condition, Dad sends us children downstairs. When we reach the landing, Sophie plucks a pack of cigarettes from her pocket and shakes them enquiringly at me and Pete. Without a word, we grab our coats and head for the front door.

When we reach the garden, I glance up, startled to find the sky already cloaked in navy blue. Sophie tries to light a cigarette, but one match goes out and then another. I take the box from her and light one myself; it flares up and she leans close to it, one hand cupped around the flame and the other resting gently on my wrist.

'I hope it happens tonight,' I say. 'I don't want her to go on any more.'

Sophie sighs, her Lambert and Butler trembling between her lips. 'I hope so too.'

'I never expected to see her like this,' Pete says. 'When I remember how beautiful, how full of life she always was. It's just... cruel.'

Sophie takes one final draw of her cigarette and pitches it into the lawn like a dart. 'Yeah, well. Welcome to the world.'

When we step back inside, Pete and I head automatically for the stairs, but Sophie touches a hand to our shoulders. 'No,' she says, when we turn to face her. 'Let's leave them be. Give them some time alone.'

The minutes that follow tick by with torturous slowness. Pete takes to pacing in front of the living room fire, prowling restlessly back and forth like a cat, while Sophie sits on a chair with a cup of coffee, staring sadly out of the window. I pick up a book, try to read it, but my mind can't hold the words. I don't have the reservoir of space to take anything else into my brain. I lose track of the time, lose track of my thoughts. Outside, a light rain begins to fall.

Finally, the doorbell rings. It's Sophie who answers, though Pete and I are only a second behind her. Dr Sullivan steps inside, shaking the rain from her coat, her expression serious.

'How is she?' Pete asks, anxiously.

Dr Sullivan touches his arm. 'I'm not sure yet, Peter. I'll need to go up and see her first.'

Which, I have to admit, is a good point.

I return with Pete and Sophie to the living room, and for another excruciating hour, nothing happens. Then, finally, Dad wafts in through the living room door, so pale he seems translucent, and drifts to the couch, where he stands, trembling.

'Is she...?' Sophie asks.

Dad's jaw clenches. He nods once, then covers his face and a terrible whine comes through his hands. I didn't know how Dad cried. I'd never seen it before. It sounds physically painful for him. We all hurry towards him, throwing our arms around his shoulders. Dad returns the embrace, for a second. Then, clearing his throat, he pulls back and rubs at his nose. 'Right,' he says, recovering his composure. 'Well. Would you like to go and see her?'

We go upstairs to find Mother on her bed. Dr Sullivan has removed the pillows from under her head and drawn the covers up to her chest. Dad takes her hand and holds it against his mouth for a minute, looking at her. When he steps aside, Sophie and Pete take his place, leaning forward to kiss her forehead, her cheek, her tousled hair falling across her face. I tell myself to join them, but a strange feeling of numbness has spread over my body. It's not until a hand touches my shoulder that I feel able to move. I raise my eyes to find Sophie ahead of me, her tear-soaked face providing a near-perfect reflection of my own grief and sadness. 'It hurts, Sophie,' I whisper, as if speaking any louder will break me. 'Oh god, it hurts.'

Sophie pulls me into her. 'I know,' she says, weeping into my shoulder. 'I know.'

'I should have done better,' I say.

'Sssshhhhh,' she says, rubbing my back. 'Ssssshhhhh.'

'All that resentment. All those things I said.' I feel my throat tighten a bit, but I push the words through. 'But I did love her. I loved her so much.'

Sophie takes my shoulders, holds me at arm's length. 'And she knew it, Tommy. She knew.'

'It hurts so much worse than I thought it would. I just –' And then my throat closes entirely and there's nothing I can do to force it open. Sophie stares at me and nods into the silence between us, as if I am still talking and making perfect sense.

TWENTY-FOUR

IT'S FIVE O'CLOCK ON WEDNESDAY EVENING. I'M SITTING ON the sofa next to Sophie and Pete. None of us have slept in the twenty hours since my mother's death. The hours since then have been filled with those important jobs that kindly anaesthetise grief and numb shock, the phone calls and paperwork and filling in of forms. My body aches with tiredness. My eyes are sore and tender. I'm pretty sure I've never been so wiped out in my entire life.

The house has been steeped in silence for so long that we're all a little stunned when the doorbell rings. I answer it to find Emma standing on the porch with a tray of lasagne. 'Is this a bad time?' she asks.

'No,' I say, taking the tray from her, before I frown and make some effort to clarify my previous statement. 'It is a bad time,' I say, 'but I'm still glad to see you.'

'I wasn't sure whether or not to come,' she says, a flush spilling over her pale cheeks. 'I just wanted to make sure you were okay, that you were all eating enough. Not that I'm the best judge of that or anything, but still...' She shakes her head, annoyed by her attempt at humour.

'It's really nice of you,' I tell her. 'Thank you.'

Emma relaxes slightly, takes a deep breath. 'I'm just... I'm so sorry, Tom,' she says, her eyes glistening. 'It's an awful thing.'

'Yeah. It's pretty crap. But I'm glad for the time I had with her.'

Emma smiles. 'It meant the world to her to have you here.'

I feel the burn behind my eyes, the pressure of tears, and blink wet eyelashes. 'Will you come in for coffee?'

Emma shakes her head. 'Best not. Just... give my love to your family. And... Tom? You'll call me if you need anything, won't you?'

I rest the lasagne in the crook of my arm and reach for the door handle. 'Yeah,' I say. 'Course.'

Emma's not reassured. She grabs hold of my sleeve. 'Promise that you'll call me if you need to talk.'

She doesn't let go until I say, 'OK.'

After Emma leaves, I traipse through to the kitchen and exchange the lasagne for three steaming mugs of coffee, which I take back to Pete and Sophie in the living room.

'You and Emma seem to be getting on well,' Pete says, as I hand him his drink.

'Friends generally do that,' I say, taking a sip of my own coffee. It burns the roof of my mouth, but I don't mind. It's a relief to feel something palpable, something immediate and aching to distract me from everything else, even if it's only for a moment.

'You don't think she could be the new Lena?' Pete asks, raising a brow.

'Not while the old Lena lives and breathes.'

'You could do worse, you know.'

I give a wry laugh. 'That's quite an endorsement, Pete.'

'Oh, come on. I just mean, there's nothing wrong with her.'

I stare at him blankly. 'Well, I'll be sure to tell her you said so.'

We return to silence until, finally, Dad joins us in the living room. For the past six hours, he's been in his office calling friends and family from his address book, repeating over and over the funeral arrangements he made earlier today. I'm relieved to see that his face is not so dull, but the grief is still there, the heavy knowledge that his wife is dead. He'll wake up with that thought for a long time, I suppose; the thought makes me almost unbearably sad.

Sophie makes her way to Dad, and when she wraps her arms around him, he rests his hand on hers. 'How are you?' she asks.

Dad sighs, and shakes his head. 'Not so great,' he says. 'I really wish she hadn't gone and left me alone like this – not so soon.'

'I'm sure she didn't want to.'

'No,' Dad says. 'I suppose not. But still – the fact remains she's upped and left me.'

'I know, Dad,' Sophie says, rubbing his arm in sympathy.

Dad remains thoughtful. 'You know, I always thought I'd be the first to go. After all, I was the one with the shorter life expectancy. That's the one great inequality we men are truly allowed to moan about to women. And yet, here I am.'

'If it helps,' I say, 'We're glad you're still here.'

Dad manages a chuckle, before falling silent once more. Finally, he says, 'Still. I think she'd be happy, on the whole. We'd expected a great deal more pain in the end. To have been spared all that was... well, it was kind.'

Sophie, Pete and I all smile reassuringly, and a silence falls between us until the phone rings and Dad is forced to make his way from the room to confirm the rumour or accept the condolences and live my mother's death once more. We three children exchange uneasy glances, before returning to our seats, praying for an end to the nightmare in which we've unwittingly found ourselves.

The following morning, the flowers begin to arrive. The first, an enormous bunch of white lilies, arrives just after nine with a card that reads, 'Sending love at this time, Auntie Alison and Uncle Ben.' I haven't even found a vase before the doorbell rings again. Roses this time, from the Maxwells, who've lived in the village for longer than anyone can remember: 'All our love at this sad time'. Within three hours, the hallway's filled with flowers from cousin Jasmine, and old Mrs Davies, and the bowling club, and Norma bloody Bates, all of them sending their love at this tragic fucking time.

It's not yet noon when Sophie steps into the kitchen with bouquet number eleven. I'm standing by the sink, trying vainly to restore some order to its predecessor, which arrived only ten minutes ago. It looked marvellous when it got here, but I seem to have made rather a hash of the stem cutting and the arrangement is now more 'dog's breakfast' than 'awesome orchids.' It's making my blood boil.

When Sophie reaches my side, I give her flowers a catlike stare of disdain. 'Bloody do-gooders,' I say, with an impatient shake of the head.

Sophie raises an eyebrow. 'Well, indeed. Isn't it just awful when people are so kind?'

I mash another white rose into the vase, which, it now occurs to me, is far too small. 'You know what I mean.'

'Yes, I do,' Sophie says. 'Mum's dead and you're pissed about it. But there's no point blaming the neighbours.'

'I just don't see why we need so many.' But I feel rotten to be caught sounding so ungrateful.

By the early evening, we have more bunches of flowers than things to contain them, so I make my way through the gloom to our garden shed in search of more. When I arrive back, I find Chris waiting for me by the side of the driveway.

'Don't even start,' I tell him.

Chris begins to approach, his head lowered menacingly. I wave my arms, making myself as big as possible, which stops him in his tracks. He tilts his head and gives me a quizzical look.

'I'm not joking, you dumb pigeon. You don't want to mess with me today.'

Eyes narrowed, we begin inching carefully towards one another – participants in the world's slowest game of chicken. This continues for a while, until Chris opens his beak and starts to hiss at me. Then I lose my patience. 'Will you just... fuck... off,' I shout and, picking up a piece of gravel, throw it towards him. I was aiming right, I swear, but somehow it catches him on the head with a dull thud. Chris lets out a sort of 'Bakawk!' and runs in a tight little circle before collapsing to the ground.

I stand, staring at him. 'Chris?' I ask. 'Chris? Are you okay?'

Chris doesn't answer.

'Chris?' I edge nervously towards him. 'Chris? You better not be shitting me.'

But he isn't. He is, in fact, very, very dead.

I'm still attempting to come to terms with what's just happened when Sophie steps outside for a cigarette. When she sees me, she stops dead in her tracks. 'What's wrong with you?' she asks. 'You look as though you've seen a ghost.'

'I killed Chris,' I say, staring at Chris in confusion.

Sophie stares at the lump of feathers on the driveway, and then at me, a frown of bewilderment pulling her brows down. 'What on earth did you do that for?'

'I didn't mean to. I just wanted to frighten him.'

Sophie walks over to Chris' other side, prods him a few times with her shoe.

'I feel a bit guilty,' I tell her.

Sophie looks up to me, still frowning. 'Yes, I imagine you do.' Then, after some consideration: 'Do you want a cigarette?'

Shaking, I take the pack from Sophie, and for the next few minutes we smoke in silence, our eyes fixed on Chris, whose eye stares back at us. Then, finally, I say, 'What if this means something?'

Sophie peels her eyes away from Chris. 'What do you mean?'

'Well, I... I just killed him. With my anger. Maybe it's a warning of how destructive my temper can be. Maybe it's saying I need to hold my temper in future. Or... or maybe my anger's *already* been responsible for all kinds of destruction.'

Sophie narrows her eyes at me. 'This is about Mum, right?'

I look back at her. Say nothing.

Sophie bites her lip, suppressing a laugh. 'Hmmm. So, you're saying that Chris sacrificed himself so that you might understand you poisoned your mother with hatred, thereby forcing you to live out your remaining years consumed by guilt and regret.'

'Maybe,' I say, but my voice doesn't fall quite right, leaving an implied 'Am I?' hanging in the air.

Now Sophie's laughing for real. 'Tom, he was a fucking peacock.'

'I know, but... Yes, it does sound a bit silly when you put it like that.'

Sophie nods and returns her attention to her cigarette. It's just reached her lips when I speak again. 'But then... What if it's true?'

Sophie raises her eyes and hands to an Attendant Spirit hovering above, who presumably sympathises. 'Not the Chris part,' I add, quickly. 'But you know... about Mum.'

Sophie looks at me, serious now. 'Tom, you did not cause Mum's cancer.'

'No, I know. But I wasn't exactly... kind. I hate to think I made things more difficult for her.'

Sophie sighs. 'She knew you loved her.'

I nod.

'Plus, she wasn't exactly an easy woman to get along with.'

I nod again.

Sophie clears her throat. 'By which I mean...well, the tensions between you weren't *your* fault. Do you understand what I'm saying?'

'Yes,' I say, and though I try to stop it, a tear runs down the side of my nose. I slap it away with the heel of my hand. 'Even still. I think I'm going to miss her. Not just her presence, but her. You know?'

Sophie nods, and we return to smoking, and to staring at Chris. It's while we're doing this that another thought occurs to me. I'm not sure Sophie's going to like it. But still.

'It's sort of a metaphor, when you think about it. I mean,

Chris was the last of the cocks, wasn't he? Now all we're left with are seven hens, with their dull, brown feathers.'

'So?'

'So, with Chris dead –'

'– murdered –'

'– dead, the flock's been drained of its colour. The place won't be the same without him.'

Sophie's silent for a moment. 'Tom,' she says. 'You're such an idiot.' But tears are welling in her eyes.

TWENTY-FIVE

BILL ARRIVES THE FOLLOWING AFTERNOON. BETWEEN HIS JET-lag and Sophie's grief, it's hard to say who looks the more exhausted, but they're clearly overjoyed to see one another as Sophie runs to greet him by his car. 'You dummy,' Sophie says, as she throws her arms around him. 'You weren't supposed to get here until tomorrow.'

'I know,' Bill says. 'I know. But I *had* to see you.'

If anyone else had said this, Sophie would have met the line with gagging sounds. Coming from Bill, though, it only makes her hug him all the harder. Bill rubs her back for a few seconds more, then clasps her by the shoulders, holding her at arm's length, looking into her eyes. 'Has it been very awful?' he asks.

'A little,' Sophie admits.

'But you're... alright?'

Sophie nods.

'And Mum?' Bill continues, nervously. 'Was there any suffering? At the end?'

'Not too much, no.'

And with that news, Bill bursts into tears. 'Oh god, I feel just horrible! I should never have left you alone.'

'Oh, Bill,' Sophie says, rubbing his arm in sympathy. 'Don't be silly.'

'I never even had the chance to say goodbye!'

Sophie pulls Bill into another hug. 'Shh. It's alright. Really, it is. She knew she was in your thoughts. And you were always in hers.'

Bill considers this, and sniffs. 'Really?'

'Course you were,' Sophie says, winking at me from over Bill's shoulder. I stifle a giggle.

Bill seems happier, then. 'I missed you so much,' he says.

'I missed you too, sweetie. Shall we go inside?'

Bill takes a couple of steps across the drive before he spots me standing a few yards away. Dabbing at his eyes with a tissue, he walks towards me and plants a wet kiss on my right cheek. 'I'm so sorry for your loss, Tom,' he says, his chin wobbling precariously.

'Thanks, Bill.' I squeeze his shoulder, then pluck the case from his hands and start towards the house.

'And... Tom?' he says, grabbing my elbow. 'Thank you, for everything. You've made these horrible weeks so much easier for Sophie than they might have been. She's incredibly lucky to have a brother like you.'

I glance bashfully towards the ground. *Ah, Bill,* I think, a flush creeping across my face. *If there's a nicer person alive in the world today, I've yet to meet them.*

∾

In the evening, I decide to pay a visit to Rose and Pete. My argument with Pete's been playing heavily on my mind for over a week now, and I'm eager to test the waters between us. I arrive at eight, confident that the kids will now be in bed, but when I reach the door, I can hear screaming coming from inside.

There's no answer to the doorbell, and so I follow the noise to the kitchen, where I'm met with carnage. Ellie is twisting and screaming as Pete struggles to fasten her into her highchair, while Crawford is perched on the top of the table, drawing an elaborate pattern on the plastic tablecloth with a purple Sharpie. Crawford's toys are strewn everywhere, while the worktops, usually spotlessly clean, have become a temple of unwashed dishes. Pete's face, always so calm and collected around Rose, is covered in thick beads of sweat. Between Ellie's shrieks, I can practically hear his sanity cracking.

'I don't know what's wrong,' he moans, when he sees me standing by the door. Pete's as cool as a cucumber in a financial crisis, but a kiddie meltdown is obviously more than he feels qualified to handle.

'There's nothing wrong,' I say, stepping into the room. 'She's just tired. It's an hour past her bedtime.'

'But... she hasn't even had her bottle yet.'

'She gets that in bed,' I say. 'Didn't Rose tell you?' Then, looking around: 'Where *is* Rose?'

'Gone,' Pete says with a giggle, a panicked, almost hysterical laugh that dies in a whimper. 'Upped and left as soon as I got back home.'

'Gone where?'

'Out with friends, she said. Just left me here to babysit.'

'Oh,' I say. 'But... is it even possible to babysit your own kids?'

Pete doesn't answer, just continues to stare helplessly around the room. He says, 'I don't know where to start, Tom. It's all going to shit.'

Crawford looks up from his artwork, eyes wide. 'Unco Tom, Dada said a sweary-word!'

Pete looks at me imploringly. Sighing, I pluck Ellie from her highchair and feel her nappy bulging beneath a soiled sleep suit. 'Jesus, Pete, when did you last change her?'

Again, that imploring look. 'Once after every meal, isn't it?'

'That's for brushing teeth,' I say.

Pete stares at Ellie, confused. 'She's only *got* two.'

I bounce Ellie on my hip. She rests her head on my shoulder and her wails fade to pathetic moans. 'Let's just get them upstairs, and take it from there.'

Pete nods. 'Come on then, Crawford,' he says, pasting a strained smile to his face. 'Let's go find your PJs, shall we?'

Crawford's face drops. 'But my not finished my painting.'

'You can finish it tomorrow,' Pete says, snatching Crawford from the table. 'It's bedtime.'

Crawford looks stricken. 'My can't go to bed,' he argues, as he attempts to squirm from Pete's arms. 'Mummy's not here.'

'Daddy's – ouch! Crawford, would you stop... Ow! Daddy's going to sit with you tonight.'

'But you can't,' Crawford says, tears brewing in his eyes. 'You no' even know the words to *Hugless Douglas*.'

Pete says nothing more, just pinches the budding headache between his eyes and turns in the direction of the stairs.

In the kids' bathroom, we set about the gruesome task of changing Ellie's nappy. Small as she is, she's produced what looks like a half-pound of chocolate mousse, which she's somehow contrived to smear up her back. Pete takes the first shot at scraping the crap into the nappy, but gags when his finger vanishes through the wet wipe and into the mess. 'Oh, bloody hell,' he says.

Again, Crawford's eyes snap open. 'Another naughty word!' he says, jubilantly. 'Free strikes and you're out, young man.'

I take charge of nappy duty while Pete readies Crawford for bed. When both kids are in their pyjamas, I clap Crawford on the shoulder. 'Right,' I say. 'Sleepy time. I'm going to give Ellie a drink of milk. Are you going to let Daddy read your story?'

Crawford crosses his arms dramatically. 'Fine. But if he does it rubbish, my not going to sleep.'

I grin at Pete. 'You see? No pressure.'

With Ellie splayed on my shoulder, I grab a bottle of formula from the kitchen before returning upstairs to her darkened room, where I press play on her white noise CD and snuggle down to feed her on the armchair by her cot. 'You're not to worry about your silly old Daddy,' I tell her, as she sucks on her bottle. 'He loves you dearly, even if he is a stupid old fool.' She looks up at me, and I think she understands.

When she's finished her milk, I lay the bottle on the floor and begin to rock her in my arms. I watch in wonder as her eyelids grow heavy, dipping closed, then snapping open like a paper window shade, until, at last, she falls asleep. I kiss her forehead before laying her down in her cot and creeping quietly from the room.

It's another ten minutes before Pete re-emerges from Crawford's room. He closes Crawford's door silently then tip-toes down the carpeted stairs, a burglar in his own home. 'How did it go?' I ask.

'Not bad,' Pete announces, proudly. 'He said I'm nearly as good at *Hugless Douglas* as Rose.' He glances at his watch and heaves an exhausted sigh. 'I can't believe it's nine o'clock already.'

I shrug. 'Time flies when you're having fun.'

Pete grins sheepishly. 'I did get myself into a bit of a tizz, didn't I.'

'Well,' I say. 'It'll give Crawford something to talk about tomorrow.'

Pete allows himself a small chuckle before turning serious. 'Not that it was all my fault, mind you. The situation could have been avoided completely if Rose hadn't gone and left us alone.'

'No question,' I say. 'How very dare she.'

'Well, indeed,' Pete says.

'Cruel, is what it was.'

'Absolutely! She might at leas–' He stops talking then, eyes me suspiciously. 'Are you taking the piss out of me?'

I can't help but laugh, then. 'Pete, just listen to yourself. All this talk of being punished, abandoned, by Rose. Haven't you even stopped to think that maybe she just needed a few hours to herself?'

Pete seems momentarily startled by this suggestion. I take advantage of the silence and forge ahead with my argument.

'I'm pretty certain Rose never expected you to freak out like this. After all, she only asked you to put your children to bed.'

'She didn't ask,' Pete says, huffily. 'She ordered.'

'Fair enough,' I say.

'And anyway,' he adds. 'She's used to it.'

'Yes. Well, she should be by now.'

Pete turns to me, offended, and opens his mouth to complain some more. But then my point appears to hit home and his shoulders slump. 'Oh god,' he says, miserably. 'I'm being a dickhead, aren't I.'

I nod. 'Little bit.'

Pete covers his face and groans into his hands. 'Oh god,' he says again. 'I'm such an idiot.'

I choose not to argue the point. But even so: 'It's not like Rose to leave the kids like this. Did something happen?'

Pete rakes a few loose strands of hair from his eyes, rubbing them as if he hasn't slept in a week. 'We had a bit of a falling out last night. I'd promised her I'd be home for dinner, but Head Office needed someone to stay behind and push through a last-minute deal, and... well, I guess I volunteered.'

'And you missed dinner?'

Pete nods, his cheeks colouring. 'Rose was furious. She says the job's consumed me completely. She said it's killing our relationship, and my relationship with the kids. She... she called me *obsessed*.'

I try my best to look shocked by this, but it's hardly news. Anyone who knows Pete at all is perfectly aware of his preoccupation with work. Everyone, that is, except for Pete, apparently.

'It's like you told me last week, Tom. I should have listened to you. She's exhausted. And she's lonely.'

'So, what are you going to do?'

'I don't know. Rose said I should take a step back at work, but... I'm just not sure I can. This is the only person I know how to be.'

'Does it make you happy? Your job?'

'It's what I was born to do.'

'Says who?'

Pete looks to me, and although neither of us say it, we both know the answer: *Mum*.

'Pete, you need to listen to Rose. It's either your job or your marriage.'

Pete tries to laugh. 'I think you're being a little dramatic there.' But almost immediately he rubs a hand across his face, and from the way he does it it's clear he knows I'm right.

'You can fix this, Pete.'

He shakes his head. 'It's just... what if I fail?'

I blink in confusion. 'What are you talking about?'

'I'm not like Dad was. It doesn't come naturally to me, family life. It scares the shit out of me when I'm left alone with the kids.'

'So, you just need some practice. You're a good man, Pete, deep down. Just be yourself, and the kids will love you for it. And remember, you won't be on your own. If you have any problems or worries, Rose will be right there to help you. She really does love you, you know.'

Pete nods miserably, and for a moment I think he's going to cry. Then he turns to me and in a choked voice, says, 'I do hate it, you know. The job. I'm drinking down a bottle of Gaviscon every day just to keep myself from puking with stress.'

I nod understandingly. 'Well, that settles it, then. Do what you gotta do. Life's too short, Pete.'

Pete considers this, and then – in a rare display of affection – squeezes me gently on the knee.

We stop talking then, and in the ensuing silence Pete grabs the TV remote and begins hopping through the sports channels. Taking this as my cue to leave, I grab my coat from the table and set off out of the house. I'm halfway down the garden path when, to my surprise, Pete bursts through the front door and, in a hoarse shout-whisper, beckons me back over to him.

He looks almost shy when I reach his side. 'Tom,' he says. 'I've been' – he clears his throat like the words are hard to get out – 'erm, thinking. About what I said in the park.'

I shake my head. 'If it helps, I'm pretty sure everything you said was true.'

'No,' Pete says. 'I was harsh.'

'Pete,' I groan, pressing a hand against my forehead. 'You don't have to apolog–'

'Yes, I do!' Pete interrupts. 'Of course, I do. For Christ's sake, Tom, I've treated you like shit for years. It's no wonder you've kept your distance from me.'

'It's not just your fault. I've been angry, too. I guess we all have.'

Pete stuffs his hands into his pockets, rocks back on his heels. 'Yeah, well...' He clears his throat again. 'Even still... You know I love you, don't you?'

I look to Pete, stunned. 'Actually, I was never sure.' I shift awkwardly from one foot to the other. 'But... thank you. It's nice to hear. And, uh... yeah. I love you too.'

We stand in the dark, and there are no more words. The silence is enough. Finally, he reaches out to clap me on the back. After he goes in, I stay out there a while looking up at the stars. When the chill gets to be too much, I turn my collar to the wind and head back to the house to sleep.

TWENTY-SIX

Mother's funeral takes place in Myreton Church on a cold and dreary Thursday morning. The building is crowded with people, some I've known my whole life, some I've never seen before. Our family takes up the entire front pew, end to end. I'm sitting between Sophie and Pete. Rose, sophisticated as ever in a black dress, is next to him, and then come Crawford and Ellie, who's seated on my father's lap. They look like two miniature adults, Crawford in a little shirt and tie, and Ellie in a dress. Emma arrived with her family a few minutes ago, and they're seated next to Mike a few rows back from us. Lena's taken a seat in the back row, where she sits alone, dabbing her eyes with a tissue. I watch her for a long moment, my heart aching, before forcing my eyes forward once more.

Before long, the whispers of the two hundred mourners are silenced as the minister takes his place at the pulpit. 'Good morning,' he says. 'And thank you for coming here today to celebrate the life of Lorraine Halliday. I feel, as I'm sure many of you do, that a book could be written about

Lorraine's life. She accomplished so much, and meant a great deal to all of us in this room.'

Sophie and Bill have already begun to cry. Pete, I see, is taking it hard, too, swallowing big enough to make his Adam's apple bob above his tie knot. I watch this for a moment, fascinated, and am horrified to feel the tickle of laughter in my throat. I swear quietly to myself; all my life I've struggled with this impulse to laugh at the wrong time. Clearing my throat, I pick up a Bible from the floor and attempt to distract myself with a story or two of infanticide or cannibalism.

Sophie looks towards me, then. 'Tom, what on earth are you doing?' she whispers.

'Nothing,' I whisper back, but then it comes. A chuckle.

Sophie's eyes widen in shock. 'Oh my god,' she says. 'Stop giggling.'

I look helplessly towards her. 'I can't help it,' I say, then burst into tears.

And that's how I spend the entire service, laughing and crying in the presence of my family, a few yards from the stone font in which I was baptised and surrounded by stained-glass windows whose pictures told impossible stories I puzzled over every Sunday of my childhood.

After the service, my family and I stand for a moment or two in the knife of the wind as people shake hands with us, sorry for our trouble. Then the undertakers load the coffin into the back of the hearse and drive it the fifty yards or so down the gravelled lane to the grave. The procession shuffles behind it in a long, snaking line.

The grave is almost unspeakably horrible, a blind clayey hole with a pile of raw earth on one side and my mother's coffin sitting dumbly on the other. There's some talk, by the minister I think, but I'm too numb to listen to anything that's being said. I'm aware of nothing, in fact, until Pete touches my shoulder and leads me to the graveside, where I stand with the other pallbearers.

Then suddenly I'm four again, and feeling indescribably heroic as I step, for the first time, onto the top platform of the old metal slide on the village green. It's a huge moment for me – in the past year, I've made countless attempts to reach the summit of this rusting giant only to find my legs turning to jelly as I reached its uppermost steps. But I've done it now, and as I gaze fearlessly into the distance, I can't understand why I ever felt afraid.

Then I look down.

By the time Mum arrives, I'm so frozen by fear that she has to prise my fingers one by one from the railings before lifting me back to safety. The line of kids who were caught behind me laugh and jeer as she sets me down on the tarmac, though they immediately shut up when Mum spins around and fixes them with a terrifying glare.

There's a touch against my shoulder. It's the undertaker, who presses a length of white cord into my hand.

Standing by the foot of the slide, my chin's beginning to wobble. 'Oh, Tom,' Mum says, staring down at me. 'Are you having a pity party?' I hold back my head, trying to force the tears back down. I've always cried easily. I hate myself for it, which makes me cry even more. I let out a few sniffles. After a moment, I find the courage to look up at Mum, and am surprised to find her smiling kindly at me. 'Well,' she says, gently. 'Even pity parties call for ice cream. Shall we go to the shops and buy one?'

The cord tightens against my palm. I look up to find my fellow pallbearers lowering the coffin into the grave. I follow their example, forcing myself to watch as the strap slides slowly from my grip.

Mum helps me on with my jacket, then crouches down until

our faces are level. 'You're such a sausage,' she says, passing a hand through my hair. 'But you're my *sausage.'*

And I realise – it's true. I *was* hers. She might never have invited intimacy the way other mothers did, but she loved me. I was her sensitive one. I cared about things. I felt things more than other people. And I made her proud.

The undertaker removes the cord from my hand, forcing me back to the present, and to the minister's sermon. 'We therefore commit her body to the ground,' he says. 'Earth to earth, ashes to ashes, dust to dust. In the hope of resurrection unto eternal life, through the promise of Our Lord Jesus Christ, we faithfully and victoriously give her over to your blessed care. Amen.'

The first spadeful of earth. The thud on the hollow lid gives me a sick, empty feeling. Pete drops the rope and buries his head in his hands, sobbing monotonously. Dad, standing soberly to his side, places a hand on his shoulder. Sophie steps forward and throws a little bouquet of roses – my mother's favourites – into the grave.

I'm going to miss her so much.

After the burial, we walk the short distance to the Myreton Inn, where Dad has arranged for the usual provision of tea, coffee and alcoholic refreshment. There are far too many sandwiches – too much food altogether, including a tray of those horrid, greasy vol au vents that never fail to appear at funeral teas. The mourners step inside, rubbing their cold hands, stamping the mud from their shoes. There's a strange euphoria about the room, the release of afterwards and the illusion that the woman we have come to remember must be about the place, somewhere.

I pour Sophie and Bill a cup of coffee and then one for myself. We stand in a corner of the room, drinking and not talking. Our fellow mourners seem to understand that we need some space, and leave us be, until Mike and Emma wander over to offer their condolences. Emma is dressed in a long black dress, while Mike is wearing a tie and black jeans with trainers. His hair is all combed down.

'How's it going?' Mike asks.

'Pretty poorly,' I say.

Mike nods understandingly. 'Yes. I remember. But it does get easier.'

I smile, touch a hand to his shoulder. 'I'll look forward to that.'

I move among the wake, offering drinks, receiving sympathy. People have their memories, and are eager to share them. Uncle Davy remembers a trip to the hospital after Mum challenged him to see how many beads he could fit up his nose. An old school friend, Wendy Collins, remembers the impromptu trip she and Mum took to Paris the week before they set off for university. Sarah Pearce, who studied with Mum in Edinburgh, remembers when Mum got so drunk at a bar that she stole a girl's birthday crown off her head, went to another bar, and made everyone there buy her birthday drinks. A dozen stories, just like those. I learn as much about Mum in an hour as I have in the past ten years.

By noon, the party seems to have its own momentum. I place down my glass and set off in search of Lena, praying that I haven't missed her completely. Instead, I find Dad wandering the back corridor of the hotel in a sort of agonized daze, searching for a quiet nook or cranny away from the guests who continue to bound out of the shadows to present their sympathies.

'Ah, Tom,' he says, his voice small and weary. 'How's it going back there?'

'They're happy as Larry. Especially now the free wine's kicking in.'

Dad smiles. 'Has Old Bates cornered your Uncle Davy yet?' It's one of those old family jokes that Norma Bates is in love with Uncle Davy.

'Not yet. He's keeping a safe distance by the end of the bar.'

'Sensible man,' Dad says. 'He's had a horrible enough week. An indecent proposal from Bates might just finish him off.'

We laugh a little, then fall into a companionable silence, which lasts until Lena spots us from the foot of the corridor and hurries towards us, pulling Dad into a tight hug. 'I'm so sorry,' she says, tears sliding unchecked down her cheek. 'I'm so, so sorry. And I hope you don't mind me... I mean, I didn't want to cause a drama, but... oh, Jack, I *had* to come.'

Dad touches a hand to Lena's cheek. 'Darling,' he says. 'You are *very* welcome.' Lena presses her face to his hand, her shoulders wrenched with violent sobs. Dad waits until the worst of the crying is over, then kisses the top of Lena's head and, with a sigh, says, 'Anyway, I should be getting back to the party. Take care, won't you?' When Lena nods, he takes a deep breath, squares his shoulders, and sets off to rejoin the party.

After Dad leaves, there's a moment's silence between Lena and I. 'If it helps,' I say, 'I'm happy to see you, too.'

Lena nods tightly, smiles through her hankie.

'Bit of a shame that Jeff's not here as well, mind.'

Lena barks out a laugh. 'Yes, I'm sure that really would have made your day.'

There's another silence while Lena wipes the trails of mascara from her cheeks. 'In any case, he had no reason to come. Jeff and I are no more.'

'You broke up with him?'

Lena shrugs philosophically. 'Well, it was never going to work, was it? I mean, the guy's more in love with himself than he could ever be with some *woman*.'

'I'm delighted to hear it,' I tell her.

'I'm sure you are,' she says.

'It's going to be a little awkward at work from now on.'

Lena nods. 'Pretty nightmarish, I'd say. That's why I've asked for a transfer.'

I swallow. 'What?'

Lena smiles sadly. 'I'm done with London, Tom. Too much has happened there. It's not the home it once was.'

'Where will you go?'

'I don't know. Back to Sweden, in the first instance.'

I shake my head, confused. 'How on earth are you going to transfer to Sweden? They don't have any offices there.'

Lena looks at me like I've missed the point completely and starts to say something, but she's stopped from doing so by Rose, who appears from the main party, looking flustered. 'Oh, *there* you are,' she says, touching my arm. 'Your Auntie Mary was all ready to send out a – oh, Jesus, I'm sorry, Lena. I didn't see you there.'

Lena smiles kindly. 'It's alright. I should get going anyway.'

'You won't stay?' I ask.

Lena shakes her head. 'My train leaves in less than an hour. And anyway, it sounds like you have plenty to be getting on with.' She takes my hand, presses her lips to my cheek. 'Take care, Tom. And be happy.'

I watch her walk the short distance to her car, where she falls into the front seat and rests her forehead on her hands on the steering wheel. There's still time to run outside and talk to her, but I'm not sure I have the words to bring her back to me. Eventually, in desperation, I take a couple of steps towards the door, but by then it's too late. In the next moment, she pulls out into traffic, and within seconds her car disappears around the bend where the main street ends.

All your life this moment will haunt you, I think. It sounds a lot like my mother's voice.

TWENTY-SEVEN

FOR TWO DAYS AFTER THE FUNERAL, I BARELY LEAVE MY ROOM.
I eat little, and the only thing I drink is the water from my
bathroom taps. There are long stretches of time when I
don't know what I am doing, or what I have done – nothing
mostly, but it would still be nice to know what sort of
nothing that was. From time to time, I hear little bursts of
conversation, footsteps on floorboards, birds chattering in
the garden; but for the most part, I'm aware of nothing –
nothing but the gaping holes that have been left by my
mother and my wife.

Finally, on Saturday evening, I go through to the bathroom and shave and wash the sleep from my eyes and look
at the same mirror that has reflected my face for twenty-five
years or so. I've aged at least a decade since my mother's
burial, I think. But there's nothing to be done; I take a deep
breath, then turn away to go and face my family once more.

I find them perched around the coffee table in the living
room, picking away at a collection of bowls and dishes that
hold the remainders of the food our friends and neighbours
delivered in the days after Mum's death. I stand quietly in

the doorway, examining the remnants of my family. It takes them some time to notice me, but when they do, they let out a collective sigh of relief. I feel guilty then for making them worry.

Crawford's the first to greet me. 'Unco Tom! Dada buyed me a Paw Patrol Paw Patroller!'

'Ooh,' I say. 'What's Paw Patrol?'

This makes everybody laugh. They think I'm joking.

Sophie pats the sofa, beckoning me over to her; when I take a seat, she lays a hand on my shoulder and pours me a cup of coffee. It feels nice to be back in the land of the living, even if my heart's still aching.

'It's good to see you,' she says. 'I was beginning to wonder if I'd get the chance before we set off for home.'

'Well, you got lucky. When are you leaving?'

'Tuesday morning,' she says. 'But we'll be back again for Christmas.'

Christmas. I can hardly believe it's only two weeks away. I never thought when I arrived here in October that I'd still be around seven weeks later.

I turn to Pete. 'What about you? When are you heading back to work?'

Pete clears his throat. 'The sixth January.'

Sophie's head snaps around to Pete. 'The sixth of what?'

Pete nods. 'I've taken the rest of the month off.'

Sophie looks enquiringly to Rose, who confirms the news with a happy nod. 'Oh my god,' Sophie cries. 'What did you do with my brother?'

Pete shrugs and looks down at the floor, breathing heavily through his nose; he's wearing a slightly embarrassed expression on his face. 'Actually, there's more. I've decided to take a step back at work for a while.'

There's a distinct popping sound as every mouth in the

room drops open. On hearing it, Pete breaks into a big dopey grin. 'Well, let's be honest, it's not before time. My work life balance has been a mess for years. I don't even remember the last time I took an entire weekend off.' Pete tugs self-consciously at the collar of his shirt. He's definitely blushing now. 'Fortunately, it's not too late to change, and rediscover a bit of perspective. So, as of today, I'm done with chasing rainbows and unpaid overtime. We're going to be a family again.'

A slightly stunned silence greets the end of this speech. Then Sophie blows out her breath and stares hard at Pete. 'Jesus,' she says. 'I'm almost proud of you.' Which is hands down the kindest thing she's ever said to him.

We fall into another silence, which is friendly at first; then the atmosphere becomes less comfortable, and I realise my family's begun to decide how best to address the Tom-shaped elephant in the room. Naturally, it's Sophie who speaks first. 'What are your plans?' she asks.

I shrug. 'I guess I'll head off on Tuesday as well.'

'To where? London?'

I chuckle nervously. 'Where else?'

'I don't know,' Sophie says. 'Anywhere? I mean, there's nothing waiting for you in London, is there. Unless...' She looks at me curiously. 'Unless there's a chance for you and Lena?'

I shake my head. 'No. Lena... I... We...' Fuck it, I might as well tell them. 'She's moving back to Sweden.'

Sophie's mouth moves, but her tongue is slow to follow. It might be the first time I've ever seen her speechless. 'Shut the fuck up,' she says, at last.

I shrug my shoulders. 'It's true.'

'But... where will she go?'

'To Stockholm, I suppose. She wants to be closer to her

parents.' This sentence creates an image in my mind – Lena in her parents' house, laughing, is the thing I picture – and for a minute I feel panicked. I grab a fork and eat a mouthful of Mrs Gardner's beef stroganoff, because casually digging into a plateful of food feels like the best way to convince everyone that this is just another of those things, which it is not.

'I just don't understand,' Sophie says. 'Why would she do that?'

'I don't know.'

'She worked so hard to get where she is. Why would –'

'I don't *know*,' I say, sharply. 'I don't *want* to know. I just want to stop thinking about it. I can't bear it any more. So, can we just drop the subject? Please?'

Sophie's head snaps back, but I can tell she's surprised rather than offended by my outburst. The fact that she's not offended makes me realise how terribly worried she must have been about me. I drop my eyes to the floor and Sophie, bless her, changes the subject completely. 'What about you?' she asks, turning to Dad. 'Are you going to be alright?'

Dad sighs. 'Oh, you know me,' he says.

Sophie nods. 'That's why I'm asking.'

Dad considers this. 'I see your point,' he says. 'But I'll be okay.' Then, noticing the uncertainty in our eyes: 'I'll be fine. I promise.'

Sophie sighs. 'I just can't imagine you rattling around in this big house on your own.'

'Well, no,' Dad says. 'Neither can I. Which is why I've decided to sell it.'

Sophie drops her fork. Pete nose-burps his drink. Rose's eyes open so wide I can see inside her skull. I'm too stunned to react.

Dad laughs. 'I don't know why you're all looking so

shocked. This house was already too big for your mother and I. It'd be ridiculous if I decided to live here alone.'

'But… you can't sell it,' Sophie says.

'Why not?' Dad asks. 'Do you want it?'

'Well, no…'

'Tom?'

I shake my head.

'And what about you, Pete?'

Pete looks to Rose and smiles. 'We're fine as we are.' Rose beams at him, and places her hand in his.

'But won't you miss it?' I ask.

Dad shakes his head. 'This house was your mother's. It was filled to bursting with her energy. Now, it just feels empty and meaningless.'

'Still. It's your home.'

'She was my home.'

A silence descends on us, then, and for a time I think we might never break it. But then, finally, Sophie puffs out her cheeks. 'I know I like a bit of gossip, but this is just ridiculous.' She shakes her head. 'Is that it now? Are we done for today?'

Rose raises a finger. 'Actually, I should probably tell you. I'm pregnant.'

There's another of those popping sounds as we all gape at Rose. She takes a moment to study our frozen expressions, then begins laughing and slaps her knee with her hand. 'Ah, I'm only kidding,' she cackles. 'Sure, what would I be wanting with another child? I've quite enough on my plate just keeping these three lunatics amused.'

There's a deep well of silence before Sophie and I start giggling. Bill and Dad follow. We sit there, cracking up. When one of us starts to calm down, we look over at Rose, and to Pete's stunned face, and it starts all over again. Eventually, even Pete starts to laugh. And I realise, not for the first time this week, that he might not be quite such a bad egg after all.

TWENTY-EIGHT

THE FOLLOWING EVENING, SOPHIE, BILL AND I MEET UP AT THE Myreton Inn for a final drink with Mike and Emma. We arrive to find Norrie, Merv and Gary in their usual stools by the bar. One of them has selected 'Sweet Caroline' on the jukebox, and they're all singing along, tapping their hands on their beermats to the little 'ba, ba, ba' refrain in the chorus. Sharon's writing tonight's specials on the specials board, and when she sees us, she lifts a hand to her temple and pulls the trigger of an imaginary gun. These men have something of an obsession with Neil Diamond, and she's heard this song more times than she can remember.

'Quiet, for a change?' Mike asks, as Sharon puts her gun away.

Sharon raises an eyebrow. 'Not for long. We've got five Christmas parties tonight, so you can expect some fireworks between now and midnight.'

We grab a table as far as possible from the jukebox just as 'Sweet Caroline' makes way for 'Forever in Blue Jeans', which provokes another groan from Sharon.

'So, Emma,' Sophie says, when we're settled. 'I hear

Dad's asked you to stay on and help in the house for the next few months.'

Emma beams. 'I can't tell you how happy I am about it.'

'You're not the only one,' Sophie says. 'I'll sleep better knowing he has another familiar face around him. He really does appreciate your help, you know.'

Emma shrugs. 'I enjoy offering it. So, it's a good deal for both of us.'

Sophie turns to Mike. 'You're awfully quiet, sir.'

'I just can't believe you're all heading home tomorrow,' Mike says. 'It feels like only yesterday since I bumped into Tom again.'

Sophie smiles. 'Well, you needn't look so glum. Tom'll be back here for Christmas, so you've only another two weeks until you see him again.' She turns to me and finds my gaze. 'You *will* be back here for Christmas, won't you Tom.'

This is not a question; I give a half-smile, nod my head obediently.

'There you are, then,' Sophie continues. 'And, hey, maybe we could all go to Edinburgh when we're here, find you a nice guy to keep you company while Tom's away.'

'What?' Mike says. He looks at me, aghast.

I raise my hands. 'I didn't say anything.'

Sophie looks confused. 'Well, it's not as though there's anyone here in Myreton to...' She stops talking. 'Oh. Was it supposed to be some kind of secret?'

Mike's too busy cringing to hear the question. I nod my head on his behalf.

Sophie looks to me desperately. 'But... it's so *obvious!*' She turns to Emma. 'Did you know?'

Emma nods shyly. 'I never said anything, but... yeah.'

Sophie turns to Bill. 'And you?'

Bill clears his throat nervously. 'Well, I only just met the guy, but, yeah, it seemed obvious enough. Though, in fairness,' he adds, proudly, 'I've always had a very impressive gaydar.'

'What's that about a gaydar?' asks Sharon, who's chosen this moment to deliver our drinks order. Then she notices Mike's horrified expression and begins to laugh. 'Oh, thank goodness,' she says. 'The cat's finally out of the bag.'

The rumpus at our table has caught the attention of the oldies at the bar. 'What the hell's a gaydar?' Merv wants to know. He looks at his friends, who both shrug, and then back to Sharon.

'We're having a little coming out party,' Sharon grins, too wired to notice Mike's desperate attempts to stop her from answering.

'A comin' oot party?' Norrie asks. 'What the hell are you talkin' about?' But before Sharon can answer, Gary punches him on the arm and lets out a victorious cackle. 'Here, I told ye, didn't I?'

Norrie bristles. 'Naw, ye didnae,' he says. Then, after a moment's reflection: 'Told me what?'

Gary points a finger at Mike. 'That he's a poofter,' he says, triumphantly.

'Who?' Norrie says. 'Mike? A poof? Naw he's no'. Is he?'

The three men stare, fascinated, at Mike, who's studying the floor with great interest. 'He doesnae look like yin,' Merv says, after careful thought.

'That's right,' Norrie says. 'He's no' –' He searches carefully for the right word '– Girly enough.'

Merv nods. 'His voice isnae right.'

'Neither's his wrist,' Norrie adds. 'It's too strong. He could never carry thon heavy drinks around a' night if he was a woofter.'

Sharon stares warningly at the three old men. 'Language, gentlemen.'

The men cackle, completely unabashed. 'Ach, c'mon, Sharon, you know we're only teasin'. So long as he keeps feedin' us beer an' listenin' tae oor shite, we couldnae care less what he does wi' his tadge.'

Sharon rolls her eyes, then turns back to Mike, who looks as shocked as if one of the creamware figures by the bar had started talking. 'You should know,' she tells him. 'Most of the village already knows, or at least suspects. You might want to think about relaxing your hold on your secret. After all, it's not 1955 anymore.'

'Absolutely!' Sophie says, delighted by the chance to put a positive spin on her recent blunder. Flushed with relief, she puts a hand on my knee and uses it as leverage to raise herself from her seat. 'Right,' she says, clapping her hands together. 'I think this calls for some Sambuca, don't you?'

Any remaining nerves within our little group are quickly settled by Sophie's round of shots. In fact, it leaves us feeling so warm and fuzzy that we decide to have another, and then another again. By the time the fourth round arrives, three of the Christmas parties have arrived, all dressed to the nines for their nights out, and the mood within the place has turned celebratory.

At around nine, I make my way, unsteady but happy, to the bar for another round of drinks. I've just placed the order when a voice behind me says, 'So, I finally found you.'

It's Daryll. I can feel his presence. The coldness of him seeps into my back and settles over me like ice water. Sighing heavily, I turn slowly around to face him. As soon as I see his hard eyes drilling into mine, I wish I could disappear into the floor.

Daryll takes another step towards me. 'I was starting to

worry you'd sneaked off back to London before I had a chance to congratulate you.'

'Congratulate me?'

'For the little prank you played on me last week.' Another step closer. 'You should know, it cost me over two-hundred pounds to get that little artwork of yours fixed.'

'*My* artwork?' I ask, with genuine surprise.

Daryll doesn't answer, just presses his face into to mine. His sour breath is hot on my face as he hisses in my ear: 'Do you think I'm fuckin' stupid? Did you think I wouldn't know it was you? You dumb piece of shit. I was always going to figure everything out. This was always going to come back and bite you. And it *will* bite you. I *will* have my revenge. And when it comes, it'll make what happened at Greywalls look like a –'

'Shut up.'

Daryll stares at me, his eyes wide. 'What did you say to me?'

I take a step closer to him. I can feel a vein throbbing in the middle of my forehead. I can't remember the last time I felt so angry. 'I told you to shut up. Just... shut your mouth and stop talking.'

This throws Daryll, for about a nanosecond. Then he smiles, grimly, and steps so close towards me that our chests are practically touching. 'Well, well,' he says. 'Little Tommy Halliday, playing the big man for his skinny wee girlfriend. But I know your knees are shaking, you little cunt. I know you'll piss your pants if I lift a single finger towards you.'

I have to hand it to him; his insights are spot on. I've never wanted to piss so bad.

'You think you're some fucking god around these parts,' Daryll growls, through upper and lower teeth that are still clenched together. 'You're nothing but scum. And how fucking dare you interrupt me when I'm –'

'Leave him alone, Daryll.'

Daryll and I look around to find Emma staring at us from the side of the bar. Standing there, with her shoulders back, she suddenly looks like a warrior, not a victim. 'I mean it,' she says calmly. 'Leave him alone, or I'll tell everyone what you've been up to.'

Daryll's cheeks and brow flush a patchy red. 'I've done nothing wrong.'

'Are you sure?' Emma asks. 'You don't think people want to know how many nights you've sat outside my house in your van, how many times I've seen you spying on me as I walk through the village?'

Daryll tries to snicker, but it doesn't quite work. 'You're talking nonsense,' he says. 'You're a fuckin' fruit loop.'

'Are you sure about that, Daryll?' This last question comes from Sophie, as she makes her way to Emma's side. Her face is set, and she's staring hard at Daryll. 'I'd say she's perfectly sane, myself. The story sounds believable, too. In fact, it sounds a little bit like *our* story. Do you remember that one, Daryll? When we ended up in your room, and one thing led to another and... actually, I don't remember. Did you fuck me that night?'

Daryll glances around nervously. Everyone in the place is listening. 'That... that was consensual!' he stammers.

'Was it?' Sophie asks. 'Of course, I wouldn't remember, would I, because I was asleep the whole time.'

The room is filled by a collective gasp.

'You fucking monster,' Sharon says.

Bill, I notice, has made his way to Sophie's side. He's a big guy, Bill. A nice guy, but still, I wouldn't want to get on the wrong side of him.

Daryll stares at Sophie, desperation consuming him. 'Women shouldn't get so stinking drunk if they don't want these things to happen to them.'

Sophie's eyes narrow to tiny slits. 'Because, what? If they get drunk, they're fair game?'

'That's not what I meant,' Daryll says, frantically. 'You're twisting my words.'

'No, I'm not.'

'I did nothing wrong!' Daryll cries. He's pleading now.

But Sophie just shakes her head. 'Yes, you did. And you know it. And now you'll have to live with the fact that everyone else knows it, too.'

Daryll throws his wild eyes around the room, where thirty stunned faces stare back at him. Sophie's right; the news will be around the village by Monday morning. He drops his gaze to the ground and heaves a sigh. Bill takes a step forward, touches a hand to his arm. 'I think you'd better leave now, don't you?'

Daryll says nothing, just turns wearily around and begins to trudge towards the exit.

'And, by the way,' Sophie says. 'The writing on your van? It had nothing to do with Tom. That message was all mine.'

Daryll's shoulders hunch. His hand, which had been reaching for the door handle, freezes. For a few long seconds he stands, motionless, facing the door. Then, very slowly, he turns his great bulk around to face Sophie once more. 'You bitch,' he says, his eyes horrible, searing into her. 'You dirty fucking whore.'

What happens next takes place so quickly that even I don't see it coming. Sophie lunges towards Daryll and, with her right forearm, pins him against the door. 'You FUCK,' she growls. 'If you ever go near Emma again, I'll kill you.

Truly. Say one bad thing to her and I'll come back here myself and kill you. Do you hear me?'

Daryll stares at Sophie, a stunned expression on his face.

'Do you understand me?' she asks. 'Yes, or no?'

Daryll swallows, then nods. 'Yes.'

'Good. Now get the fuck of this building. I don't ever want to see you again.'

Sophie glares at Daryll, daring him to argue, but all the fight's gone out of him. He glances once more at the faces that glower at him from around the room, then drops his head and walks in silence from the building. And then there's actual applause. It makes me jump a little – the room rippling with whistles and hoots. Every single person joins in, thrilled by the drama, delighted by Emma and Sophie's courage. Sophie joins Emma by the bar and gives her arm a squeeze, before turning to the room once more and sinking into a curtsy.

We return, triumphant, to our table, where we drink and drink and reminisce and laugh. We've been lit by a glow, which lasts through the night, beyond the bar's closing, when we move out into the car park to say our farewells.

It's Mike who turns to me first. 'Let's not leave it another twenty-five years,' he says.

'Christmas,' I say. 'I promise.'

Mike nods, reassured. 'It's been really something getting to know you again. I love you, man.'

'Aww, Mike.' I look away, rubbing the back of my neck. When I look back, I see that Mike's doing the same thing. A mirror image of awkwardness. This, at least, makes us both smile.

I touch Mike's shoulder, and then turn to Emma. 'Thank you for rescuing me tonight,' I tell her.

Emma shrugs. 'It was nothing.'

'No,' I tell her. 'It was unbelievably brave. I'm so proud to know you, Emma.'

Emma looks to the ground, prods shyly at the gravel with the toe of her shoe. 'Take care back in London, won't you? And don't worry about things here. I'll look after your dad.'

'That's not your job,' I say. 'Just look after yourself. Okay?'

Emma considers this and nods.

'I'll see you at Christmas?'

'Yes,' Emma says. 'I'll look forward to it.' And with that, she kisses me quickly on the cheek and darts away, like a rabbit making a sudden dash for its burrow.

Sophie wakes me up from a sweet dream some hours after we arrive home from the pub. There was nothing too complex about the dream, just me and Lena sitting in a park, surrounded by happy families and smiling children and the sound of wind in the trees. She was talking to me, and although I heard her perfectly in my sleep, I'm unable to remember a single word the moment I'm forced into consciousness.

'Come on, Mr Sleepyhead,' Sophie says. 'Open your eyes.'

I let out a disgusted groan and try dragging a pillow over my head, but Sophie reaches under my sheet and digs a fingernail into the arch of my foot. I let out a painful yelp and throw myself into a seated position. It takes me some time to force my eyes open; when I do, I find Sophie sitting at the foot of my bed, grinning mischievously. 'Oh!' she says, with mock surprise. 'You're up.'

I lean back groggily against the headboard. 'What time is it?'

'Half one,' Sophie says. 'Not perfect, I know, but I need to talk to you.'

'And it couldn't have waited until breakfast?'

'Not if I wanted to sleep tonight.' She clears her throat. 'So... May I?'

With a sigh, I tilt my head slightly in a half-nod.

'Okay,' Sophie says. 'So, I'm just going to say it.' She clears her throat, sits up a little straighter. 'Don't go back to London.'

'What?'

'Don't go back,' Sophie says. 'There's nothing there for you.'

'Sophie, I –'

'No, I know,' Sophie interrupts. 'London's your home. You've made a life there. But is that true? When did you last meet up with friends? When did you last even speak with one of them? Yes, I know you have your books and your films and whatnot, but... are they enough? Do you really think they provide all the nutrients you need in life? Do you honestly consider that a healthy diet?'

I open my mouth to speak, but no words come out.

'You know what I think?' Sophie continues. 'I think you believe the only reason you were miserable down there is because Lena left you. I think you've convinced yourself you were as happy as you could be in the circumstances, that you'd have felt the same anywhere. But it's not true. You've changed since you came back here, Tom. You've been happier around us, around your friends, out of doors. It's not just Lena you've been missing; it's life in general.'

'But...'

'What? Your flat? The small reminders of a life you once had?'

'So, what am I supposed to do?'

'Give them up,' Sophie says. 'Give them all up. Take some time to consider your options, to heal.'

There's such hope in Sophie's eyes that I promise to think about it, but I know my mind's already made up. I will return to London tomorrow, and once there I will set about the task of arranging myself, my life, without Lena Sandberg at its core. It's devastating, of course, this new knowledge that the woman who's played such a huge part in my life is truly gone. But in time, surely, I'll find my feet again. Until then, I will allow my life to return to the way it was before, living quietly, with my books and my films and my whatnot by my side. And I'll be fine.

I'm fine.

I'm absolutely fine.

TWENTY-NINE

THE FOLLOWING MORNING, I OPEN THE FRONT DOOR OF THE house and step out into the cold with Sophie, Bill and Dad. Fragments of birdsong are beginning to mingle with the murmur of the North Sea, but the world is otherwise silent as we make our way towards the foot of the driveway.

'You're all set, then,' Dad says, when we reach Bill's car. I hear an unmistakable tremor of emotion in his voice. 'Give us a call when you get home, won't you?'

'Just two weeks, Dad,' Sophie reminds him. 'We'll see you for Christmas.' She gives him a long hug, then stands aside so Bill can do the same. With Dad distracted, Sophie grips my arm and forces my eyes onto hers. 'Remember what I told you,' she says.

'I do,' I say. I do not add that I'll try to forget it again as soon as she leaves.

Sophie nods, not entirely convinced, before climbing into the passenger seat of the car. 'And you *will* be here for Christmas. Remember?'

'Of course,' I say, as Bill starts the car. Two of the peahens are standing cluelessly a few inches from his bonnet, so he has to swerve wide and drive on the grass before pulling out onto the street and driving away. Dad and I just stand there and watch.

After some moments, Dad pats a tissue against his eyes. 'Well, I think I'll go and pay a visit to your mother.'

'Mind if I join you?'

'The more the merrier,' Dad says, which, given the circumstances, isn't remotely true, but I'm glad to find company on this, my first visit to the graveside since the funeral.

When we reach the grave, I'm shocked by how fresh it looks. The mound of earth above the grave has barely begun to settle, and its grassy surface perches above it like a bad toupee. Naively, I'd expected a headstone, and am surprised by the small wooden cross that stands in its place. I wonder how long it will take for the stone to arrive, but don't trouble Dad with the question. Instead, I ask, 'What will you do?'

Dad studies the grave for a moment, his eyes sad. Then he says, 'Oh, lots of things.' He looks back at me. 'There's the house to sell, and the attic to clear, and papers to arrange. I'll cook, and read, and no doubt I'll be down here each morning, whispering to your mother, filling her in on all the news like I used to on the days before she died.'

I glance down and suddenly feel wretched. 'You'll be lonely,' I say.

Dad sighs. 'Yes,' he says. 'Yes, I will. But it won't always be this raw. I'll get used to it, Tom. I'll find other ways to live.'

We fall silent, then. I think about the rest of the day and what I'll do. All of the days, all empty in front of me. The thought is terrifying. But then, just as I become aware of a panic forming in my chest, there's a voice behind me.

'I thought I'd missed you when there was no answer at the house.'

Slowly, I turn round. A few feet away, Lena is smiling, her eyes filled with tears. Then: 'Oh.' That's all I can think to say. *Oh*. Less a word than a sound. I drop my hands to my side, feel my stomach muscles contract as if I've had a shock. But it's joy. 'I thought I'd never see you again,' I tell her, simply.

Lena lets out a half-laugh. 'You were never going to get rid of me that easily.'

I feel Dad's hand on my shoulder, turn towards him. He smiles gently at me, gives my arm a strengthening squeeze. Then, stopping only to kiss Lena's cheek, he turns away and sets off towards home. I watch him leave for a few seconds before turning back to Lena. 'You said you were going back to Sweden,' I say.

Lena nods. 'I'm leaving on Saturday. But... Tom, I'm only going for two weeks.'

I look at her, stunned. 'What?'

'I've quit London, but I've no plans to leave Britain.'

'Oh,' I say. 'But... but...'

'You want to know why I'm here?'

I nod, too surprised to talk.

Lena tucks her hair behind her ear, looks solemnly at the grass, 'I miss you, Tom. I miss you so much. I've tried so hard to get along without you, but it's been six months and... Things just aren't the same as they were.'

'You...? Right. Oh god, I'm sorry.'

'You don't have to apologise,' Lena says.

But I'm crying, so I feel like I should.

'I spoke to the Director,' Lena continues. 'There are plenty of opportunities for me outside of London. There's even one in Edinburgh. If you wanted that.'

I swallow. 'You want to try again?'

Lena shrugs. 'I never stopped loving you, Tom.'

I let out another sob. This is getting embarrassing. *Pull yourself together*, I can hear my mother chide me. *Pull yourself together and give her a hug.* And, for once, I decide to listen.

As soon as my arms are around Lena, she begins to cry as well. 'That morning, before you left for Myreton... I thought then you wished you'd never met me. I thought you blamed me for ruining your life.'

'I know,' I say. 'I've been so angry with you.'

'We've been angry with one *another*. But we can get through this. I *know* we can.'

'You said you needed a fresh start,' I say.

Lena looks up, manages a bleary, red-eyed smile. 'So, let's start afresh.'

'I still have so much healing to do,' I warn.

'We can heal together,' Lena says.

I look into Lena's eyes. 'I'd like that.'

Lena smiles, rests her head back against my shoulder. 'What are you thinking?' she asks, pulling my arms more closely around her.

'Just that I'm glad you're here.'

'Me too,' she says. 'I'm glad I'm here, too.'

She raises her head from my shoulder, looks at me through gleaming eyes, and lifts herself onto her tiptoes to kiss me. Then, stepping back, she asks: 'Shall we go?'

'Yes,' I say. 'But... go where?'

Lena smiles a tender smile. 'Does it matter?'

And I realise; it doesn't. As we make our way from the churchyard, I feel my heart beating in my chest like a rising phoenix. And for the first time in a very long time, the world around me begins to look incredibly beautiful.

ACKNOWLEDGMENTS

The towns of Myreton and Cranston live only in my imagination, but the setting is very real; the beautiful expanse of fields, woods and beaches that make up the coastal area of East Lothian, a few miles to the east of Edinburgh. Locating my stories there is an act of self-indulgence on my part; it is the area I think of when I think of home, and writing about it allows me to revisit it in my mind.

I am hugely indebted to the following for their faith and hard work and good advice; Ingrid Bell, Lisa Brinklaus, Mark Fearne, Dee Groocock, Steve Hales, Michael McLellan, Ellen Maloney, Kate Maré, Catherine Morrison, David Sodergren and Elyse Walters.

Heartfelt thanks, as always, to Mum and Dad, for their continued support and encouragement.

Above all, my thanks to my wife, Conni, and my beautiful daughters, Malin and Anja, for their endless love and support. I couldn't have done it without them.

ABOUT THE AUTHOR

After finishing university, Andy Marr took a job in a bank, but he hated it, so he stopped and became a writer instead. He is the author of two novels: *Hunger for Life*, which is closely based on the life he shared with his amazing little sister, and *A Matter of Life and Death*, which is entirely fictional.

Andy lives in Edinburgh with his wife and two daughters, where he spends his days writing and his nights fantasising the downfall of Boris Johnson.

 facebook.com/AndyTheActualAuthor

 twitter.com/AndrooMarr

 instagram.com/andy_the_actual_author

Printed in Great Britain
by Amazon

17452921R00167